ASHES OF ROSES

CHRISTINE POPE

DARK VALENTINE PRESS

ASHES OF ROSES

ISBN: 978-0-9883348-5-4
Copyright © 2013 by Christine Pope
Published by Dark Valentine Press

Cover art by Nadica Boskovska. Cover design and book layout by Indie Author Services.

To learn more about this author, go to
www.christinepope.com.

To my mother, for teaching me the importance
of having a dream

CHAPTER ONE

Torric Deveras, Emperor of Sirlende

Lord Keldryn Tylande, my chancellor, had always reminded me of one of my father's old hunting dogs, with his drooping jowls and sad dark eyes—and never more so than when he was attempting to cajole me into an enterprise he knew from the start I would never agree with.

"Linara Tharne, youngest daughter of the king of Purth," he said desperately, setting a miniature portrait in a jeweled frame on my desktop.

I didn't even bother to look at the portrait. As if a painted picture could be counted on to tell the truth. Portrait painters had to eat, that much I knew, and so of course made sure that the richer their subjects, the more flattering the portrait. And even if this Linara were fair in actuality and not merely on a tiny piece of canvas, I already knew she was not at all suitable.

"By my calculations, the girl is barely twelve years old," I replied, and set down my pen before pushing the inkwell off to one side. It was rare that I should have an uninterrupted hour, and I had been attempting to use it to some purpose, examining the sketches the architects had brought for the renovation of my quarters and making what notes I could for any alterations and improvements. Typical that Lord Keldryn would sniff out that idle time and thrust his own intentions upon it. "Surely you do not expect me to marry someone half my age, a child who will not be ready for the marriage bed for at least another five years?"

I could tell from the brief tightening of his fleshy lips that he had, indeed, expected me to do that very thing. After all, even an emperor had little choice when it came to who might sit on the throne next to him. So few who were suitable, let alone appealing.

"Your Majesty—"

A raised hand was enough to silence him. "You will have to do better than that, Keldryn."

"Your Majesty, there is no one else. Anyone of acceptable rank has been betrothed almost since birth. As you were, with the princess who met her death so shockingly. The King of South Eredor has only sons, as did the Mark of North Eredor. We do not treat with Seldd, and the Hierarch of Keshiaar's two sisters were married off years ago. Even Princess Linara of Purth is only free to marry because her own betrothed died of the plague two winters ago."

A scowl creased my brow, but I did nothing to prevent it. I saw no reason to hide my irritation. Did my chancellor really think that by reciting facts to me I already knew, I would somehow capitulate, take some child I had never seen as my wife? At least that poor girl from Farendon had only been three years my junior.

Even princesses were not immune to accidents, and that was how I had lost my intended bride—in a terrible tumble down the stairs that had left her with a broken neck, her family without a daughter, and I, the Emperor of Sirlende, without a bride. I cannot say I grieved overmuch, except for the loss of what might have been, as I had never met her. Some might say that was cold, but the ruler of an empire is often not allowed much space in his heart for warmth.

Apparently wishing to take advantage of my silence, Lord Keldryn pressed on, "Your Majesty, it has been almost a year. It is time to make a decision. Sirlende deserves stability, an heir. It—"

At once I stood, pushing my chair back as I towered over him. Perhaps it was not entirely fair to use my height against him when my rank would do well enough, but by that time I had lost all patience. "Are you presuming to lecture me on what I should or should not do, Keldryn?"

The color drained from his face. "N-no, Your Majesty. Of course not, Your Majesty. It is only—"

"It is only that you think you can manage Sirlende's affairs better than I."

"N-no, Your Majesty—"

Suddenly weary of his stammering, of his shuddering hangdog jowls, I said, "Enough, Keldryn. We will speak of this no more. I realize I have a decision to make, but it is one I will make in my own time. Understood?"

He bowed. "Of course, Your Majesty. I will take my leave, then."

And he bowed once more, as if hoping that would mollify me, before he turned and exited my study. I remained standing, staring at the door through which he had just left, then reached up and plucked the gold circlet from my head before tossing it carelessly onto my desktop. The metal clanked against the inkwell, but did not knock it over.

I ran my hand through my hair, although the gesture didn't do much to ease my roiling thoughts. Yes, some of what Lord Keldryn had said was true, even if I didn't want to admit it to myself. Now, at the beginning of Sevendre, I was closer to my twenty-sixth birthday than to my twenty-fifth, far past the time when I should have been wed, should have started a family, done my part to ensure the royal succession.

That had not yet happened, through no real fault of my own. And yet I knew Keldryn's remarks only echoed what was likely being said throughout my court and indeed up and down the length of my realm. Such things could only be let go for so long.

My study began to stifle me, although no fire had been lit, and the windows were open to let in the fickle late afternoon breeze off the River Silth. I knew then where I needed to go, to find the one person who would listen to me reasonably and calmly, and offer only useful advice, not browbeating and foolish attempts at guilt.

Not looking at the crown I left on my desktop, I exited the chamber.

My sister was, as I had expected, in her suite high atop the East Tower, her windows open as well to the fleeting afternoon winds. Most young ladies of her age and rank would most likely have been occupying themselves with an embroidery frame and needle, or perhaps practicing upon the lute or mandolin, but of course Lyarris was not engaged in such frivolous pursuits.

She sat at her own desk, dark head bent over sheets of paper filled with her even, slanting hand. But she laid her pen aside at once as her maidservant let me in, and an impish smile pulled at my sister's mouth as soon as the serving maid had curtseyed deeply and shut the door behind me.

"My, Torric, that is quite the thundercloud you have hovering about your head."

"Is it that obvious?" I inquired, and flung myself into my favorite chair, the one by the hearth with the leather ottoman. No fire here, either, not on this warm afternoon, but the room still felt cozy, on a friendlier scale than my own admittedly grand suite.

"I'm afraid so." She picked up a scrap of cloth and blotted her pen, then set both items down on her desktop. Always so careful, my sister. A scattering of sand across the still damp ink, and she set the paper aside and stood, coming to take her own seat on the velvet-upholstered chair that was a match to the one in which I sat. She tilted her head to one side and regarded me with some curiosity, her dark eyes keen. "What is it this time?"

I let out a noise probably closer to a snort than any sound an emperor made should be. "Keldryn again, badgering me about getting a wife."

Her mouth twitched. "Oh, *that*."

"Yes, *that*."

For the space of a heartbeat or two she said nothing, but only stared at the empty hearth as if seeing the ghosts of winters' fires past within the surround of carved black marble. Finally, and with a little prefacing sigh of her own, she said, "He means well."

"Ah, well, then, that excuses all the nagging and cajoling, doesn't it?"

"Perhaps not excuses, precisely, but explains."

I shifted in the chair and set my booted feet on the ottoman. Staring at the shining black leather encasing my toes did little to ease my mind, however, no matter how comfortable my body might be at the moment.

Lyarris seemed to sense that I did not feel like replying, for she continued, "He is only saying what many are thinking. Even I, actually. True, you needed to let a respectable interval pass after the death of poor Princess Lisanne, but we have gone beyond that now, I think, especially since the lady involved was someone you did not even know."

Again, I was being told something I already understood all too well. "So you would have me marry a girl of only twelve, someone who could not be a true wife to me for many years?"

A lift of the shoulders, and a brief shake of her head. Then she ventured, "It is not as if you could not keep yourself occupied during that time…"

My mouth tightened at those words, and at their implications. Lyarris, sheltered as she might be, was not a complete innocent. She knew I was nowhere near as chaste and cloistered as she. Oh, I was careful not to repeat the mistakes my father made. I took no mistresses from among the wives and daughters of my courtiers, choosing instead those women who had made the pleasuring of men their trade, although of course these liaisons were only with the courtesans who practiced their profession from their own elegant salons, and did not freely give of their charms to just anyone.

So I supposed in a way my sister was correct in saying that I would not be suffering much denial of the flesh by waiting for a child bride to reach the proper age for bedding. However, the notion did not much appeal to me. I had thought—I had hoped—that when I took a wife, I would put those other women aside. If nothing else, my parents' bitter marriage had taught me a very good lesson in how not to treat a wife.

"Do you really think I would do that?" I inquired, not bothering to keep the anger from my tone. "Do you think me no better than Father?"

Something flickered in my sister's eyes then, something that came and went so quickly I couldn't quite tell what it was. Regret?

"I did not say that, Torric," she replied, voice calm enough. "Indeed, I am glad to hear that you plan to treat your wife with respect, even in a match made for politics and not for love. But I doubt anyone would think ill of you for doing what you required during a time when you were waiting for your wife to gain a few years."

Politics. I felt my mouth thin, and wished it were a little later in the afternoon, so I might call up for some wine to clear my muddied thoughts. Then again, I was the ruler of this land. I could do whatever I wished.

No, that was not true. Not true at all.

Some might call it an irony, that the lord of the greatest realm on the continent could not do exactly as he pleased. But I knew in many ways I had far fewer freedoms than the drovers who brought their cattle to market each day, or the women who sold flowers on street corners. Everything in my world was ordered precisely, from the days I heard the petitions of the people to the guests I invited to the balls and suppers hosted every night at the palace. *It is as it always has been done* were words that had become the bane of my existence.

I said, "It is foolish, don't you think, that the rulers of our land should always look outside its borders for their spouses?"

"But the alliances—"

"Oh, those are more empty words, and you know it. Every treaty of any import was signed into existence hundreds of years ago. Even during the war, those treaties were honored."

Lyarris nodded. She did not look altogether convinced, even though she most likely had no true arguments to present on the subject. The various lands of the continent had been at peace for many years, perhaps because most everyone knew, even if they would not utter the traitorous words aloud, that they could not hope to defeat Sirlende in open warfare...even the divided Sirlende my father had inherited.

Civil war had not been visited upon the empire for many centuries, but when my grandfather died of a sudden fever when he was barely thirty-five years old, leaving a twelve-year-old son to inherit the throne, greedy factions rose up to claim it for their own. Almost a decade of fighting ensued, with my father and his supporters finally gaining the upper hand. It had seemed wise at the time that he should take the eldest daughter of his bitter foe, Duke Harvald of Darlast, as his wife in an attempt to seal the breach.

It had all sounded well and good in theory. In practice, however...

I shook my head to free it of the memories of bitter arguments and slammed doors that populated every recollection of my childhood. "At any rate," I went on, "if I am deemed able to govern an empire, then I do not see why I cannot be allowed to select my own bride."

My sister raised an eyebrow. "I daresay that particular notion will not go over very well."

"What do I care for that? Besides, what you really mean is that it will not go over very well with my advisors. I daresay the people might have a very different opinion."

"Perhaps," she replied, and I was relieved to hear that now her tone was musing rather than derisive. "Although how on earth would you even go about such a thing? Put a crier on every street corner, announcing that the Emperor of Sirlende is in need of a wife?"

This time there was a note of gentle amusement in her voice, but I took no offense. Her words had gotten me thinking.

"Something very like that, yes," I said. "Of course, I will need some boundaries. Naturally, she must be of gentle birth—"

"Naturally," my sister cut in, her mouth lifting in the half smile I knew all too well. "I think your advisors might very well put their foot down if you took it into your head to marry a barmaid, or a girl from one of the weaving factories."

I ignored this statement, partly because I knew Lyarris was teasing me, and partly because of course I would never do anything so mad as to put a flower-seller on the throne beside me. "All the way down to baronet...or do you think that's being somewhat too generous?"

"The daughter of a baronet is still of gentle birth, if not nearly so lofty as the daughter of a duke."

"True enough. Very well, then, down to the daughter of a baronet." I paused, thinking of what other requirements would be important. "And of a suitable age—say, between the ages of eighteen and twenty-two."

"Because of course any young woman of twenty-three who is yet unmarried is a hopeless old maid."

My sister smiled as she said this, but I thought I noted a crease of her brows even so. For of course she was twenty-three and still unwed, although through no fault of her own. My father, instead of having her betrothed to some foreign prince, had arranged her marriage with the son of one of his greatest supporters, the Earl of Fallyn. All should have been well—except that the earl's son fell violently in love with the daughter of one of their neighbors, and the earl came to Iselfex to beg for his son's release from his promise. My father granted the wish of his old friend, one of the last actions he took before dying just a few days short of his forty-eighth birthday.

Very noble of him, I supposed, save that his decision left my sister the Crown Princess in the unenviable position of being quite possibly the continent's greatest matrimonial catch…with no one to claim her. Princes from South Eredor all the way east to Purth had been promised since birth, and although I had no doubt most of them would have cheerfully abandoned their intended brides the same way the earl's son had discarded my sister, they did not have understanding fathers to deal with the way the earl had. At any rate, all but one of them were married already anyway.

Lyarris' unattached state was another of Keldryn's favorite topics when he wasn't harping on me to find a suitable wife. But while there were other possibilities—several dukes without wives, or men of equal rank in Farendon and Purth—I found myself reluctant to hand her over so blithely. Her counsel was often better than that of my advisors, and I knew I would miss her terribly if I sent her away. If she had come to me with violent declarations of love for some noble or another, I suppose I would have made myself listen to them, but she seemed to have formed no real attachments as of yet, and so for the moment I was content to allow matters to remain as they were.

"Not a hopeless old maid," I told her. "But I am not ashamed to admit that I would like my wife to be a few years younger than I. Besides, by limiting eligible young women to a four-year span, it makes the pool of candidates a bit more manageable. As it is, how many do you think might be suitable?"

A tilt of her head to one side as my sister considered my question. "I cannot say for certain, but I believe it might be as many as several hundred. What on earth are you going to do with them all?"

Good question. Once the word had gone out to all those young women of gentle birth, how was I to meet them all, to form any kind of opinion of their character...to determine which of them might be a match for me, not merely by accident of birth, but by temper and humor and intelligence?

"We are always hosting entertainments," I said, speaking slowly as the plan formed in my mind. "Foolish parties and suppers and musicales and tournaments and hunts. Why not use one of those occasions to bring everyone together?"

"I suppose so." My sister stood and moved away from me to look out the window, as if by seeing all of Iselfex spread out below her she could somehow better grasp what it was I proposed. "Not too lavish, though, Torric. Remember, some of these families, though noble, are not wealthy. Trying to outfit a daughter so she can catch the emperor's eye might be enough to bankrupt them."

Her words took me aback, for until she mentioned it, I hadn't even considered such a thing. Those courtiers who maintained townhouses in the capital certainly seemed to have enough of the ready to throw about at a moment's notice, but I supposed a country baronet might take a very different view of the expenses involved.

"Very well," I said. "What do you propose?"

She turned away from the window, the late afternoon sunlight painting a golden outline around her sleek dark hair.

"It will take more than a day or two for you to make your decision, I assume?"

"Well, yes, especially if there are very many young women for me to acquaint myself with."

"All right. Then why not five days? A full week might be too much, but I should think five days would be manageable."

That seemed sensible enough. "Very well. Five days it is."

"And only one event each day. That is, perhaps start things with a tournament, and then have a dinner, and then a hunt, then a musicale, and finally end the five days with a grand ball."

The progression also made sense to me. But... "Why only one event each day?"

A grin and a shake of her head, as if she were amused by my male ignorance. "Because at an affair such as this, no young woman will wish to be seen in the same gown twice. If there is more than one event each day, then that will double the number of new gowns required, and that would be quite a burden for each family."

Reasoning like this was precisely why I had come to my sister for counsel. "Of course. As always, you are eminently sensible. I wouldn't wish to create a hardship for anyone if it can be avoided."

"Oh, it might still, if the family is poor enough, but that will be their decision to make. There will be no repercussions if a girl chooses not to participate, for whatever reason?"

"Of course not," I said at once. "The whole point is to find someone willing, someone I enjoy spending time with, and who, I hope, will enjoy spending time with me."

"Some may be more willing than others, depending on how insistent their families are, but I suppose you cannot control every aspect of the situation." A wry little smile, and she added, "Although I am sure you will do what you can to manage things."

I lifted my shoulders. Truly, now that I had come up with the plan, it would be on my advisors and my staff to arrange the thing. "When would be best? I was thinking the first week of Octevre."

"I think that is a good plan. It should have cooled down by then, so the days will be pleasant, and it will also give everyone almost a month to prepare."

"Excellent." I went to her then and gave her a quick hug, catching a brief waft of rose perfume before I released her. "Now to go and tell Keldryn what I have planned. I can't wait to see his expression."

"You mean to do *what*, Your Majesty?"

As I had hoped, my chancellor looked close to an explosion, one he was somehow managing to hold in, even though his eyes bulged and an apoplectic flush tinged his sagging cheeks. In tones of supreme unconcern, I replied, "I am going to choose my wife from among the good people of Sirlende. Surely you cannot find fault with that? Or do you think a Sirlendian girl is not fit to sit upon her own country's throne?"

"I—no, that is—of course not, Your Majesty. I did not mean to imply—but—"

"Very well, then. From here on it is merely a matter of logistics. We have five weeks until the first of Octevre. Surely that is enough time to plan such simple amusements, especially as we hold similar ones almost every night here in the palace? Well, perhaps not a tournament, but the last one was only a week ago, so I don't imagine my seneschal can have completely forgotten how to organize one in so short a period."

"No, of course not, Your Majesty, but—"

Somehow I managed to keep myself from smiling, but it was quite difficult, as one corner of my mouth seemed to want to twitch at his discomfiture no matter what I did. "In fact, have him sent to me as soon as we're done here, as I want to make sure he understands exactly what I intend. In the meantime, though, you can start the preparations to have the proclamations drawn up. I want criers sent to all the districts of Iselfex—"

"*All*, Your Majesty?" Lord Keldryn inquired, a wealth of meaning in that one simple word.

True enough. There were several districts in my capital that couldn't possibly possess any suitable candidates. "Very well, Keldryn, all the districts where noble houses are located. Then send messengers to any towns with a population of more than five hundred, and, well, you can manage the rest," I added blithely, as I did not quite have a grasp of how this was all to be accomplished. "But I do want to make sure that word is sent to all the corners of the empire."

"Yes, Your Majesty," my chancellor said, the words not quite a sigh, although close enough to one that I raised an eyebrow. His eyes widened, as he hastened to say, "It will be done with all haste, Your Majesty. I will make up a draft of the announcement and have it ready for your approval within the hour."

"Excellent." By then I was willing to be magnanimous, as it was clear Lord Keldryn would offer no further arguments. Perhaps he had told himself he should be happy, for at least he now knew that I planned to do something about getting a wife...even if my means of doing so were unorthodox, to say the least.

As to that, well, perhaps it was time to overturn some of those old traditions.

CHAPTER TWO

Ashara Millende

Today is going to be a good day.

It was a charm I had begun to repeat each morning, a few simple words to convince myself that things surely weren't as bad as they had seemed the night before, when I had curled up on my mean little pallet in front of the remains of the kitchen fire and attempted to sleep. True, some days were better than others, and many far worse, but just as the sun rose each morning, my hopes would rise with it, the thought that perhaps this day something would be different, that something would change.

As for this particular morning on a bright day in early Sevendre, it did offer some promise, with no river mist to mute the sun's rays, and make the air thick with moisture. It was a time of year when many of the great families who dwelt in Iselfex would retreat to their country manors and castles, escaping the damp heat. We, however, did no such thing. Indeed, my stepmother had fled the country for the city some ten years earlier, and showed no signs of ever wanting to return.

To be sure, part of my anticipation of its being a good day was that she and my two stepsisters would be gone for all of it, as they had departed the afternoon before to spend a few days at the house of a friend. Not exactly a country ramble, but Mistress Theldrin's home was outside the borders of the capital, in a pleasant location at the edge of the River Silth… upstream from the capital, and so untouched by the waste any great city generates. While I might have entertained wistful thoughts of spending some time away from Iselfex, away from the noise and the smoke and the ever-present crowds, of rolling down my stockings and taking off my shoes and walking barefoot through the cool water, I knew I would never be allowed such liberty.

No, it was enough to look forward to the prospect of several days passing with no demands that I iron a chemise, or heat water for a bath, or fetch a hair ribbon, or blister a finger preparing the curling rods for my stepsisters' hair, or—well, I will not bother to list all the tasks they could dream up to keep me running from morning to night. Yes, I would still have to dust, and mop, and empty the refuse bins, and peel the potatoes for the cook's unending soups and stews, but at least I would not have to do all those things and attempt to fulfill my stepfamily's unceasing demands.

At first glance anyone who saw me must think me the lowest of the small staff who kept the household going, but in truth, I had not been born to this life. This grand house, with its shining wooden floors and windows of stained glass and four marble fireplaces—all of which had to be cleaned regularly—should have been mine.

My stepmother, who loathed country life as much as my father had loved it, removed us all to Iselfex, to the town-house my father had inherited along with his title and the lovely estate some three days' ride north of the capital. The estate, I gathered, my stepmother leased to a prosperous wine merchant who had dreams of living the life of a landed gentleman, and it was the money from those rents, along with what she had inherited from my father, that enabled her to set herself up in some style in town.

As for myself…

I sometimes wondered, in the depths of the blackest nights, when sleep would not come and my thoughts went down dark pathways, whether my stepmother would have had me killed outright, if she thought she could get away with it. But although I was reduced to being the meanest of servants in my own home, she could count herself as being virtuous in that at least I still had a roof over my head, and was fed regularly. She constantly complained about being in debt, and how we all just barely struggled to get along, as if that were excuse enough for me to "earn my keep," as she liked to put it. Never mind that my stepsisters had new gowns at least once a month, and that my stepmother hosted grand dinner parties every fortnight. No, she couldn't possibly afford to give me the same treatment she lavished on her own daughters.

Ah, well. My pallet was a poor one, but the kitchen was generally warmer than the drafty bedrooms upstairs, and the cook, a good-hearted woman who spied the lay of the land, even if she did not have the courage to protest my treatment, tried to sneak me what morsels she could in addition to my own meager meals. With all that, she still sighed over how thin I was. I did not bother to point out that some extra scraps of cheese and a stolen bit of bread here and there were not enough to offset all the running about I had to do to keep my stepmother, if not precisely happy, at least quiescent.

It was time to draw water from the well. Our house was situated on a small cul-de-sac that it shared with four other homes, and in the center of the street where it dead-ended was the well where we got all our water. That was one thing about Iselfex—fresh water was easy enough to come by. Indeed, the very name of the city meant "place of the wells" in the language of those who had founded it.

I fetched the two heavy wooden buckets from their place by the back door and went out. At once the smells of the town met my nose—smoke, and spent grease, and beneath it the damp, warm scent of the river, which lay only a hundred yards or so from the house. The sun was already hot, despite it being barely the fourth hour of the morning. I could feel the perspiration start under the kerchief that bound my hair and begin to trickle down my neck.

Nothing for it, though. I grasped the buckets more tightly and made my way to the well, keeping my gaze studiously downcast. I had been scolded more times than I cared to recall over being what my stepmother called too "bold"—which apparently meant looking about me as I walked. Perhaps she wished me to be invisible altogether, and believed that if I did not gaze at other people, then they would not look at me.

Even so, only a few months earlier one of the footmen from the Marenhalls' household had offered to carry the buckets for me, declaring I was far too frail for such a chore. I had tried to demur, for in fact I was stronger than I looked, but he had insisted, taking my burden from me and walking with me to the back door. Oh, what a row that caused! For my stepsister Jenaris saw the whole thing, and went tattling to her mother, and I was most vigorously chastised for encouraging male attention. Of course I had not, but I knew there was no point in trying to explain that to my stepmother.

She must have said something to Mistress Marenhall, for the tall young footman never approached me again. Perhaps in my heart I experienced a small pang, as kind words were few and far between for me, and that was the first time a young man had even dared to approach me, but any protests would have resulted in punishment far worse than a harsh scolding and a hungry night with no supper.

I went to the well, and attached my first bucket to the rope there and lowered it. A splash as the pail met water, and then I began to haul the heavy bucket upward, my hands hardened by now to the rough hemp rope, the dead weight of it as I slowly drew it back toward me—slowly, for if I spilled too much, I would only have to go back and fill it once again.

With care I set it down at my feet, and began to attach the second bucket. I had just dropped it over the side of the well when a rider on a fine blood bay came clattering down the street, unrolled a piece of heavy paper, and called out in a strong, commanding voice,

"Hear ye, good people of Iselfex! His Imperial Majesty, Torric Deveras, has let it be known that he wishes to seek a bride from among his own people. All young women of gentle birth between the ages of eighteen and twenty-two are hereby invited to attend a series of celebrations, beginning with a tournament on the first of Octevre, and culminating in a grand ball on the fifth of that month, so that his Majesty may make the acquaintance of these young women and make one of them his wife. So he has said, and so will it be done."

And with that the rider dismounted. Only then did I realize he wore the silver and black of the Imperial house, his doublet of black velvet slashed with silver tissue, a brooch in the shape of the Imperial device, an eagle with wings outstretched, holding his cloak closed at his throat. All in all, it must have been an uncomfortably hot ensemble for such a warm day, and I found myself pitying the young man somewhat.

He went to the wood and stone wall that enclosed our property, and proceeded to nail the proclamation to one of the wooden posts there. I reflected that perhaps it was a good thing my stepmother was away and couldn't see such deface-ment of her property, but then I realized she most likely would not consider such a thing to be an act of vandalism, but rather welcome attention from the Crown.

Even from where I stood I could see the flush on the rider's brow. It had to be thirsty work, going from street to street and making his proclamation. I lifted my buckets and went toward him, barely staggering under my burden, as I had grown accustomed enough to it by that time.

"Some water, good sir?" I asked, and indicated the buckets I held. "I have no dipper, I fear, but—"

A most unofficial grin spread across his lips, and he took the bucket from my left hand, drinking deeply. Indeed, he drank so much I feared I would have to go refill the bucket, but at length he set it down by my feet.

"Many thanks, miss," he said, his smile even wider now, if that were possible. "I can only hope that the young woman His Majesty chooses is half as thoughtful as you."

Not knowing what else to do, I bobbed a curtsey. "You are too kind, my lord."

His gaze sharpened slightly. I knew my accent was not that of a servant girl, and I had been trained in manners and courtesies while my father was still alive. I held my breath, hoping he would make no further comment, and hoping I hadn't attracted attention that might get me in trouble.

But the moment passed, and he shrugged. It was clear to me that he had many more stops to make, and the puzzle of a servant who sounded like a nobleman's daughter was something he would have to leave aside for another day.

A nod, and "thank you again, miss," and he turned away from me, going back to his horse and swinging up into the saddle with a smooth, practiced movement. Then he was gone, and I was left to stare at the paper nailed to the fence post.

So the Emperor was seeking a bride. On the face of it, I met the requirements—I was nineteen, and of gentle birth, my father having been a baronet. But I knew there was no chance of participating in the planned festivities. Even if I had somehow managed to scrounge one halfway present-able gown, my stepmother would never allow me to leave the house and abandon my duties for a single day, let alone five in a row.

Indeed, she made sure that I did not venture beyond the little cul-de-sac where the house was located. Any errands were entrusted to Mari, the other maidservant, or Janks, the young man who performed everything from footman duties to minor repairs, as needed. My stepmother did not keep a carriage, hiring a coach as required, and had many of the household's necessities delivered.

Perhaps in a perfect world Mari might have been a com-panion to me, someone I could commiserate with over my stepmother's harsh treatment of us all. But Mari had adopted the general tone of the household toward me, thinking her-self my superior because she had the lighter duties of man-aging the wardrobes of my stepsisters and stepmother, and doing their hair, and dusting the bric-a-brac with which my stepmother had cluttered the interior of what once had been quite an elegant house.

If I had not once caught Mari and Janks indulging in behavior that most likely would have gotten her dismissed— and which gave me an education in relations between men and women that I would not soon forget—she very likely would have treated me even worse than she did. Although I had sworn not to say anything, knowing how hard it would be for her to get a new situation with no reference, still I thought she did not completely believe me, and that I held the information in reserve against a day when I might have need of it.

So I sighed, and gathered up my buckets, and returned to the house. Mari had gone with my stepsisters and stepmother, leaving Janks and me to manage the place on our own. I actually rather liked him, even if I didn't care much for his taste in young women. But he always treated me with a rough kindness that was a welcome respite from Mari's cattiness and my stepsisters' scorn.

He grinned at me now, and came to take the buckets from me, hoisting them easily and depositing them on the kitchen's stone floor. "Heard the news, ay?" he asked, clearly ready for some gossip, with the lady of the house gone and not much to occupy his time…well, except keeping an eye on me. I had no doubt my stepmother had left strict instructions for him to make sure I ventured no farther than the well.

"I did," I replied, and lifted one bucket to pour some water into the basin I used to scrub the vegetables. Claris, our cook, would be returning from her marketing soon, and I knew better than to not have things ready by her return, even if the meal she prepared would be modest enough, as it was only the three of us who would be eating it.

"Think they'll try for it?"

I shrugged. "Most likely." I did not want to say more than that. Just because I liked Janks didn't mean I would trust him to keep my opinions between the two of us. I could have added that the preparations would send the house into an uproar, and that my stepsisters only had the barest claim to fit the parameters of the Emperor's summons, as their own father had been merely a knight. However, I had no doubt that my stepmother would use my father's title to get them in, even if such machinations stretched the borders of what was actually allowed.

Nor would I say that neither of my stepsisters was nearly pretty enough to catch the eye of the Emperor. He could have his pick from hundreds of eligible young women, after all. Although Shelynne, my junior by a year, was an attractive girl—taking after her mother, luckily, who was still handsome—she did have a tendency to wear an unfortunate expression half the time, owing to her extreme near-sightedness. And Jenaris, the elder, was really not pretty at all, although her mother tried to hide her shortcomings with elegant gowns and perfectly curled hair and the slightest touch of stain on her lips. Even so, Jenaris still looked to me like a pig wearing silk and curls…and her disposition did little to dispel that impression.

Janks frowned a little, and retrieved an apple from the basket that sat on the sideboard. After crunching into it and taking a few contemplative chews, he said, "It'll be a right old mess, won't it? Running about all over town, ordering new gowns…they'll probably drive Mari to distraction, poor girl."

Somehow I managed to refrain from saying that I did not feel a great deal of pity for Mari. Another lift of my shoulders, and I said cautiously, "I believe it will create some extra work for her. I suppose we should be glad it's a month off."

"Ha. So that'll be a month full of more work. Typical, isn't it? The grand lords and ladies have their brilliant ideas, and it's dropped on the likes of us to manage it somehow."

I smiled and shook my head, and was saved from making a reply by the arrival of Claris, who bustled into the kitchen laden with baskets of vegetables and fruit, and precious little linen bags of nuts and spices.

"I doubt the mistress would appreciate you standing around idle, just because she happens not to be here," the cook snapped. "Janks, I thought you were supposed to be taking care of the creaking floorboards in the small salon."

"Yes'm," he said with a grin and a laughing light in his dark eyes. A slight bow, and he went out into the rear court-yard, no doubt heading for the small shed where he stored his tools and other necessities for keeping the house in repair.

Her gaze moved to me, and I stiffened, waiting to be scolded for my shiftlessness. But her expression softened, and she only said briskly, "I see you have the water ready for me. Scrub these vegetables, and chop them into small pieces. I thought we would have soup tonight, as it will do well for our luncheon tomorrow also. The mistress won't be home until tomorrow night, so I'll figure something out for us by then."

I didn't recall letting out a sigh, but something in my expression must have changed, for Claris added, "Ah, well, enjoy it while you can, Ashara. At least they won't be back for another day."

Embarrassed that I had been so transparent, I nodded, then went to the vegetables. At least in doing something so mindless, I could keep myself from dwelling on what was to come, and instead focus on making sure the pieces I cut were uniform and to the size Claris desired. She might have pitied me, and did what she could to make my life more comfortable, but that did not mean she would tolerate any sloppiness in her kitchen. Not that I minded.

At least she was honest, and did not hide her thoughts. I found I appreciated that quality in a person.

Somehow I seemed to have a more difficult time than usual falling asleep that night. Perhaps it was merely the damp late-summer warmth, which lingered in the kitchen more than any other room of the house. Or perhaps it was that I had not had nearly as many tasks to complete that day as I normally would, and so my body was not drooping with exhaustion.

Whatever the cause, I tossed and turned on my pallet, seeming to feel every unevenness in the floor beneath it, every sharp end of the straw that filled the heavy, rough mattress. At last I opened my eyes and stared up at the beams of the ceiling, darker lines against the dim plaster.

For some reason I could not stop thinking of the proclamation posted on the wall only yards from where I lay. How many would answer its summons? Of course there would be some who would not attend, those who were already betrothed, or whose families perhaps could not bear the expense of a venture with such low chances of success. Even so, I guessed it must be hundreds, and wondered how the Emperor would ever choose from among so many.

Still, it would be quite something to see so many noble young women gathered in one place, and something even more to see the Emperor himself. He was young, only some six years older than I, and I had heard he was the handsomest man in all of Sirlende. This I guessed must be an embellishment, for of course those wishing to curry favor would say he was a veritable paragon, even if the reality did not quite match their compliments.

But it would have been nice to see for myself.

I sighed, and rolled over onto my side, although I knew that position was even less comfortable than lying on my back. Long ago I had given up trying to sleep on my stomach, for then it seemed as if I only inhaled the musty odor of the straw, and ended up sneezing for half the night.

Something seemed to move in the quiet kitchen, and I thought I heard a whisper of my name. "Ashara..."

I sat up, clutching my blankets to my breast, telling myself it must be Claris coming in from her quarters down the hall. But I had never heard the cook sigh so, and as I blinked into the darkness, I saw that the woman who now stepped out of the shadows near the back door was far more slender than Claris, who had an unfortunate tendency to over-sample her own wares.

"Who's there?" I asked in a harsh whisper, even as I reached out for the fireplace poker. My fingers wrapped around the cool metal, but I stopped at the stranger's next words.

"I am your Aunt Therissa."

Startled, I still managed to say, "I don't have an aunt. Neither of my parents had any brothers or sisters."

She stopped by the sideboard, and the candle in its holder there was suddenly alight, although I had not spied her picking up a match. Despite the dimness of the room, I could see enough of her, see a pretty woman of perhaps forty-five, her dark hair in a long braid wrapped like a crown around her head, drops of silver hanging from her ears. From what I could see of it, her gown appeared to be of good quality, although not overly elaborate.

All in all, she looked quite respectable. That didn't explain what she was doing in my stepmother's kitchen in the middle of the night.

"No, Ashara," the strange woman replied, and her tone was sad, even though I could not guess at the reason why. "I am your mother's older sister, although I suppose she never spoke of me."

"No, she did not." Pushing away my one thin blanket, I got to my feet and faced her. We were of a height; my eyes met hers directly. "So why should I believe that you are who you say you are?"

She did not reply directly, but only looked at me for a few seconds, then said, "Ah, you are so like her, Ashara. What a beauty she was, and that hair! Oh, how I envied her that hair. I always hoped a child of hers would inherit it."

Without thinking, I ran my fingers down the thick braid which hung over my shoulder. It was a dark, rich red, exceedingly rare in Sirlende, where not one child in ten thousand would have locks of such a hue, where most everyone had hair in shades of brown and black. My stepsisters resented my hair, and my stepmother made sure I covered it with a kerchief every day of my life. It was too distinctive, I supposed, something that a person would remember. And if someone ever recalled that Lord Allyn Millende's lost daughter had hair that color...well, it might lead to questions my stepmother would no doubt not wish to answer.

"So you say you are my mother's sister," I said, keeping my voice barely above a whisper, lest we awake Claris where she slept just down the short hallway off the kitchen. "Why, then, have you come to me now? For I daresay you would have been of far more help to me ten years ago, when Father died and I was left to the mercies of my stepmother."

Surprisingly, tears glittered in the woman's dark eyes. "If I had known, I would have come. I have just returned to Sirlende after traveling the continent for the past twenty years or so. When I left, my sister had just married her beloved Allyn, and I thought all was right in her world." A sigh, and she added, "Now that I am here, I find that nothing much is right at all. But I wish to repair things, if I might."

She spoke clearly, and I winced, sure she would bring Claris down upon us at any moment. Whispering, I said, "We must be careful, or you will wake the cook. She sleeps not twenty paces over there." And I pointed in the direction of the corridor that led off the kitchen and to the pantry and the small chamber the cook occupied.

Incongruously, my aunt smiled, and waved an airy hand. "Oh, you needn't worry about that. She will not wake any time soon, and neither will that amiable but none-too-bright young man out in the room off the stables."

I wondered how she knew they wouldn't wake—and how she knew where Janks slept at all. My stepmother, following her own odd notions of propriety, would not allow her footman to sleep in one of the cramped rooms just below the attic, but had him reside in the small lean-to attached to the stables, where once upon a time the horse-boys must have lived. But we kept no horses, so that space was empty enough.

"I wouldn't be so sure," I replied, keeping my voice pitched low. "Claris is quite the light sleeper. More than once she's caught my stepsister Jenaris coming down to raid the larder at midnight."

A little tinkle of a laugh, and my aunt said, "Truly, there is no need to fear. I have made quite sure that they will not wake before morning."

"You have?" A sudden fearful thought went through my mind. "You didn't—that is, you haven't *drugged* them, have you?"

"Of course not. I only worked a simple sleep charm."

A—I stared at her, and backed away slowly. "You're—you're a *witch*?"

"Oh, for goodness' sake." Her dark eyes flashed. "But of course I suppose I shouldn't be surprised that you would have the same narrow-minded beliefs as the rest of your countrymen, with no one around to teach you differently. My fault, perhaps, but I think no one with an open mind could blame me for leaving Sirlende to go to more…accommodating…locales." She crossed her arms and gazed at me frankly, then said, "I am not a *witch*, Ashara. I am a user of magic, mage-born. Some might call me a sorceress, but I fear my talents aren't quite grand enough for me to claim that title."

These revelations left me staring at her, open-mouthed. Magic was something never discussed, the penalty for its use death…here in Sirlende, at least. I had been told that all those who bore the taint of magic in their blood had long since died off, but there were always whispered rumors of those who could still cast spells, if you knew where to look. Since I could not even venture beyond the street where I lived, I'd had no opportunity to go seeking these illicit users of magic…assuming they even existed.

But here now was this woman who claimed to be my aunt calmly announcing that she possessed such powers, and had in fact charmed the only other two occupants of the property into a deep sleep…so we should not be disturbed. And there had been the matter of that candle which had mysteriously lit itself…

"What do you want?" I asked, and told myself that my voice hadn't shaken that much, not really.

"To make things right, my child. I had to leave, lest anyone discover what—who—I was. And I do not regret the knowledge I gained while I was away. But to find that my sister has been dead all these years, and her child practically a slave in the household of a woman not fit to wipe the soles of her shoes—well, that has caused me a good deal of regret. And I want to repair things."

"How on earth can you do that? Are you going to take me away from here?" It was perhaps an indication of my desperate desire to get away from my stepmother that I would even entertain such a notion, user of magic or no.

"No, my dear." She smiled, and looked on me with fond eyes. "Something even better.

"I'm going to make you Empress of Sirlende."

CHAPTER THREE

Ashara

I stared at her, thinking she must be mad, or at the very least possessed of a warped sense of humor. Finally I found my voice, although all I seemed able to say was, "You're what?"

"My dear child, it really is the most perfect opportunity. The Emperor seeks a wife among his own population—an excellent notion, I think, because it will only endear him to the people, that he would not set a foreign princess on the throne to rule over them. And your father was a baronet, and you are nineteen, so there is no reason in the world why you should not go present yourself to him, and win his heart."

"No reason—" I began, then broke off, shaking my head. "I fear I am in no position to approach His Majesty. That is—just look at me!" And I waved a hand at my patched chemise, my no doubt smudged face.

"Ah, well," my aunt replied, still smiling. "That is no great matter. I did tell you that I was a user of magic, did I not? And while I cannot tell the future, or bring down the storms, or shatter the walls of a castle, I do have my own particular talents." She lifted her hand and spread it toward me, as if offering me something on her empty, outstretched palm, even as she murmured some words I could not understand under her breath.

I lifted my own hands, as if to ward off whatever spell it was that she cast...and stopped dumb, staring at my raised arms in shock.

For I did not see my ragged chemise, nor the bare, thin arms that should have emerged from its dingy cuffs, but rather sleeves of a rich amber silk, worked with thread of gold and nuggets of dark honey-colored stones. And on my fingers were rings of gold, set with amber and garnet and tiny warm-tinted river pearls.

"W-what?" I stammered. "How?"

"An illusion," my aunt said calmly. "Oh, a very real one— if someone were to take your hand, they would feel the rings on your fingers, and if the Emperor, perchance, were to put his arm around your waist to dance the *verdralle*, he would feel silk. But none of it is real, and none of it will last forever. But it will last long enough."

I dropped one trembling hand to touch the heavy skirts that now seemed to encase my legs, felt the rich silk under my work-roughened fingertips. How could such a thing be possible? How could she cast a glamour that not only looked real, but *felt* real?

"You see?" she said. "You can go among them, and no one will know that you sleep on a pallet in front of the kitchen fire, or that you spend your time scrubbing floors and heating water and emptying chamber pots. All they will see is the beautiful gentle-born girl you are—would have been, if your poor father had not passed so unexpectedly."

Was it possible? Could I go to see all those noble-born young women, catch a glimpse of the Emperor himself? I did not flatter myself to think he would take any particular interest in me, but…

I shook my head. "You can put a fine gown on me, and curl my hair and clean my face, but I still can never be one of them. I am only a plain, simple girl, with no knowledge of the manners required to pass at court."

Her dark brows drew together. "Is that truly what you think? Are you going to let yourself believe the lies told you by your stepmother—although I think she should not use the word 'mother' at all to connect herself with you, because she is nothing of the sort. Anyhow, don't let the poisoned words she has uttered over the years sway you, Ashara. I believe you do not understand exactly what power you could command, if you only had the heart to take it for yourself. Do you see?"

And she spread her hand in front of me, although this time it seemed she cast a very different sort of spell, for her upraised palm became shimmery and reflective, clearer and brighter than the silvered looking glass in my stepmother's chamber. In that mirror-like surface I saw my reflection, saw the rich gown and how it seemed to enhance the deep russet tones of my hair, the warm topaz shades of my eyes. I saw how

my nose was delicate and straight, my chin small and determined, lips full and rich with color, although of course I wore
no cosmetics. I was not brave enough to use the word "beautiful," but somehow I thought I was not quite as ugly as my
stepmother had tried to convince me over the years that I was.

I opened my mouth to reply, but somehow the words
became caught in my throat. And that choking sensation
seemed to overwhelm me as the tears rose in my eyes, and
I bent my head and sobbed, sobbed in a way I hadn't done
since I lost my father. Then I felt my aunt's arms go around
me, smelled the sweet rose scent of her perfume as she held
me close, not saying anything, as if she understood that I
needed to weep, to let that part of myself break down before
I could go on with any part of her mad plan. At last, though,
my tears were spent, and I pulled away, sniffling.

Any expectation that she might materialize a handkerchief out of thin air was dashed when she fished one prosai-
cally enough from a pocket in her gown and handed it to me.
I blotted my eyes, even as I began to stammer an apology.

"None of that," she said. "You've been through enough
to make a lesser girl weep for a year, so I think I can excuse
five minutes or so of it. But now you've seen that I can make
this happen for you—if you will let me. Will you not take
the risk? I have seen this Emperor of yours, and for once the
stories do not exaggerate. He is a very handsome man, and
the sort any girl might fall in love with, even were he not the
ruler of the greatest country in the world."

Oh, the tumult that raged in my breast then! For I did
want to go and see him, and perhaps, if I were very lucky,

share a dance. I did not possess the sort of vanity which would allow me to think it would be anything more than that, but it would be enough. Only—

"There is no way it will work," I said sadly, loath to abandon that hope, brief and short-lived as it was. "My stepmother watches everything I do. Even now while she is gone she has set the others to keep a watch on me so that I might not run off. There is simply no way I could disappear for hours and hours to these tournaments and dances and whatnot without her knowing I was gone, and punishing me for my absence when I returned."

Despite these depressing words, my aunt did not appear to be terribly dismayed. She smiled, and shook her head, and uttered more words under her breath. Then it was as if I looked upon myself, saw the messy braid and the meager chemise, and, yes, the dark smudge on the tip of my nose. Even her voice when she spoke sounded like mine, lighter in tone, soft, with none of the heartiness she had displayed only moments earlier.

"You see?" she said. "She will never know that you have gone. I will mind the house for you while you are off attracting the Emperor's notice. The only chancy part will be trading places when you return, but even that can be managed. So fret not, Ashara."

I stared at her, stared at words I had not spoken coming from what appeared to be my own mouth. So this was magic. In that moment I saw why it might have been suppressed, why wars were fought over it so many years ago. For if my aunt could imitate me so precisely, what would have stopped some long-ago mage from taking on the semblance of a great lord...or even the Emperor himself?

A shiver went over me. My aunt must have seen it, for she reached out and placed a gentle hand—*my* hand, complete with calluses and broken fingernails—on my arm. "It can be a little unsettling, I know. But you must also know that I am doing this for you."

The words burst from me. "But—but *why*?"

"Because I was not there when you needed me. I had my reasons for leaving Sirlende, and they were good ones, but I stayed too long away. I should never have let things come to such a pass. This is my chance to make it right. I have watched you for a while, actually...seen how you can still laugh with Janks, when you think no one is looking. I've seen the way you pause at the well to watch the sky if the sunset is especially beautiful. And I saw today how you offered that messenger a drink of your water, even though giving him too much would have meant more work for you." She lifted her shoulders, and the semblance of myself melted away, leaving behind the pretty bright-eyed woman she actually was. Those eyes were not so bright now, but sad, and somehow pleading. "Let me do this for you, Ashara."

I found I could not tear myself away from that earnest gaze. This meant a great deal to her, I knew. And was this not something I had dreamed of, finding a way to tear myself from the bonds my stepmother had placed upon me? Now such an escape seemed to be handed me, wrapped up with bright ribbons the way presents had been long ago, back when I had been lucky enough to receive such things.

But oh, the consequences if we should be caught! It had been a very long time since anyone in Sirlende had been put to death for using magic—long, long before I was born—but the laws still existed. If anyone caught me in the lie, discovered that I had been using magic to attract the Emperor's attention...

So what? I thought then. *This life you live is not even half a life. How precious can it possibly be? Better to risk all, than condemn yourself to the prison your stepmother has created.*

Put that way...

"All right," I said firmly. "I will do it."

I had a hard time falling asleep after that. My aunt left, promising that she would make all the necessary plans, and that all I had to do was wait—and, if possible, watch my stepsisters as closely as I could, that I might soak up as many bits of etiquette and courtly behavior as I could.

That probably wouldn't be too difficult. I had no doubt that as soon as my stepmother returned to Iselfex and heard the news, she'd be drilling Jenaris and Shelynne on which fork to use and which forms of address were proper and how deeply to curtsey to a duke as opposed to a baron. All I would have to do is lurk in the background, listening and watching while pretending to scrub the floor, and I had no doubt I would have my own education easily enough. Probably more easily than they; neither of my stepsisters was particularly quick of mind, although Shelynne did have a facility with numbers that rather astonished me, given that she was not much of a scholar otherwise.

No, I lay there on my pallet, and stared at the ceiling and wondered if I had signed my own death warrant by agreeing to my aunt's mad plan. After all, so many things could go wrong.

...And so many things might, just might, go right.

Escape was something I had dreamed of over and over again, hoping I might find the perfect opportunity, the one chance that would allow me to escape servitude to my stepmother. Some might say it had been foolish of me to stay under her roof for so long, to suffer the abuses visited upon me, but I was not completely naïve—I knew the sorts of perils a young woman alone in a great city might face, and they were far worse than being forced to empty chamber pots or polish the silver until one's fingers were red and aching.

Even so, I had tried to plan for that day by picking up the odd coin in the street and secreting it among my meager possessions, or collecting odd items that might be of some worth to a tinker or metalsmith—a brass button, a silver hair comb with several of its tines of deer horn broken off. Small things in and of themselves, but I had hoped against hope that perhaps one day they might be enough to allow me to run away, to give me enough security that I would not have to fall prey to the hazards which usually dogged young women on their own. It had never been enough, not yet.

And now...well, now I had truly put my foot in it, as Claris might say. Perhaps when my aunt appeared on the fateful day, on the first of Octevre, my resolve would fail me, and I would tell her to go, and leave me to my miserable existence. Better that than to take such a terrible risk.

I would only have to hope I had more backbone than that.

My stepmother and stepsisters returned late the following day, sending the household into a frenzy of unpacking and cleaning and cooking. It appeared the news of the Emperor's quest for a bride had reached all the way to my stepmother's friend's estate, for she was plotting almost as soon as she alighted from her hired carriage.

"I'll be having the dressmaker in tomorrow, Ashara, so make sure the front steps are well-scrubbed, and do get rid of those dreadful cobwebs in the entry hall. Are you blind? They should have been knocked down days ago. And dust the second salon and polish the floor. We want to make a good impression."

Knowing I would attract attention if I did anything more than bob my head and drop a curtsey, I hastily did both those things. Perhaps there was a little too much ready acquiescence in my manner, for her eyes narrowed as she looked at me. But then she appeared to be distracted by yet another thought, because she went on, directing her next words to her daughters, "And the day after I must have a dancing master in. Oh, I knew I should not have neglected teaching you the steps! Well, we must do what we can, and luckily only one of the Emperor's gatherings involves dancing. I know he will be too distracted by your pretty faces to note any particular clumsiness."

This was too much, even for me, and I let out a sound rather too close to a snort. At once my stepmother's piercing dark eyes were upon me, and I pretended to cough, and wipe my eyes, as if some bit of dust had irritated my throat. She glared at me for a long moment, and I worried she would use this excuse to manufacture yet more tasks for me. But apparently the excitement of preparing for the Emperor's bride-hunt overcame her dislike for me, and she turned to her daughters and said, "Well, there will be more, but I must decide which must take precedence. In the meantime, it will be dinner soon. Speaking of which…" She trailed off, and appeared almost hesitant, for her.

"What of dinner, Mamma?" inquired Jenaris, her tones weighted with suspicion.

"Only that—well, I believe it might be good for you to not have any bread, or potatoes, and only one piece of meat and some field greens. I have heard that the Emperor likes slender girls, and—"

"And what?" Jenaris demanded, hands on her ample hips.

"And Mamma thinks you are too fat," Shelynne helpfully supplied with a giggle. "I daresay she is right. Not that it is necessarily a bad thing—at least I don't have to worry about you borrowing any of my gowns, as none of them would fit."

"Ma-MA!" Jenaris shrieked in outrage, and reached out to give one of her sister's shining dark curls a sharp tug, eliciting a howl of pain.

"Girls," my stepmother said in quelling tones. "None of this is behavior that befits a lady, let alone a future Empress. Jenaris, you are not fat, but I do think that it behooves you to be careful in what you eat for the next several weeks. And

Shelynne, it is not ladylike to point out another's shortcomings. You may one day find yourself on the receiving end of such observations."

While these were fine, salutary words, they did not appear to have the desired effect. Jenaris stuck out a mutinous lower lip; I had no doubt she planned a few more midnight raids on the larder. And Shelynne only rolled her eyes, as if to indicate that she didn't believe she had any shortcomings in need of pointing out.

As usually happened when my stepmother lost patience with her daughters, she turned her ire on me. "And you, miss, standing there as if you hadn't a care in the world. You have work to do, so why are you still here?"

"I was only waiting to see if you had any further instructions for me, ma'am," I replied meekly.

"Get to the kitchen and help Claris with dinner! No doubt she's been missing you these five minutes, you lazy, idle girl!"

I bobbed my head and made my escape to the relative refuge of the kitchen. My stepmother rarely ventured in there, as she thought it more genteel to call for Claris and have any necessary consultations with her in the dining room.

The cook was bending over a saucepan as I entered, her greying hair wisping in the steamy heat of the kitchen. "Goodness, what a ruckus," she said. "And of course she would be wanting pork medallions in wine sauce right off, as if she were having company."

"Perhaps she missed your cooking," I suggested, at which Claris shot me a very jaundiced look.

"Wanted to remind me who was in charge, more like," she responded. "Ah, well, at least we had a few days' rest. There's some who don't even get that."

I nodded, not quite trusting myself to speak.

"Well, don't stand there bobbing your head like one of those foolish dolls in the marketplace. Those greens need to be shredded, and Miss Jenaris's must have no sauce, so hers has to go in a separate bowl."

No sauce? My stepmother really must be serious about this. Somehow I thought it would be difficult to reverse years of indulgent sweet-eating in only a few short weeks, especially if I knew my stepsister. She would find a way to sneak the things she wanted, no matter that her mother had forbidden that she touch even a single piece of bread.

But I knew better than to say such a thing aloud, even to Claris. Word had a way of getting around, especially in a household as small as ours. I realized then that I had not caught a glimpse of Mari—our resident tattletale—but guessed she must have been up in the room my stepsisters shared, unpacking their things and setting aside the ones that needed to be laundered.

I went instead to the pile of field greens and began to rinse them off, setting the clean ones aside to drain as I did so. This was a relatively simple task, so my mind began to wander as I worked, imagining what the inside of the palace might look like, and what the music played at the balls would sound like, and what sort of food would be served at these gatherings. My stomach fairly rumbled at the thought. My stepmother did not precisely starve me, but I ate last, and of everyone's leftovers, save for the bits that Claris slipped to me here and there.

Well, at least the Emperor liked slender girls, or so the rumors said…

Master Mellenden, the dancing instructor, arrived promptly at ten in the morning the next day. I heard my stepsisters groaning about the time scheduled for their lessons, as neither of them preferred to be up and dressed much sooner than luncheon, but on that point my stepmother put her foot down.

"That is the only time he has available!" she'd snapped, as I lingered in the background of the large salon, studiously dusting her collection of small enameled birds. They'd been quite the fad some years ago, apparently. In fact, the whole house had become quite cluttered due to her tendency to latch on to the newest and most fashionable mode, no matter how frivolous it might be. "Master Mellenden is highly in demand! It was either ten o'clock or nothing! Do you want to look like left-footed fools in front of the Emperor?"

Apparently neither of my stepsisters did, for at that comment they'd muttered and sighed and rolled their eyes, but did not offer any further argument. And so it was set that Master Mellenden would come three days a week for the next month.

He was a handsome fellow, somewhere in his early thirties, I thought, and I could see why he would be so in demand among the ladies of the town. My stepmother was lucky to get him, even at the unfashionable hour of ten in the morning.

Our house was not grand enough for a ballroom, but Janks and I rolled up the rug in the second salon and moved all the furniture against the walls, leaving enough space for several couples to dance there. My stepmother did most of her receiving in the main salon, and so having the smaller room out of commission for the next month probably would not discommode her too much.

Janks's service was not done there, either, for Master Mellenden declared that the only way for a young woman to learn to dance properly was with a man, and so the poor footman had to suffer through learning the *verdralle* and the *linotte* and the *padrane*, all the while handling both of my stepsisters as if they were made of eggshells. For their part, they tended to wear a look of disgust any time they were unlucky enough to be partnered with Janks rather than the dancing master, which I thought exceedingly ill-mannered of them...even though such behavior was only to be expected.

I, of course, could take no part in these proceedings, but could only pretend to be useful by fetching fresh water for them to drink, or to run and get Jenaris a new pair of slippers when she tore the stitching on hers, or to be there to open the windows when it became too warm and the girls declared they couldn't dance another step without some fresh air. To be sure, the air in Iselfex was none too fresh in early Sevendre, but I wasn't about to say such a thing out loud.

No, I only wanted to be present as much as possible so I could see how one was to place a hand on one's partner's shoulder during the *verdralle*, or how to do the complicated underhand turn during the *linotte*, or the way one must always start a dance with one's right foot first. All this, and so much more, catching a faint whisper of what the tunes must sound like when played by a full quintet and not the one pointy-faced young man Master Mellenden brought along with him to play the flute as accompaniment.

It all seemed so complicated, and yet wonderful at the same time. I was not completely unschooled; my father had had a dancing master for me when I was young, as well as a tutor to teach me how to read and write and figure. He had taught me how to ride a horse himself, not trusting anyone else to do it—and also because I thought he wanted any chance he could take to ride the fields of his beloved estate, and taking his young daughter out on her pony afforded him the opportunity to be out in the wind and the sun, and not cooped up in the house.

Even so, it had been many years since my last dancing lesson, and I drank in what I could and prayed it would be enough. I wished there were some way I could coerce Janks into practicing with me, but of course he would think it foolish of me to want to dance, and if Mari should ever catch us at it, even if he were to agree—I shuddered at the thought. No, best to commit the various steps to memory, the same way I had learnt my multiplication tables, and to hope I would be able to recall the *padrane* as easily as I could remember six times nine.

Besides Master Mellenden, there was Mistress Rhandil, the seamstress, who was in and out of the house so often I rather began to wonder whether she could have saved herself some time and taken up residence in one of the unused bedrooms on the third floor. And I didn't even want to think what all those bolts of shining fabric were costing, and the trims woven with precious metals, and the silk stockings and embroidered purses and feathered fans! True, last year had provided a bountiful harvest, and my stepmother always took the lion's share of such income from her tenants, but even so, I could not see how she was possibly able to afford all this.

Manners and etiquette cost nothing. That is, my stepmother's younger sister, who apparently had been quite the beauty in her day, had married a baron, and actually spent a good deal of time at court. Since she had borne only sons, she had no daughters who would be rivals for the Emperor's hand, and so she took it upon herself to pass on her own knowledge of the court.

"'Your Majesty,' of course, for the Emperor, and the dowager Empress. 'Your Highness' for the Crown Princess, 'Your Grace' for any dukes or duchesses who might be present. Anything below that, and you're safe with 'my lord' or 'my lady,' thank goodness," said Lady Khorinne, sipping from a delicate etched glass filled with rhubarb cordial. "If you are very lucky, and His Majesty takes a particular interest in you, then he may give you leave to address him by his given name, but of course you should never do such a thing unless you have a very clear invitation."

"And is he so very handsome?" sighed Shelynne, who apparently did not care much for titles and wanted to get to the heart of the matter.

"His Majesty is the handsomest man I ever saw," the Baroness declared at once. "Begging my husband's forgiveness, for of course he is a very fine man as well, but nothing next to the Emperor. You must count yourselves very lucky, girls, that he is being so magnanimous in giving this opportunity to the young women of his own land, instead of ignoring them in favor of a foreign princess."

Of course my stepsisters chimed in at once that yes, he was being so very generous, and that they could not wait to see him for themselves.

"Ah, well, not much longer," said the Baroness. "Only a week left, and so much to do!"

"Yes," my stepmother put in, with a significant glance at Jenaris' waistline, which had not diminished much over the preceding three weeks. "We must do everything we can to be ready."

At that point she sent me to the kitchen to fetch some cakes—"but none for you, Jenny!"— and so I missed the rest of the lesson. Just as well, for my mind was churning. Only one week left! And unlike my stepsisters, I had nothing I could outwardly do to prepare. My prayers, and my worries, I kept to myself.

The fateful day dawned cool and misty, a good sign, and a welcome respite from the heat that had dominated most of Sevendre. Almost from dawn the house was a flurry of frenzied activity, from drawing baths for my stepsisters to helping Claris prepare a morning meal that would provide sustenance without bloating them too much, to helping to lay out the elegant gowns prepared by Mistress Rhandil. As this first event was a tournament and would take place outdoors, the dresses were not quite as elaborate as the evening gowns and ball gowns they would wear later in the week, but still very fine—a dark blue dress trimmed with wheat-colored embroidery for Shelynne, and a burgundy one with soft gray embellishments for Jenaris. And after they were dressed, Mari spent almost an hour doing their hair, getting it to lie in sleek, shining curls over their shoulders, then setting the little caps made to match the gowns at precisely the correct angle on the backs of their heads.

Through all this hubbub I saw or heard nothing from my aunt, and began to wonder if she, too, had decided the enterprise was madness and had abandoned it. I should have known she was made of stouter stuff than that, for almost as soon as the hired carriage bearing my stepsisters rattled off down the street and I had gone out to the courtyard to pour out the used wash water, I heard a whisper from the unused stables.

"Ashara!"

I turned and saw my aunt's face peeking out from behind one of the stall doors, and quickly set down the basin I was carrying. After taking a quick look around to make sure I was unobserved, I slipped inside.

Aunt Therissa wore a hooded cloak, but she had slipped the hood back. Her dark eyes shone with excitement as she looked at me. "Are you ready?"

"I-I think so," I stammered. "That is, I have been watching my stepsisters practice their dance steps, and I know which fork to use first, and—"

"That is not what I asked," she said, interrupting me, although her tone was gentle. Her gaze met mine, and I found I could not look away. "Are you *ready?*"

My heart began to beat faster, and my fingers suddenly felt as if they had been carved from ice, but I managed to nod. "Yes, Aunt Therissa. I am ready."

A smile then, although I could not say whether it blazed forth because she was relieved I had not backed out at the last minute, or simply because I had called her by her name for the first time. "Good. You are your mother's daughter after all." Once again she murmured words I could not understand under her breath.

I looked down and saw I wore a gown of heavy russet silk, almost the color of my hair, with a subtle pattern of leaves woven into the fabric. Trim of copper and bronze edged the sleeves, and fine lace peeked above the edge of the low-cut— but not too low-cut, as this was a daytime event—bodice.

"Beautiful," she breathed. "He will see no one else, once he catches a glimpse of you."

"I rather doubt that," I said dryly, but she only laughed.

"Very well, I will leave that to the gods, but you must be off. I have a carriage waiting just down the street. Hurry!" And even as she said that last word she muttered something else, and I was looking back at myself, down to the fingernail I had newly broken that morning and the fresh burn along the edge of one hand, from carelessness with a bread pan still hot from the oven.

I stared, but she only shook her head. "'Tis nothing that you haven't seen before. Now go, and make me proud! Just be sure to be back before twelve hours have passed, for I can't hold the spell any longer than that!"

As I didn't trust myself to speak, I only nodded, then slipped out of the stables. No one was watching, no doubt still occupied with cleaning up the aftermath of my stepsisters' preparations, and so I was able to steal away unobserved. The promised carriage waited a few doors down, and I hurried toward it, accepting the hand of the driver as he lifted me into its interior as if I had done that sort of thing every day. After all, this was my first test. I must make him believe I belonged here, or certainly no one else would.

But he only bowed, and shut the door behind me, then moved on to take his perch up front. I heard him chirrup to the horses, and the carriage began to move forward. Clenching my hands in my lap, I willed myself to be calm.

No matter what happened, there was no going back now.

CHAPTER FOUR

Torric

"Well, I see you've managed to make a spectacle of things once again," my mother commented in the acid tones she'd perfected over the years. "How on earth are you going to choose one young woman from all *that*?" And she pointed with her fan of carved ebony and peacock plumes in the direction of the milling crowd, one that was far more weighted toward the female sex than any crowd at a tournament generally might be.

Of course I would never admit such a thing to her, but I did begin to wonder if she had a point. We had estimated and we had guessed, but we hadn't known for sure until we opened the gates to the tourney field exactly how many prospective brides might answer the summons. Judging by the brightly dressed throng below, it had to be at least four hundred.

Lyarris, ever the diplomat, leaned forward and smiled at Mother, something I was rarely able to do. "I daresay it looks rather overwhelming from up here. But I trust Torric to sort them out quickly enough. After all, you won't give anyone who isn't handsome a second look, will you, brother?"

I shot her a sour glance then, even though I knew she was probably right. After all, what was the point of such an exercise if I ended up with a plain wife? Certainly somewhere among that mass of young women, even now heading toward their seats in the stands, there must be one who was lovely in addition to being intelligent and charming. That couldn't be too much to ask.

However, I did not deign to reply, but instead scanned the crowds, although at this distance attempting to pick out any true details of their faces and figures was difficult. Here and there I thought I saw a girl whose countenance seemed pretty, or whose person promised to be pleasing. But none of them stood out all that much, and I began to wonder if this tournament had been that wise an idea. True, at the end, after the victor had been crowned, we would all move to a series of pavilions set up beyond the fields, where we would take refreshment, but that was some hours off. And in the meantime I would have to sit up here in the imperial box and pretend to be interested in the doings of the horses and their riders.

Ah, well, better to be up here than down there, sweating under the heavy mail and perspiring even more in concentration. I recalled those days all too clearly; my father had of course made sure I had thorough training in arms, although the chances of my ever having to lead an army into battle were slender enough. At any rate, I had enough experience that I knew it was far more pleasant to be watching the clash of arms, rather than down on the field collecting a new set of bruises that would last for days.

I did note a distinct lack of brightly colored favors fluttering from the warriors' belts or their sleeves. Most of the men gathered to display their battle prowess today were younger and unmarried, but I wagered that most of the young ladies who were similarly unattached had not wished to bestow their favors upon mere knights or even baronets or dukes' sons...not when they had set their sights on an attachment far more lofty than that.

"Ah, quite the turnout," came Lord Keldryn's falsely hearty tones from behind me. I glanced over my shoulder to see him bowing to my mother and my sister, then rising as he surreptitiously wiped at his face with a silk handkerchief, though the day had turned out to be fairly mild.

"My son is quite the prize," my mother replied, a response that would have sounded neutral to almost anyone else. However, I caught the edge of irony in her tone, and forced myself to remain silent, to act as if I were still engrossed in watching the milling crowd below me.

Although I had decided to let it go, it appeared my sister had not, for she said at once, "Of course he is a prize, and would be even if he weren't the Emperor."

My mother lifted an eyebrow, and I held myself still, wondering which salvo she would launch next. But apparently she did not wish to cause a scene in so public a place, for she said only, "Lord Keldryn, my chair, if you would."

The chancellor hurried to pull the seat out for her, and even waited to make sure her skirts were all disposed of gracefully before he bowed once again and backed away. Good gods, the man was an earl in his own right, and not one of the footmen. But no one dared gainsay Korrelia Deveras, not even the chancellor.

And, most of the time, not even her son.

Frowning, I took my own seat, and Lyarris settled herself beside me, easily and with no assistance, though her gown was quite as elaborate as our mother's. My sister wore an expression of pleasant neutrality, but I could tell from the glint in her eye and the small twitch at the edge of her jaw that she was not quite as placid as she appeared to be.

Ah, sister, I love you, but I do not need you to fight my battles for me...

By this point most of the crowd had settled itself on the long rows of benches in the stands, and I saw the first two combatants readying themselves at the far end of the field, raising their helmets in place, taking up the lances their squires had handed them. Still, there were a few latecomers hurrying to get the remaining few seats, their gowns bright against the dry autumn grass and the low fence of whitewashed wood that surrounded the ring.

A gleam of dark copper caught my eye, and I saw a young woman with an astonishing head of dark red hair making her way along the path that led to the stands. Even in profile her face appeared pure and lovely, although I could not make out any exact detail from so far away. Her gown was almost the same dark russet as her hair, her body slender and graceful. There seemed something almost hesitant in the way she looked about her, as if she were not quite sure she belonged there. Not all that surprising, if she were some nobleman's daughter freshly in from the country. Still, something about her diffidence made her immediately endearing. I found myself wanting to go down to her, to reassure her that of course she was welcome here, that someone so beautiful would always be welcome in my court.

However, I knew if I rose from my seat now, so close to the beginning of the tournament, it would be a severe breach of etiquette. No, I would have to remain here and hope to find her again, and soon. Not that it should prove all that difficult; her hair, so rare and so lovely, would make her stand out in any crowd.

"You've spied someone, I think," Lyarris murmured, her own gaze intent on the scene before us.

"I did," I replied, in equally subdued tones. "Did you see her? The girl with the red hair?"

"Red hair? That is interesting. No, I did not."

My gaze followed where she was looking, and thought I could guess at the source of her distraction. Up in the first round was Lord Sorthannic Sedassa, Duke of Marric's Rest. I had thought for several months my sister had evinced some interest in the man, although she had said nothing on the topic.

It might not be a bad match, even though the duke's mother was a commoner. But with his sister now wed to the Mark of North Eredor, there could be some political expediency there, above and beyond the weight normally given to a duke and lord of one of the empire's greatest estates.

Well, time enough to think on that later. This tournament and the events scheduled to follow it had been planned with the goal of finding me a wife, not my sister a husband, and I doubted Lord Sorthannic would marry himself off in the next week. There had been no whisper of a betrothal there, or even an attachment. He was still newly come to his inheritance, having been lord of Marric's Rest for barely a year, and no doubt he wished to feel easy in his new position before taking on the added responsibility of a wife.

But when I looked away from the field, back toward the stands, I found I had lost sight of the redheaded young woman. The stands were covered by enormous sail-like structures of canvas, and the shadows they cast were enough to dull the hair of everyone sitting beneath them, making it impossible to detect the girl I sought.

"I am sure she is still there somewhere," Lyarris said, a hint of amusement in her voice. "Be patient."

"I am patient," I replied, and settled myself back in the throne-like chair I used for outdoor events such as this. "I am just finding myself wondering who thought it would be a good idea to start off this whole thing with a tournament."

She refused to be baited. "I believe I proposed it, Torric, but you did not gainsay the idea, so I thought you found it favorable enough."

"I did…at the time."

"Well, do try to put on a somewhat pleasant expression, brother, for a scowl such as the one you're currently wearing will only make everyone who came today think you are not pleased with the turnout."

I hadn't realized I was frowning, but her gentle admonishment did remind me that I should not act like a spoiled child deprived of his favorite toy, but rather the ruler of the greatest country in the world. Settling back in my chair, I glanced past Lord Keldryn, who had taken a seat behind my mother, to where Lord Hein, my seneschal, stood watchful in a corner of the imperial box. I knew it was no use to ask him to take a seat; he would remain alert, on duty, ready to remedy anything that might go amiss during the day's festivities. Indeed, I wondered whether he had slept at all the night before...or whether he planned to sleep until the five days of celebrations were over and done.

"My Lord Hein, we are ready," I said formally.

"Excellent, Your Majesty." He moved to the front of the box and lifted his right hand—the signal to the heralds, who lifted their horns and played a brief, stirring succession of notes.

At once the first two combatants—Lord Sorthannic and another knight whose device I did not recognize, a spreading blackthorn tree on a yellow background—entered the ring and bowed to the imperial box, and to the watching crowd in the stands. Then they took their places at opposite sides of the field, lances held at the ready.

"A wager, Lyarris?" I asked in an undertone. "I believe you would place your bet on the Duke of Marric's Rest."

The smallest turn of her head toward me, and she raised her eyebrows. "Torric, you know I do not gamble. It is enough to watch and see their skills in action."

I repressed a laugh. "Very well, play it cool if you must... but I will see if you are still this disinterested come the ball four days hence, if Lord Sorthannic should ask you to join him in a *verdralle*."

This time she said nothing, but the brief color that flamed along her cheekbones told me all I needed to know.

Smiling a little to myself, I returned my attention to the field. Truly, though he was new to his title and indeed to Sirlende itself, having lived here for only the past seven years or so, I knew that Sorthannic Sedassa was a worthy foe on the field. He had been schooled in the tournament arts by none other than Lord Senric Torrival, the Duke of Gahm himself, who once dominated the field before he decided he had broken enough bones and that now a younger generation should prevail.

The marshal dropped the red flag, signaling that it was time for the battle to commence, and the two combatants leapt forward on their mounts, lances pointed outward. Of course, those lances had dulled points, guaranteeing that no warrior would be carried lifeless from the field, as had happened a time or ten in the days before we became more civilized about such things, but even so, a good solid blow could leave a combatant with bruises for some time, even if he was lucky enough to maintain his seat.

A mighty crash, and I saw that the unknown knight with the blackthorn device had already lost his shield, it being splintered by a direct blow from Lord Sorthannic's lance. The crowd applauded and cheered, and the two riders wheeled back to their respective corners so they might make another pass.

Once again the great warhorses charged toward one another, the blackthorn knight having been re-outfitted with a new shield. But that shield didn't seem to bring him any fresh luck, for once again the Duke of Marric's Rest made a direct hit, this time with such force that his opponent was knocked clean off his horse. At once the Duke pulled his own mount to a stop, so the blackthorn knight might regain his seat, but after a moment it seemed clear that the man was in no condition to continue the match.

The custom at this point was for the victor to withdraw, so the other man's squires and seconds might see to his needs, but apparently Lord Sorthannic was not one for custom. He dismounted, and went to the fallen knight, offering his hand so the man might regain his feet. The knight took it, nodding, then opened his arms to the watching audience, as if to show that he had taken no lasting hurt.

At once the crowd exploded in cheers, cheers that only grew louder as the heralds announced the Duke of Marric's Rest as the winner of the first round. After a brief exchange, the two men bowed to one another and exited the ring.

"Quite the gentleman, your duke," I told my sister.

"He is not 'my' duke, as you know all too well. Still," she added, and this time she could not quite keep the admiration from her voice, try as she might to sound neutral, "it was quite noble of him to offer assistance in such a way."

"Quite," I agreed, and covered up a smile by gesturing to one of the servants who stood nearby and asking for a glass of wine.

Lyarris muttered something just then, a word I couldn't catch but which sounded suspiciously like "impossible."

Well, I'd been called worse things, I supposed.

Some hours passed, and some of the skirmishes were quite fierce—fiercer than such an event called for, one would think—but in the end it was Lord Sorthannic who prevailed, and who took for his troubles a handsome purse of a hundred golden crowns, although I doubted he had much need of it. Indeed, I heard later that he had asked for his winnings to be distributed to those establishments throughout the city which undertook to care for the poor. If such a gesture had been made by almost anyone else, I would have questioned its motives, for it seemed a little too pure, too selfless. But the Duke of Marric's Rest, though I did not know him well, did not seem the type to be playing at politics. Indeed, I guessed he was only present in Iselfex now because it would have looked odd for such a peer of the realm not to take part in the festivities.

But after all that was done, and His Grace had retired along with the other combatants to tidy up for the reception, I rose from my seat and offered Lyarris my hand. "Time to see the candidates at last."

Almost as one the other nobles sitting in the box rose as well, for of course they could not remain seated in the presence of the Emperor. Lyarris smiled, and took my proffered fingers, getting up with a graceful rustle of her silken skirts.

"The moment you've been waiting for," she replied.

"I will admit to some curiosity."

"Only some? Then I mistook the gleam in your eyes when you mentioned the girl with the red hair."

I bowed slightly, acknowledging the jab, then straightened, my expression sobering as our mother drew near.

"Whatever you're whispering about, stop," she told us with a fearsome frown. "It is not seemly for the Emperor and the Crown Princess of Sirlende to be trading secrets like little girls passing notes in the schoolroom."

Ah, Mother, what a singular gift you have for sucking all the joy out of an occasion. But I only treated her to a bow as well, then said, "I fear you have caught me, Mother, for I was teasing Lyarris about her particular interest in the Duke of Marric's Rest."

At my words my sister's eyes widened, and she said hastily, "And teasing is all it was, I assure you."

A sniff. "Well, I suppose you could do worse, for all that his mother was a nobody out of South Eredor. At least he is a duke...and unattached."

After making this last salvo, she sailed past, Lord Hein trailing nervously after her. Gods forbid if she should find anything amiss with his preparations—the pavilions not sufficient for the crowds, the iced wine not adequately leavened with fresh fruit. I certainly could find no fault with anything so far, but my mother excelled at picking things apart until she found something to dissatisfy her.

I looked over at my sister, whose normally serene expression appeared somewhat cloudy around the edges. That "unattached" comment had been intended to wound, I had no doubt—a reference to the Earl of Fallyn's son, who had decided that he loved another.

"Never mind what Mother says," I remarked, and took Lyarris' arm so that I might help her out of the somewhat cramped box.

"I try not to, but sometimes…" She faltered, but then lifted her chin and essayed a bright, false smile, as we had just emerged into the hazy afternoon sunlight, and were in full view of the watching crowds. They would wait in their seats, as custom required, until we had taken our places in the great pavilions set up to house the festivities.

I gave her arm a slight reassuring squeeze. "Sometimes it is difficult, I know."

We made our way along the hard-packed earth of the path that followed the perimeter of the jousting field, on past the stands and into the welcome shade of the first of the pavilions, the silver and black of the imperial banner fluttering from a hard spire of dark iron at its apex. Ten guards had fallen in around us as we walked, but I was so used to such things that I hardly paid them attention anymore. Still, neither my sister nor I said anything further until we entered the pavilion, when Lyarris looked around and exclaimed,

"Oh, it's lovely!"

Truly, it was. As with the guards, I was so used to the pomp and splendor of living in the palace that I tended not to notice the luxuries around me, but here was beauty of a different sort. Autumn flowers and leaves in warm tones swagged the support braces, and more flowers and fruits had been set out in intricate arrangements on the tables, which fairly groaned with food, even though this had been intended as a simple reception and not a full meal. Apparently Lord Hein had a different concept of "simple" than I did.

I saw the gentleman himself standing off to one side, appearing to hold his breath as my mother inspected the spread for herself. Hoping to forestall any criticisms, I went to him at once and said, "You truly have exceeded my expectations, Lord Hein. If this is what you have managed to accomplish on the first day of the festivities, I can only imagine what is to come on the next four!"

He bowed deeply, relief clear on his lean features. "Your praise is most welcome, Your Majesty."

"Has the wine been properly iced, Hein?" my mother inquired. "It is such a warm day, I am sure it will all melt before an hour has passed."

A quick apologetic look at me. I nodded slightly, and the seneschal turned to my mother, saying, "We have put by a great store, Your Majesty, so I am quite sure that it will last the afternoon. Here, let me put your fears to rest."

And he fetched her a goblet himself, although of course a man of his stature should not be performing such a duty— servitors lined the canvas walls of the pavilion, standing ready to fetch and carry as need be. Then again, my mother always did take pleasure in exercising her own power whenever the opportunity presented itself.

As it seemed the offering of iced wine and fruit was enough to placate her for the nonce, I caught Lord Hein's eye and said, "And the candidates…?"

"Ah, yes, Your Majesty. My staff is directing them now to their designated locations. We have counted four hundred and twenty-seven, so we are dividing them into groups of a little more than one hundred each and guiding them to the four other pavilions. This one will be kept for the use of the

Imperial household only, should you wish to escape the crush if necessary."

My mouth twitched, but it appeared he did not notice, or at least affected not to. "Excellent plan, Lord Hein."

"Yes, you must needs have a hidey-hole to flee the throngs of adoring would-be brides," Lyarris murmured, suppressed laughter clear in her voice.

"Hush, or I'll have Mother down on you again."

This threat had the quelling effect I had hoped for, as she fell silent at once. Still, her dark eyes were dancing, and I was glad to see it. At least our mother's casually cruel remark had not made a lasting impression.

Now that the moment had come, I actually experienced a few pangs of nervousness. Foolish, of course. I was the Emperor of Sirlende, and they were merely girls, young women who of course would be on their best behavior.

But there were so *very* many of them…

Still, there was nothing for it. I took in a breath, then walked a pace or two, at which point I stopped and looked back at my sister, who had not moved.

"Are you not coming with me?"

"I am not the one in search of a wife, Torric," she said calmly. "I think it better that I stay here, in the imperial pavilion, whilst you make your rounds. It is safer, for the last thing I want is some girl from the country who has never been to the capital to think me a rival for your attentions."

"Traitor," I replied, but I winked at her, to show her that I meant for the word to have no bite.

She gave me the warrior's salute then, one fist to her breast as she bowed toward me. "Seize the day, brother."

"I have no doubt of that."

Any further exchange would be seen as a delaying tactic, so I turned away from her once again and made my way to the next pavilion over, which had been set up some ten yards from the one secured for imperial use. Four guards accompanied me, although what they could do to protect me from a horde of over-zealous noblemen's daughters, I was not certain.

As I approached I heard an excited chatter of feminine voices, a hubbub which stilled almost immediately as I entered the large tent.

Good gods, there really were more than a hundred of them. Of course I had spent my whole life at court events where those in attendance numbered far more than that, but the young women seemed so concentrated in that smallish space, especially when one considered that I, the four guards attending me, and the four other servants pressed up against the walls were the only men in the place.

Such a sea of glinting color and staring eyes and shining dark hair! Quickly I scanned the group, but I saw no flash of russet among that crowd of black and dark brown. This was only the first pavilion, I reminded myself, and I should not be surprised that she was not here.

The young women were silent, staring at me, and although I had ridden in parades and reviews, traversed the narrow streets of my capital with all eyes on me, somehow that attention had not seemed as intimate, as focused as what greeted me now. Several of the girls had their mouths hanging open slightly, as if they were not quite sure they believed what they were seeing.

Before the silence could become too awkward, I said smoothly, "Greetings, ladies. I thank you for coming, and invite you to partake of the hospitality offered. There is wine, and fruit, and sweetmeats and cheeses and breads. Come, we are here to get to know one another. Mingle, I beg you."

Perhaps the notion of the Emperor of Sirlende begging them to do anything was too much. I heard a few nervous giggles, followed by some whispered exchanges, and at least several of the bolder girls moved toward the refreshment tables. As if a spell had been broken, the servants sprang into action, filling goblets, handing over small silver plates heaped with delicacies.

Somehow I thought I would have rather waded into the thick of battle than plunge into that group of suddenly lively young women, but my sister was right—I had brought this on myself. Recalling the falsely bright smile she had given the crowds just a few moments earlier, I assumed one of my own and made my way into the throng, nodding as names were thrown at me from all sides—"Marika Tredaris, Your Majesty"—"Alanna Krendil, Your Majesty"—and knowing I would never be able to retain enough to match a face to a name.

Not that it mattered, as none of them were the girl I sought.

I spent a little less than an hour in the first tent, then made my excuses and hastened to the second pavilion. Perhaps she would be there.

But no, once again the red-haired young woman eluded me, and I was forced to spend another hour smiling and nodding and acting as if I would recall them all, when in fact they were all a blur to me. Several were quite pretty, and others seemed charming and sweet, but none of them made any deep impression. It was as if, once I had seen the girl with the gleaming dark-copper hair, I had eyes for no one else.

The third pavilion was a repeat of the first and second, and inwardly I began to despair, wondering if she had left early, had looked upon the crowds and become intimidated, had slipped away before she ever came to one of the great tents. After all, she had looked oddly hesitant, unsure of herself. I could see how a shy girl might be overwhelmed by such a proceeding, especially when she must come unaccompanied by a parent or even a maidservant.

My footsteps were slower as I approached the final pavilion, some of my eagerness gone. In my mind I had already convinced myself that she had left, and that I would have to settle for one of these other girls, none of whom had so far captured my fancy. I entered the tent, and again the voices of the young women went silent immediately as they stared at me. This group seemed more wary, and I thought I could understand why—after all, they had been waiting for some time for me to make my appearance.

"My ladies, my deepest apologies for making you wait so many hours. I do hope that you have found the refreshments pleasing, and that you have not been made too uncomfortable by the wait. It is my—"

I had been about to say that it was a very great pleasure to meet them all, empty words, if necessary ones, but my breath seemed to catch in my throat. At last I had found her.

She stood off to one side and toward the back, but by some miracle there was an open space before her, so I was able to see her face clearly this time, see the rosebud fullness of her mouth and her pretty little nose and the unusual amber-green of her eyes beneath the arched russet brows. For the time it took my heart to beat three times, our gazes caught and held. I saw her make an odd little gesture toward her throat, as if she, too, found it hard to breathe. And then a tall girl took a step or two to her right, and the young woman I had sought was obscured again, the contact broken.

Still, it was enough. She was here. She had not fled, or decided the throng was too much competition for her. Ah, no. There could have been four thousand girls here today, instead of merely four hundred, and they still would not have offered her any true challenge.

But although I wished to go directly to her, to ignore the eager faces of all the other young women, I knew that would be a churlish thing to do. Oh, I would speak to her, no doubt of that. It would have to appear unforced, however, something which occurred naturally as I made my rounds in the pavilion. How long that would take, I did not know, and the wait would most likely be excruciating, but eventually I would meet her.

And how I would have to pretend that I was interested in anyone else, after I had seen her, I had no idea.

I did guess, however, that the next four days were going to feel very long indeed, if I could not spend them all exclusively with her.

CHAPTER FIVE

Ashara

Oh, he truly was the handsomest man I had ever seen. I had thought surely the stories must be exaggerations, that everyone said the Emperor was so very attractive simply because he was, well, the Emperor. But no, now that I had seen him, I thought in truth that the stories had not been effusive enough in their praise.

The wait had been unbearable, standing in this stuffy pavilion for the greater part of three hours, sipping sparingly at the iced wine so I should not get tipsy, eating just as carefully of the foods put out, which were far richer than what I was used to. The last thing I wanted was to make myself ill with sweetmeats and cheese.

I had hoped to make the acquaintance of some of the other girls, to help pass the time a little more comfortably, but none of them seemed inclined to be friendly, and indeed several of them had flashed me openly hostile glares. Perhaps it was that none of them knew me; I saw several of them chattering with one another, and guessed they must know each other from court, or perhaps if their families' estates bordered one another. I had no such acquaintances to fall back upon, and so tried to make myself as inconspicuous as possible, staying away from the refreshment tables and trying not to think of the hours passing, and of my aunt having to suffer my stepmother's whims. I could only hope that my stepmother had been so wearied by getting Jenaris and Shelynne ready that she had taken to her bed soon after they left, thus leaving Aunt Therissa to manage only my kitchen duties.

At least you have had some luck, I told myself, *for neither of your stepsisters are here, and it would not have been much fun to attempt to avoid them for the greater part of three hours.* True, with so many girls divided amongst four pavilions, the odds had not been terribly high that we would end up in the same place. Still, it was a relief, not having to dodge them.

But then I knew the weary hours of waiting had been worth it, for he entered the pavilion at last. All conversations stopped dead as he apologized for the wait, and told us that he hoped it had not been too terrible. And he paused suddenly, his dark eyes seeming to pierce the crowd to meet mine. I could scarcely breathe. I could do nothing, but stare back at him, taking in the fine sculpted lines of his jaw, the straight strong nose, the sooty black hair held back from his brow by a circlet of gold. How tall he was, and how broad the shoulders under the doublet of fine figured silk in a deep wine shade!

The moment passed, and he seemed to find his voice, to speak quite normally to the girls to either side of him, some commonplace about being glad that the day was not too warm, and that he hoped they found the iced wine to their liking. They giggled and simpered and hastened to say that everything was just so, and how kind of him to be so concerned for their comfort. And I found my hand tightening around the stem of the silver goblet I held as a wave of irritation passed over me. Did they know how foolish they sounded, how empty-headed and silly?

I was surprised at myself, for I had never been the jealous sort. Then again, what opportunities for jealousy had ever presented themselves to me? Oh, I envied my stepsisters their warm beds and their pretty clothes and new shoes, but that was different. Some might say I had only been desiring things that should have been mine as well. After all, it was my father's wealth, the rents from my father's estate, that paid for their gowns and shoes and hair ribbons.

This feeling, though—this was different. I wanted to be the one talking to him, although I hoped I would not tilt my head in such a silly way, nor giggle and blush, if I should be lucky enough to exchange words with him.

He passed through the crowd, smiling as he went, although as he drew closer I thought I could see some strain in his face, some weariness at having to maintain so many conversations at once. And I thought of how many other such exchanges he must have had this afternoon, in all the other pavilions, before he ever came here. The poor man must want nothing more at the moment than to get away from all of us, to be someplace where he could have some peace at last.

But then he was there, standing only a few feet away. Immediately I dropped a curtsey, and hoped it did not look too clumsy. I had been practicing, but without a mirror or anyone to give me any direction, I had no idea whether the honor was passable or not. "Your Majesty," I murmured.

"Ah, I had told everyone that we might dispense with such things, but it appears you all are determined to maintain the proprieties." His voice was warm and rich, with an edge of amusement to it. "Your name, milady?"

"Ashara Millende, Your Majesty."

He nodded. "A lovely name for a lovely young woman."

I could feel a flush rise in my cheeks, and I saw several of the girls in my vicinity shoot dagger-sharp glares at me. He had been universally pleasant and charming so far, but this was the first time I had heard him utter a compliment to anyone. And for it to be directed at me—

"I thank you, Your Majesty."

"And have you been enjoying yourself, Ashara?"

Of course I could not tell him the truth, that I had been alternately bored and uncomfortable for most of the afternoon. It was not his fault—if I had not been so late, then perhaps I could have been in the group included in the first pavilion, and therefore not had to wait until the very last to see him.

A pleasant lie seemed the best response. "Yes, I have, Your Majesty. Everything has just been lovely."

"Excellent." He paused, and it seemed as if he intended to say something more, but then he smiled at a pair of girls standing a few paces away from me, and turned to them to ask how they fared.

Disappointment flared in me, but I knew he simply could not spend any more time with me than he already had. I would have to be satisfied with that brief exchange— and really, it was far more than many of the other girls had gotten.

Indeed, it appeared I was not the only one who thought so, for as soon as the Emperor was out of earshot, two girls turned on me with sour expressions, the taller one demanding, "How is it that you should command so much of his attention? For I have never seen you at court."

Her tone was imperious, and, judging by the matched set of rubies around her neck and hanging from her ears, she was clearly from a family of some importance. For a second or two I wanted to cower, sure that she would catch some whiff of the kitchens about me and turn me in for the impostor I was. But then I reminded myself that I certainly appeared to all watching eyes to be as well-dressed as she, and she could have no idea of my true situation.

"As to that, my lady, I cannot say. I would not presume to second-guess what His Majesty does." I shrugged, and I could see the strange girl's eyes narrow as she took in the richness of my gown. "Perhaps you will be luckier tomorrow, and he will wish you a good day then."

Her mouth tightened. Under most circumstances I would have said she was pretty enough, with her long-lashed dark eyes and rosy cheeks, but her expression was anything but pleasant. "Do you have any idea who I am?"

"As to that, I do not...although I am sure you are about to enlighten me."

She drew herself up. Standing thus, she was perhaps an inch or two taller than I, although I did not care too much for such minor differences. "I am Brinda Aldrenne, daughter of Baron Lhastir Aldrenne. And who are you?"

I made myself shrug, although inwardly I found myself glad that she was the daughter of a baron, and not a duke. Yes, she outranked me, but not by as much as I had feared. "If you did not hear me when I gave His Majesty my name, then I shall repeat it for you if I must. I am Ashara Millende, and my father was Allyn Millende, a baronet."

A little light of triumph gleamed in her eyes. It seemed she thought the difference between baron and baronet to be somewhat greater than I did. She sniffed. "I have never heard of him."

"No, I suppose you wouldn't have. He was never overly fond of town, and so we did not travel here often." I paused, then looked her up and down before adding, "And now I am beginning to see why he did not care to spend much time in the capital. If you will excuse me."

I sketched a curtsey and hurried away, moving to the refreshment table as if that were the sole reason for my leave-taking. In truth, though, my heart pounded, and I could feel my hand shaking as I extended it to one of the servants so he might refill my goblet.

Whence had come such boldness, I could not say. Certainly I had not been trained to stand up for myself. My existence heretofore had depended on staying in the background, on never uttering a word that might seem forward, let alone impertinent. But I found I did not much care for how Brinda Aldrenne had addressed me, and it seemed quite a natural thing for me to stick up for myself. Here there would be no consequences; indeed, it might have been a wise move for me to assert myself early on, so that those watching would know that I was not some meek milksop to be trodden upon in their quest to catch the Emperor's eye.

Even so, I took a large swallow of wine to steady my nerves, and was glad then of the crush around me, so I was hidden from Brinda Aldrenne's no doubt narrowed eyes.

"Nicely done," came an unfamiliar voice, and I turned to see a girl with tip-tilted dark eyes and quite beautiful curly black hair grinning at me.

"I beg your pardon?" I replied. My tone was probably sharper than it should have been, but that exchange with Brinda had put me on edge.

"The way you put Miss High-and-Mighty Aldrenne in her place. That's something a good number of us have been longing to do for years." Another quick flash of a smile, and she dipped a hasty curtsey. "I'm Gabrinne Nelandre, daughter of the Earl of Kelsir—but I promise I won't mention it again after this. And you said your name was Ashara?"

"Y-es," I said uncertainly. True, the girl seemed friendly enough, but after witnessing Brinda's hostility, I did not know quite what to expect.

"Splendid," Gabrinne replied. "And that hair of yours! I saw how he was staring at you—the rest of us might as well pack up and go home. Not that I care. I'm only here because my father said I must, but I certainly don't want to marry the Emperor."

"You don't?" After seeing him, I could not understand why anyone wouldn't wish to be his wife.

"No, I have far better prey in mind. But—" She broke off then, for there was some commotion in the pavilion, and we both paused to see what was happening.

It appeared the Emperor, having made his circuit, was now taking his leave of us. A low murmur of discontent ran through the crowd, and he raised his hand and said, "It has been quite the afternoon for all of us, but we will all meet again soon—tomorrow evening at the palace, for a great feast. But until then, my ladies." And he bowed, then smiled, his features illuminated so by that smile it seemed as if the very sun itself shone within the pavilion.

Then he was gone. Almost at once the exodus began, everyone eager to be out of the stuffy tent, now that the reason for being there had left. Gabrinne turned to me and said, "Well, it appears that is that. But I will look for you tomorrow night, and you must look for me, so we might sit together. It will be amusing to have someone new to talk to. I am so dreadfully bored by most of the girls at court. You, however—you seem different somehow. Until then!" She reached out and gave my hand a quick squeeze before making her way through the crowd.

I stared after her, a little startled by her brash comments, then shook my head. At least she was friendly, and had not seemed to notice anything terribly out of place about me. It would be good to face a grand dinner in the palace itself with an amiable companion at my side.

For now, though—now I would have to get myself home, where I knew the atmosphere would be far from amiable.

My aunt had left instructions with the coachman to wait until I had emerged, and so he was still there when I approached, in an area off to one side of the tourney field choked with other carriages and open hacks and the odd horse, apparently belonging to some young women whose families had not the means to maintain a coach. Whence mine had come from, I did not know, but I was glad that my aunt had foreseen that need and managed it somehow.

The man handed me up into the carriage, and I settled myself on the worn leather seat, at last allowing myself a sigh of relief as he shut the door and went forward to take up the reins. I had survived my first day, and no one had called me out as a fraud, or indeed found anything particularly exceptional about me.

Well, save perhaps the Emperor…

A shiver went over my body as I recalled the warmth in his dark eyes as he had gazed at me, thought of the rich timbre of his voice and the easy courtesy with which he had treated everyone. Truth be told, I had not expected that of him. Somehow I had thought an Emperor must be haughty and cold, certain of his position, his utter superiority. That notion had some basis in fact, for I had heard he could be short of temper at times, hasty with those who displeased him, with little patience for fools. But I had seen none of that today.

Well, of course not. He would be on his best behavior, wouldn't he, when seeking the young woman who would become his wife?

True. Somehow, though, I thought it was more than that.

And while Brinda had been anything but kind, Gabrinne had seemed as if she might be someone I would enjoy spending time with. It had been so very long since I had a friend. There had been Alysse, many, many years ago, before my father died, but I had not seen her these ten years and more. Of course I could never tell Gabrinne the truth about myself. Even so, it would be enough to have someone to talk to, to help me face the next four days. I did not flatter myself that I would be the Emperor's eventual choice—yes, he seemed to have found me pretty, but I was not quite so unworldly as to believe he would not eventually choose someone of higher status, the daughter of a duke…or perhaps an earl, no matter what Gabrinne might say to the contrary.

In the meantime, though, I could at least enjoy wearing fine gowns…even if they were no more substantial than my hopes of an imperial match…and also enjoy being away from my stepmother's house. The smile that had been playing about my lips faded then, as I wondered what my poor aunt had been forced to suffer while wearing my guise. Not too much, I hoped; with both my stepsisters out of the house for a good portion of the day, the workload had to have been reduced somewhat.

That led me to wonder what would be the best way to sneak back in and trade places with my aunt, so she might slip away without anyone noticing that aught was amiss. At least now dusk was upon us, and the dimmer light would afford me a better opportunity to enter the property. Through the back gates, I decided, which were latched but never locked. It would be close enough to suppertime that Janks should be indoors, and not out in his room next to the stables. Since that was where we had met this morning, I guessed it was also where my aunt would attempt to see me...if she were allowed a free moment.

Well, I told myself, *she seems to have planned all this out more or less, so you will have to hope that she has her own means of knowing when you are back.*

More magic, no doubt...

The carriage stopped more or less where it had picked me up earlier in the day, around the curve of the street from the house, in a spot where I would not be easily seen. The coachman came around to help me out, and said, "I'll be here again tomorrow evening, my lady. Your aunt said an hour after dusk. Is that correct?"

I nodded, hoping the time was right. I had no real idea, since the Emperor had not given an exact hour for his dinner. Everyone seemed to know; perhaps there was always a set time for formal dinners in the palace, something all those noble-born girls would already be aware of. How my aunt had access to that information, I was not sure, but as she seemed to know a great many things, once again I would have to trust her intelligence on this matter as well.

After that, the coach clattered away, and I was left to huddle in the shadows along the wall, and move quickly and quietly to the back gate, my shaking fingers finding the leather thong that would lift the latch. All the while I feared this would be the one time Claris sent Janks out back to fetch something, and he would find me, and all would be lost.

But he did not come, and I was able to make my way without incident across the uneven flagstones of the courtyard and into the stables, where I shut the door quietly and then leaned against the wall, taking in deep breaths of air that still smelled faintly of straw, and wondering how on earth I could possibly go through all these machinations four more times.

"You look so wearied, one would think it was you who had been scrubbing floors and beating rugs all day," came my aunt's wry voice.

I started, and turned to see her standing in the doorway, her arms crossed and an amused expression on her—on *my*—face. Even as I watched, however, I saw her features seem to shift and melt, and then it was my aunt looking back at me, now in a simple but well-made gown of dark grey silk...silk which now appeared to have several fresh spots on it, though I could not tell for sure, with only the faint light from the kitchen windows to keep the rapidly approaching night at bay.

She seemed to notice where I was looking, and reached down and spread her stained skirts. "Oh, bother," she said in rueful tones. "I hadn't even stopped to think about that. I shall have to make sure I wear my oldest gowns the rest of this week. But never mind—how was it? Did you meet *him*?"

I nodded. "Yes, and you were right, for he was so very handsome—and kind, too—and he even said I was lovely, when I did not hear him give a compliment to any of the other girls!"

Her face lit up at my words. "Oh, that is excellent news, and precisely what I was hoping for. I can only imagine that it will get even better from here, for now he seems to have noticed you particularly, and will no doubt seek you out tomorrow as well." She went past me and into one of the empty stalls, where apparently she had hidden her cloak, for she plucked it off a hook there and placed it on her shoulders, then pulled up the hood. "I will be back tomorrow just before dusk. I know it will be difficult, what with the way your stepmother manufactures work for you where there is no need, but do what you can to preserve your strength, for a dinner at the palace can go quite late."

None too sanguine at the prospect of avoiding my stepmother's innumerable tasks, I nonetheless nodded. "I will do what I can. Truly, just the thought of being able to see him again will be enough to keep my energy up, I am sure."

My aunt patted me on the shoulder. "That's my girl. Then, until tomorrow—and do take what care of yourself you can."

With that she drew the hood even further over her face and hurried out of the stables. I went to the doorway and watched her as she seemed to melt into the shadows—seemed almost to *become* one of the shadows. Perhaps it was more of her magic. A useful trick, one I wished I might be able to employ myself.

No such luck, however. I heard Claris calling my name out the kitchen door, and looked down to see that my rich russet gown was now gone, and the familiar greyish-brown linen, much faded and patched, in its place.

Sighing, I shut the stable door behind me and hurried toward the kitchen, calling out as I did so, "Coming, Claris!"

Truly, it would be a very long night, and day, to follow. I would have to hold his face in my mind, and hope it would be enough to help me through to tomorrow evening, and my next chance to see him again.

CHAPTER SIX

Torric

"So who was this paragon?" my sister inquired, setting down her goblet of wine and slanting me an amused look.

"Her name is Ashara Millende, and she is the daughter of a baronet. I cannot say if she is a 'paragon' upon such short acquaintance, but I do think she is certainly the loveliest of the girls I met today. Her voice is sweet, too, and there is something in her eyes that tells me she has a quick mind as well."

"A paragon indeed!" Lyarris sat back in her chair, ignoring her roast pheasant for the moment. "I am surprised you did not send all the other girls home at once, since it seems clear that you have already made your choice."

Of course I knew she was teasing, but even so I frowned a little. Would that I had such an option! However, even an emperor must follow the rules…especially if they are rules he invented in the first place.

My sister and I dined alone—or as alone as we could be, with no fewer than five servants waiting to accommodate our every whim. But I had already decreed that I wanted a quiet supper this evening, as such an elaborate one was planned for the following evening. By the good grace of the gods, my mother pleaded a sick headache from being out of doors for too long, and retired to her rooms as soon as we entered the palace. Her absence meant that Lyarris and I could more or less converse freely; I had long since stopped worrying about whether the servants would gossip. Of course they would, amongst themselves, but over the years enough servitors with loose tongues had lost their positions…or worse…that they knew better than to spread their stories any further than the palace walls.

"Ashara Millende," my sister mused. "'Tis a pretty name, albeit one I have not heard before. Has she never been to court?"

"I think not, or I would have recalled her. No doubt she's from a family who keeps to the country. I shall have Keldryn look into it on the morrow, to see what he can learn of her and her people." I lifted my own neglected wine before asking, "And what of you, sister? I was gone for some hours—did you have the opportunity to spend any of that time with Lord Sorthannic?"

"I did not," she replied calmly. "He did not attend the reception at all, but went home directly after the tournament. Although he was the victor, he feared that his horse had pulled a muscle, and wanted it seen to as soon as possible. Or at least that is what I heard," she added, in a casual tone that did not fool me at all.

"Poor luck…for you and the horse."

She shook her head and lifted a forkful of roast fowl, though she did not put it in her mouth at once. Instead she remarked, "I think it would be better, Torric, if you focused your energies on your own future spouse. I most certainly do not need you playing matchmaker."

Fine words. However, that was precisely what I would have to play at some point, for I was the only one with the power to oversee such an undertaking. A decision would have to be made one day, of course. Oddly, the thought of marrying off my sister did not cause quite as much of a pang as it had even a few days ago. Perhaps it was that I had seen the woman I wanted, envisioned now a future with someone by my side, and therefore did not need to cling as tightly to my one sympathetic companion as I once did.

But in one thing Lyarris was right. Now was the time for me to focus on my future wife, and that meant finding out as much about her as possible.

"There is not much, Your Majesty," Lord Keldryn said, spreading his hands in apology. "Yes, there was an Allyn Millende, who died some ten years ago. His second wife has the management of his estate, by all accounts, although she has her primary residence here in the capital, and has let out the holdings in the country. There was a daughter—or rather, daughters. I believe the second wife had at least one, but it is difficult to tell for sure, as records concerning daughters are often not as complete as those involving sons."

"But are they a good family, Keldryn?" I asked, folding my hands on my desktop and fixing him with an expectant stare.

My chancellor lifted his shoulders. "As to that, Your Majesty, certainly there is no hint of scandal associated with them, and the lands have been in the family for hundreds of years. Some good connections, as it appears the second wife's younger sister is married to the Baron of Delanir. Nothing exceptional in any of it, as far as I can tell so far. A quiet household, from what I can ascertain. Their circle is… ahem…not quite elevated enough to have brought them to court ere this time."

I thought I detected the slightest note of disapproval in his tone but decided not to comment on it. Keldryn had not been pleased that my invitation had extended all the way down to daughters of baronets, and now that it seemed my attention had fixed on one of those undesirables, I surmised he was even less satisfied with the situation. Not that I cared; Ashara Millende was still of gentle birth, if not the daughter of a duke or earl, and her family seemed respectable enough.

"Very good, Keldryn," I said. "That will be all."

He bowed, but I noted something reluctant in his manner, and his progress to the door was a good deal slower than usual.

Oh, these games—how I wearied of them. For of course he could not come out and say directly what was bothering him, but had to engage in the sort of foot-dragging one might expect from a reluctant five-year-old. "Out with it," I said. "What bothers you, Keldryn?"

The droopy hound expression was back with a vengeance. "Only that—perhaps, Your Majesty—perhaps it would be wiser not to show such a preference quite so early in the process. Baron Lhastir Aldrenne was...somewhat disturbed... to hear from his daughter that you singled out this Ashara Millende with a compliment, when you did not pay one to any of the other girls in the pavilion."

Lhastir Aldrenne. The man was odious, puffed up with his own importance, not only because of the size of his barony, but also because it happened to encompass lands that contained the richest gold mines in Sirlende. Those mines had made his father think he could hold his riches over my own father, in order to fund the campaign to regain the crown from the usurper. And yes, that wealth had come in useful, but the debt had been repaid in more land, and not the elevation to earl or even duke that the current baron's father had hoped for. Apparently that sting had not been forgotten, even a quarter-century later. No wonder he was nettled by the news that I had preferred someone of lesser birth to his own precious daughter.

"As to that," I drawled, leaning back in my chair and fixing Keldryn with a hard stare, "I would rather have a viper in my bed than that sharp-tongued daughter of his, so they might as well give up any hopes they may have in that direction. I'll admit she's more or less pleasing to the eye—that is, until she opens her mouth. At any rate, if *Baron* Aldrenne has any problems with the way I am comporting myself, then he can bring them to me directly, instead of using you like some schoolgirl carrying tales. That is all, Keldryn."

He bowed at once and hurried out of the room, no doubt wishing to be gone before I uttered any more choice words on the subject of Lhastir Aldrenne...or his unpleasant daughter.

After my chancellor had shut the door behind him, I sat up abruptly, and then pushed my chair away so I might go to the window. Not that the prospect there was so very pleasing; a grey mist hung heavily on the city, so thick that most likely it would not clear at all. I supposed I should be glad that the weather had stayed fair until the tournament was safely over, but Keldryn's words had nettled me, and I found myself restless, wishing it were this evening, and not barely two hours past noon.

Many floors below my suite, I had no doubt the palace buzzed and hummed with activity, the kitchens working at a double pace to prepare the food for such a large crowd, even as a veritable army of maids fanned out through the rooms where the gathering would be held, dusting and scrubbing and mopping. In an odd way, I envied them their tasks, although of course I had never held a broom or a mop in my life. At least they had something to occupy them, whereas I...

It is your own fault, I told myself. *You told Keldryn to clear your calendar for this week, so you might focus on your search for a bride. Is it any wonder that now you find yourself idle?*

Not that listening to ambassadors from South Eredor or Farendon droning on about trade agreements and shipping disputes would have been a very attractive alternative.

At least it was good news that Keldryn had brought me. He had not found anything exceptional about the Millende family, so it seemed I was safe enough to pursue this Ashara… if that was what I truly intended to do. Perhaps for once Keldryn was right, and it would be less than wise for me to exhibit such an interest so early in the game.

No, that was foolish. If the girl had taken my fancy, why should I not increase the acquaintance, see where things might lead? I was the Emperor of Sirlende; no one should be dictating to me what I could or could not do.

Then I let out a bitter laugh. Once, when I was very young, I might have believed such a fairy tale, but nearly five years on the throne had taught me otherwise.

A knock at the door to my suite, and Kraine, the burly guard-cum-footman who was on duty that day, went to it to reveal my sister. She nodded at him and smiled, then came further into the room and paused a few feet away from me, one eyebrow arched.

"Goodness, Torric, you're looking positively sour. Should I check to see if any of the lemons are missing from one of the trees in the kitchen gardens?"

"Very amusing."

She hesitated, and cast a quick glance at Kraine. He bowed immediately and stepped outside, giving us as much privacy as we would ever have.

"Truly," she said, once he had shut the door behind him, "I thought to see you brimming with excitement over this evening, and yet you appear instead to have the aspect of someone awaiting an appointment with the tooth surgeon."

I made an offhand gesture, then turned away from her and stared out the window once more. "It is nothing. I am merely impatient for this afternoon to be done with, so that I might be at the dinner."

"And see her again?"

"I suppose that will depend on the seating arrangements," I said, my tone deliberately indifferent.

"And of course you have no say in those."

My sister had me there, for of course all I had to do was drop a word in Lord Hein's ear, and Ashara Millende would be seated as close to me as propriety allowed. Not beside me— no, those places of honor were reserved for my sister and my mother. But the young woman might be ensconced very near, even directly across from me, if I made my wishes known. I could only imagine the expression on Baron Aldrenne's face at such a maneuver, and almost sent for my seneschal then and there, so I might let him make the arrangements.

But no, that would not be wise. The baron was doomed to disappointment in this matter, for his daughter was the very last I would ever wish to choose. Even so, there was no need to purposely antagonize him. I would let fate decide. There were so very many young women, and there would be many tables set up besides the high table at which I, my family, and certain high-ranked lords and their wives would be seated. If, in spite of all that, Ashara Millende still was seated within speaking distance, then I would know there was some greater power at work here, and I would let it do as it willed.

"Apparently my conduct toward the Lady Ashara has already been noted in certain quarters, so I will have to be more circumspect in the future. And that means leaving the seating arrangements strictly alone."

A slight shake of her head, and my sister replied, "Circumspect? That is so unlike you."

I shot her a pained look. "Truly, I have very little opportunity to be anything but circumspect, as my entire life is governed by etiquette and tradition. As is yours."

The amused glint disappeared from her eyes, and she watched me carefully. "Too well I know that, even if I try to forget it as best I can."

"And does it ever weary you? Do you ever long to escape?"

She smiled then, but it was a small, sad smile. "I think everyone does, from time to time. The bricklayer must weary of his labor in the warm sun, and the seamstress must tire of staring at row upon row of stitches, ruining her eyesight to make sure they are all even. And when I think of them, or people like them, then I think I should not be overly dissatisfied with my lot. I never have to worry about being hungry, or cold, or whether I shall earn enough to put food in the mouths of my children. So perhaps we have our own prison, but it is a very fine one, a cell that most people would happily be confined within."

I could not recall ever hearing her speak in such a fashion before, and I stared at her in some surprise. "And have you spoken with these bricklayers and seamstresses, so you might know their minds?"

"I have spoken to more people than you might imagine, Torric. I speak to my maids and my wardrobe mistress and the cooks and the footmen. You see me writing all the time, but have you ever asked me what it is that I am writing?"

To my shame, I had not. I thought perhaps she was writing letters—although to whom, I did not know—or perhaps was setting down some sort of memoir.

My silence seemed to be the only answer she required. "I am writing the stories they tell me, Torric. Sometimes it is tales their mothers or grandmothers have told them, and sometimes it is accounts of things which have occurred in their own lives. They are not merely servants, but people with their own lives and hopes and fears. They speak to me, because I encourage it, and hearing their stories allows me to live a life beyond what I have here in the palace. And so I write them down, that they may not be forgotten."

I reflected then how it was that I could spend so much time with her, speak of so many things, and yet never have discussed this with her before. I said as much, and she lifted her shoulders.

"To be fair, Torric, I did not volunteer any information on the subject, either. I did not know what you would think if I said that I was writing down so much of what those people—people you would consider common, I suppose—had told me. I thought it best to keep it to myself."

Yes, very likely I would have laughed, or at the very least questioned her judgment in cultivating such an intimate acquaintance with those so far outside her social circle. If she needed confidantes, she certainly did not lack for noblemen's daughters who would have eagerly seized the chance to become close to the Crown Princess. And I guessed it was for that very reason that she did not cultivate such friendships.

To my surprise, she came to me and took my hands in hers, squeezing my fingers gently before she released them and stepped back a pace. Her expression was very thoughtful. "I think it is a wonderful thing you are doing, you know," she said. "You are making your own fate, not the one our father imagined for you. Yes, you are the Emperor, and though you wield great power, one power has been taken from you—the power to walk away. You would never abdicate your duty. But perhaps if you follow your heart, you will find that the crown does not weigh quite so heavily." A quick, shy smile, and she added, "And I can only hope that I will be able to make such a choice when the time comes."

"You will," I promised, for it seemed clear enough to me that, teasing remarks aside, she thought the Duke of Marric's Rest would be a good match for her. I would certainly do everything in my power to see that such a thing came to pass—once my own future was settled, of course.

"And when the Emperor of Sirlende says such a thing, then I know it will happen." The teasing glint was back in her eyes. "But be of good cheer, Torric, for you will see this Ashara again this evening, and that is not so far off. Indeed, I must be getting back to my own suite soon, or Liseth is sure to chide me for not giving her enough time to dress my hair."

"Oh, I am sure the greater part of four hours is not sufficient for that task."

Lyarris only shook her head, and stood on her tiptoes to give me a swift kiss on the cheek before departing the room. After she left, Kraine once again took up his position just within the door, and I forced myself not to sigh. In that moment I wished I had an insistent lady's maid to fuss over me. It might do something to fill up my time.

Instead, I went to my desk and took up my pen, and pretended to pore over a report one of my engineers had sent me, a proposal for improving the drainage in the Marlenthe District, which was prone to flooding during the rainy season. It was not very compelling reading, but I had little else to occupy me.

In that moment I wondered what she was doing, this Ashara Millende. Was she spending the afternoon in preparations for this evening's dinner, or did she have something more worthy to fill these hours which seemed to stretch interminably?

I should have known that Lord Hein would handle the matter of the seating arrangements with the precision of one of my generals preparing his latest campaign.

"Of course it would not do to have you move your seat, Your Majesty," he told me, after I had summoned him to my office to drill him on the preparations.

Yes, perhaps I should have inquired into these details earlier, but at the time it had not seemed all that important to me, as I had never imagined that my fancy would be so caught by a young woman this early in the week. Now I was keenly interested to know what my chances of encountering Ashara tonight might be. "Of course," I said, pretending to look over the diagram he had laid before me, a diagram which

consisted of meticulously drawn rectangles and squares—
representing, I supposed, the tables and chairs set up in the
ballroom, as even the great dining chamber could not hope
to contain such numbers.

"So," he continued, "at the end of each course the ladies
will move on to the next table, giving them the opportunity
to circulate. True, they will still not all have the chance to
converse with you, Your Majesty, but at least this removes the
problem of one set of young women sitting at the high table
for the entire meal."

"Very clever, Lord Hein," I said, although I thought pri-
vately that it seemed rather foolish to make all those young
women keep moving about the room, rather like children
playing a game of Going to Karthels. However, in this ver-
sion at least I hoped everyone would have a chair to return to,
even if it were not at the high table.

He beamed. "Thank you, Your Majesty. I assure you, it
will be an affair the likes of which the palace has never seen!"

I smiled and thanked him...and reflected that his estimation of the event might very likely be accurate.

CHAPTER SEVEN

Ashara

"No, no—I told you to bring up the chamomile rinse, not the mint one. I have heard His Majesty does not care for sharp scents. Go downstairs and get the correct bottle from Claris, you stupid girl!"

Without a word I took the bottle of hair rinse and left the bath chamber. Luckily, I had not drawn the water for my stepsisters' baths yet, or I would have had to do it all over again, since of course it would have begun to cool during the time I went downstairs to fetch the proper solution.

Never mind that I distinctly heard my stepmother ask for the mint rinse, and not the chamomile. Claris made them both, along with our soap and other herbal concoctions as required, and she shook her head as I entered the kitchen and asked for the chamomile.

"Can't make up her mind, that's what," she said darkly, as she went to the cupboard where such things were stored and handed me a bottle with a pale amber liquid inside. "Not that the whole household hasn't been in a dither all day, so I suppose this is just the latest distraction…if not the last." She stared at me with narrowed eyes. "You all right, then? You look a bit peaked."

Oh, no, that wouldn't do. So much for my aunt's admonition to preserve my strength—I'd been run ragged from the time I rose from my pallet that morning, before the sun was even up. Suddenly the hem on Jenaris' gown appeared uneven, and there was no time to call Mistress Rhandil to repair it, and so I had to unpick all the careful stitching and redo the hem, all the while thinking that perhaps the gown looked a touch too short in the front because Jenaris had somehow managed to expand her waistline during the past few weeks, rather than losing the weight her mother had desired. The reducing diet had rather backfired, I thought, as it had caused my stepsister to sneak down to the pantry in the middle of the night to replace some—if not all—of the food her mother had denied her during the day.

At any rate, that was only the first of it. Then their slippers must be blacked, and the feathers in Shelynne's fan reattached, and their chemises bleached and starched and ironed, even though only the merest hint of them would be peeking out above the bodices and through the sleeves of the gowns they would wear that evening. And doing all this while attending to my usual duties in the kitchen, and the normal dusting of the public rooms, and the polishing of the floors in those rooms, quite exhausted me.

But there was little I could do about that. If I flagged while going about my chores, or showed the slightest reluctance to accept with alacrity any new task my stepmother might dream up, then I would most likely be punished by being deprived of my midday meal. That would only make matters worse, and so I struggled along as best I could, telling myself that the weariness would disappear quickly enough once I had stolen away from the house and gone to the palace.

Once I had seen him again…

I had to admit that the likelihood of such a thing felt rather slim. With hundreds of girls in attendance, how could he possibly attend to even a tenth that number? No, I should be glad that he had noticed me at all the day before. Such a thing would probably not happen again.

A more pressing concern was how I might avoid my stepsisters. True, in a crowd that size, it should be not terribly difficult to keep from crossing their paths, unless I were unlucky enough to be seated at the same table as they. But luck had never been one to smile on me, and so I could not count on such a thing to keep me safe.

Would they even recognize me? True, my hair was distinctive—a detriment rather than an advantage in this particular situation. On the other hand, here in the house it was always covered in a kerchief and kept braided and out of the way. The color might not even register with them any longer. And once I was wearing a fine gown and jewelry and had my hair down and curled…or, to be more accurate, once it had the *semblance* of being curled…surely they would see nothing familiar in my appearance, red hair or no.

Thus reassuring myself, I somehow managed to survive the rest of the day. At least it was not my responsibility to dress my stepsisters or manage the arrangement of their hair. No, I was far too lowly to be entrusted with something so important, and it was Mari and my stepmother who did those things, fussing and primping and even—when they thought I was out of the room—quietly touching some rouge to the two girls' lips and cheeks.

As befitted an evening occasion, their gowns were far more elaborate than the ones they had worn the day before. Truly, when I looked on the embroidered claret silk of Shelynne's dress, and the golden trim on Jenaris' sapphire-blue gown, I wondered again whence had come all the money for such splendor. For this was only the second event of the five, and although tomorrow's ensembles were hunting frocks, which by design were far simpler, there were still also the musicale the following night, and the grand ball to end the five days of festivities. I had seen their gowns for those events as well, seen the embroidered trim and the pearls and precious metals stitched into those decorations, and I wondered how on earth my aunt could possibly come up with anything grander, even with magic at her disposal.

I supposed I should save that worry for another day. Now it was enough to see my stepmother send the two girls off in a carriage, and be glad that she once again retired to her bedroom, wishing to dine only on a glass of wine and some cold meat and cheese—"for of course my nerves are too unsettled to manage anything more than that."

It was almost as if my stepmother colluded in giving me an opportunity to slip away and meet up with my aunt, for the wine must be fetched from the cellar, and the cellar could only be reached by a door that opened on the outside of the house. So I told Claris I would retrieve it while she put together my stepmother's plate.

"Take a candle," she admonished me, "for it's getting on past dark, and I don't need you tripping and falling in that cellar."

I assured the cook I would take care as I lifted a candle in its brass holder from the sideboard and then hurried outside. But I did not go to the cellar door, and instead hurried across to the stable. Perhaps I had been right when I told myself that I would find renewed energy once the time to go to the dinner had come, for I slipped across the courtyard as fleet and fast as if I had just arisen from my bed instead of spending the past twelve hours fetching and carrying at my stepmother's whim.

Holding the candle before me, I opened the stable door. Thank goodness Janks had lingered in the house, flirting with Mari while my stepmother was safely ensconced in her rooms, for there was little chance of him coming outside when he had the opportunity of stealing a kiss or two.

"Ah, we have a little more light this time. That is good," my aunt said as she came out from her hiding place in one of the stalls. Her smile faded a bit as she seemed to take in my appearance. "Or perhaps it is not so good, for it seems that dreadful woman must have been running you ragged today!"

"Is it that bad?" I asked, my free hand rising to my face to touch my cheek, as if I expected to find lines and wrinkles to have materialized there sometime over the course of the afternoon.

"Oh, no, not at all," my aunt replied at once. "Just a bit pale, my dear, but once you are wearing a lovely gown and have your hair done…and I've helped you out just the littlest bit…then I'm sure no one will notice."

I wondered if that "help" would include magically applied rouge and decided it really did not matter one way or another. After all, once one has agreed to the use of any kind of magic, what difference would one small additional subterfuge make?

"Something a little different this evening, I think," my aunt went on, eyeing me critically. She closed her eyes as if in concentration, then murmured a few words. "Ah, yes, most striking."

The alteration in my appearance wasn't quite as startling this time, for now I knew what her magic could do. Even so, I wasn't expecting the skirts of deep rich green damask, the intricate embroidery in paler green and gold and even soft copper, the flash of green gems on my fingers. I held up my hand, staring at a heavy ring of gold on the middle finger of my right hand. Not that I was an expert by any means, but the gem I inspected now did not seem to be an emerald—it was too dark, too close to a deep forest color.

"What is it?" I asked.

"They are called tourmalines, and they are mined to the south and west, down in the Linsmere Province, I believe. They suit you, and the gown. Do you like the ring? And there is a necklace and earrings to match, although of course you cannot see them."

I had never seen anything so lovely as that rich green gemstone on my finger, and I had to remind myself that the stone in the ring, and indeed the ring itself, was not real, but only an illusion concocted to attract the Emperor's attention. "The ring is lovely, and so is the gown. I would not have thought of this color, but now I see it, I do think it is perfect."

"As are you, child, so go and show His Majesty your perfection. At least tell me that your stepmother has collapsed again this evening."

"She has, and you must hurry, for she is expecting some wine from the cellar. The third shelf, at the back."

At once my aunt whispered the words of the spell, and suddenly it was myself looking back at me in consternation, and taking the candlestick from my hand. "Then I will go at once, and so should you. The coach is waiting, the same as last night."

I nodded, whispered "thank you," and fled, hurrying to the back gate, glad of my dark gown. One would have to be looking for the glint of its golden trim to see me slipping out to the street.

As before, the coachman was waiting to hand me up into the carriage, and I climbed in and took my seat. We clattered away at once, and I folded my hands in my lap, willing myself to look at the dark streets flashing by with some semblance of calm. I had done this before and survived. I could do it again...provided neither of my stepsisters saw me and realized who the girl in the green gown actually was.

This time I wasn't quite as late to the festivities as I had been the day before, and so I found myself caught in the middle of a long line of carriages waiting for their chance to drop off their passengers. At long last it was my turn, and

I made myself lift my chin and smile grandly as a footman resplendent in the silver and black of the Imperial household offered a hand to assist me down from the coach.

"That way," he said, and pointed—quite unnecessarily, for it was easy enough to follow the stream of young women moving inside the palace, intent on some destination I could not yet see.

But I nodded, and lifted my skirts as I moved up the steps and fell in with the rest of them. As I walked, it was difficult for me to prevent my mouth from dropping open in wonder, to somehow keep myself from staring at my surroundings in awe. For while I had tried to tell myself that of course the palace would be very grand, and so I would have to pretend as if it weren't anything hugely out of my experience, I found that resolution wavering as I gazed about me. The ceiling overhead was painted with glorious frescoes, the pillars climbing to meet them carved with twining vines and roses. Brilliant tapestries covered the walls, and in between them were sconces of gilded brass alight with blazing beeswax tapers.

Our destination was a vast chamber with a floor of polished dark oak. Enormous fireplaces of carved marble stood at either end of the room, but as the night was mild, they had not been lit. Instead, the hearths brimmed with roses, not just draped over the elaborate mantels, but within the fireplaces as well. More swags of autumn-hued roses and ivy seemed to decorate every beam and sconce and chandelier, so that the room was heavy with the scent of flowers.

"Name?" said an imposing individual standing guard at the door. He, too, wore the livery of the Imperial household, but he was older and therefore, I guessed, of a somewhat more elevated rank than footman.

"Ash-Ashara Millende," I stammered.

"Millende. Very good. That is your table," he said, pointing toward one of ten or so long tables draped with brilliant white linen and with more roses in centerpieces that marched a straight line down the center, following the line of a runner in golden damask.

My table? I supposed that made sense; they would have to have some order to where we were to be seated, or all would be even more chaos than it already was. And using our last names was probably the simplest way to manage that task. My heart sank then, for of course my stepsisters shared my last name, and so they, too, would be seated at that table.

I made my way over to the designated spot, keeping my head down, so that I might avoid making eye contact if they were already there. Because of this, I nearly jumped out of my skin when I felt someone's hand grab hold of mine and I heard a half-familiar voice say, "Ashara! How splendid that we should be placed at the same table! But I suppose it makes some sense, as you are 'Millende' and I am 'Nelandre.'"

Blinking in relief, I glanced up and saw Gabrinne smiling at me. She looked lovely, in a rich wine color that complemented her dark eyes and hair. But even as I squeezed her hand and smiled back, I let my gaze quickly shift to those already seated at the table. Yes, there were Jenaris and Shelynne, although they sat at the farthest end and were apparently squabbling over who should have the choice seat at the edge of the table.

I prayed they would stay thus occupied, and managed to say to Gabrinne, in more or less normal tones, "Yes, that is wonderful. I had worried that I would not see a familiar face here tonight in such a crush."

"Yes, one must wonder how on earth the Emperor will be able to keep us all straight. It does seem like such a larger crowd when we're all in one place rather than spread out in separate pavilions. But I suppose that is his affair."

"So we will not get to see him," I replied, some regret in my tone. For now that I followed her gaze to scan the crowd, I could see where the high table had been set up at one end of the room near a fireplace. And there he was, standing behind a chair whose back rose higher than any of the others. He appeared to be speaking with an exceptionally lovely young woman with sleek dark hair and a sweet expression.

Perhaps a frown passed over my features, for I heard Gabrinne give a little laugh and say, "Oh, no need to be jealous of that one, Ashara. That is the Crown Princess Lyarris, and although I've heard she and His Majesty are very close, she is certainly no rival."

"I am not jealous," I said immediately.

"Oh, well, that is good," Gabrinne replied, amusement clear in her tone.

Wishing to distract her, I asked, "But how does this all work? For we are seated far from the high table, and so are most of the other girls here. How on earth can His Majesty meet all of us?"

"Simple enough. At the end of each course, we are to move to the next table, and therefore will circulate around the room. Eventually we will end up at the Emperor's table, although only a few of us will be seated close enough to actually converse with him."

As I did not want her to know how ardently I desired to be one of those lucky few, I said lightly, "Well, then, we must try to get you close. For I exchanged words with him yesterday, so it is only fair that you should have the chance."

She shook her head then so that her raven curls bounced about her shoulders. "Good gods, Ashara, do you not recall that I have no wish to marry the Emperor?"

Belatedly I did remember she had said words to that effect, and also that she had someone better in mind. Who that could be, when Torric Deveras appeared to be the very peak of manly perfection, I had no idea...but it seemed that inquiring on the subject might be a good way to distract her.

"That is correct—you did say as much." I slanted her a curious look. "So who precisely do you have in mind?"

"Duke Senric Torrival of Gahm," Gabrinne announced proudly.

Of course I had heard of him, although I did not think I had yet seen him. But... "Isn't he quite old?"

"Old?" She snorted. "He is older than we, true, but still in the prime of life. He is forty-one, I believe, or thereabouts."

That still sounded quite old to me, surely more than twice Gabrinne's age. Then again, age differences such as that were not all that uncommon in noble matches...although usually it was not the young women who sought them out. "Is he here?"

"Yes, he is standing near the high table as well. There—the tall man in the dark grey doublet."

She apparently remembered enough of her manners not to point, but the jerk of her chin toward the spot where he stood was not all that less obvious. I let my gaze travel in the direction she had indicated, and saw a man of a height with the Emperor, although a good deal older. His profile was to us, and I saw a fine hawk-like nose and strong chin, and dark hair cut somewhat shorter than was currently the fashion. Perhaps there was a glint or two of grey in those heavy tresses, but certainly he did appear, as Gabrinne had protested, in the very prime of life.

"Ah, he is a very well-looking man," I told her, and she smiled at my approval. "I am surprised he is not married already."

"He was, but she died in childbed some years ago, and has never sought another wife. I suppose he must have loved her a great deal, to wait so long to marry again, but I daresay enough time has gone by. Besides, I am sure I can make him forget her."

These words were said with such conviction that I had no doubt Gabrinne would succeed in her schemes. Would that I had her confidence!

"And does your father know of your plans?" I inquired.

A toss of her splendid curls. "No, but really, I think he will be quite happy with a duke, once he gets over the disappointment of my not being Empress. Gods, that's the last thing I want! You cannot call your life your own, when you must live at court and do everything just so." My expression must have fallen, for she hastened to add, "That is, I am sure *you* would not mind, because I can tell you're at least half in love with His Majesty already, and love can smooth the way in such things. But otherwise I think it must be a dreadful bore."

I had to confess to myself that I had never thought of life at court in such terms. Seen from far away, such an existence appeared glittering and perfect. But Gabrinne's words gave me some pause, for I realized that the Empress must be the center of all attention, and that everything she did and said must be perfect. Put in such a way, it did seem that it could be something of a burden. On the other hand, I thought I would suffer a great deal to be Torric Deveras' wife…and besides, I doubted the Empress had to scrub floors or black anyone's shoes.

A lift of my shoulders that I was fairly sure did not fool her at all, and I said, "This is all entirely academic, for of course I don't believe that I will be the Emperor's choice."

Gabrinne's dark eyebrows shot upward at that remark. "You are entirely too modest. I saw how he was looking at you, and if there's one thing having five older brothers has taught me, it's that I can tell when a man is interested in a woman."

"Five!" I exclaimed, hoping to move the conversation toward safer topics. "That is quite the number."

"It is, and even worse when you are the only daughter in addition to being the last child of six. To be sure, I do believe my brothers have worn my parents down enough that they won't mind too terribly when I tell them I have no intention of marrying the Emperor…they'll only be glad that I made such a fine match as the Duke of Gahm with no assistance from them. After finding wives for all my brothers, they are quite done up."

I could only imagine. Since I had Janks in my own household, I wasn't entirely unfamiliar with having a young man about the place, but five of them at once must be quite the strain. "Well, I am glad that you will have some opportunity tonight, as the Duke is here, and appears to have a seat at the high table, so perhaps you will have a chance to speak with him when we move there."

A quick glance in that direction told me that it seemed the members of the Imperial family were taking their seats. As soon as they were all sitting, it was time for us to choose our own spots at the table and sit as well, since we were assigned to the table only, and not to any particular seat. This was accomplished with a minimum of fuss, for of course the seating arrangements here did not matter—it was only when we reached the high table that our location would be of any importance.

Luckily, Gabrinne seated herself between me and the end of the table where my two stepsisters sat, and on the other side of my newfound friend was a very tall girl who did quite a good job of blocking any view of the two of us. Because of this, I found my nerves easing a bit as the servants came 'round with great jugs of wine and filled our goblets, then retreated so they might bring forth equally oversized tureens of soup, which they ladled into our bowls. The scent that rose to my nostrils was as toothsome as any I had enjoyed in Claris' kitchen, and I gathered up my spoon.

Immediately Gabrinne's hand was on my wrist. "Not yet," she whispered. "We must wait until all at the high table have had their first taste, and then we may begin."

Chagrined, I set down my spoon and placed my hands in my lap, following her lead. Thank goodness I had found a friend as knowledgeable about such things as she was kind, or I would surely have made quite the fool of myself.

At least we sat on the side of the table that had a more or less clear view of the Imperial party, and so I was able to watch as they had their first taste of the soup. The Emperor nodded, apparently giving his approval, and then it seemed we were free to begin our own dinners.

"So what happens if the Emperor does not approve of a dish?" I whispered to Gabrinne.

She shook her head, grinning. "I have never heard of such a thing. Whether that is because he is too polite to show his disapproval publicly, or because his cooks are so excellent that turning down any of their dishes isn't even a possibility, I do not know for sure." Her expression turned sly. "You will have to tell me which theory is correct, once you are Empress."

There being no way I could sensibly reply to that remark, I lifted my spoon once again and tasted the creamy concoction within the bowl. Some kind of cream of leek soup, I thought, but with a subtle, pleasant tang I could not place, one that was noticeably absent from Claris' own recipe. Although that taste reminded me of how hungry I was, how my noon meal had consisted of only bread and cheese, and half an apple, I made myself eat slowly and delicately, taking my cue from the other young women around the table, who seemed to barely take two or three spoonfuls before abandoning their soup altogether.

"Why are they eating so little?" I asked Gabrinne in an undertone, for I noticed she had taken hardly more than the rest of the girls.

"Their gowns are laced tight, and we have three more courses to go," she replied frankly. "You are slender enough that such a thing is probably not a hardship, but I cannot say the same for the rest." My expression must have still been one of concern, for she added, this time in a murmur that no one else could possibly overheard, "There's no need to worry about it going to waste. The excess goes back to the kitchens for the servants, and if there's any left over after that, I've heard it's distributed to the poor."

I knew I must be content with that explanation, although it seemed odd to prepare so much excess, only to give it away. My stepmother had always been parsimonious with her food, unless she was having company. I had always guessed that she preferred to spend the money on gowns for her daughters or new trinkets to clutter up the house, rather than something as lowly as foodstuffs.

Perhaps a half hour later, a soft chime sounded throughout the chamber—the signal to move on to the next table, apparently. "Do I take the silverware?" I asked Gabrinne in a whisper.

"No, of course not. See, they are already coming to bring fresh pieces. Just move along!"

I did as she bade me, hanging back a little so she was in the lead, and I might follow in her shadow. This first time I had been lucky in sitting so far away from my two stepsisters, but I could not count on that good fortune indefinitely. As we approached the table where we would take the second course, things became somewhat more complicated, as I had to dodge what appeared to be a veritable army of servants laying out new flatware for us.

Even so, Gabrinne and I made it safely to the table, and I waited while she sat down before I did so as well, catching in the corner of my eye the wine color and sapphire of my stepsisters' gowns as they took their own seats a comfortable distance away. Not quite the opposite end of the table, unfortunately, but there were still at least fourteen or fifteen young women separating us, and that seemed a safe enough barrier.

Now I understood how these things worked, it was easier to sit and wait as the servants came 'round with a dish of field greens and nuts and raisins, with a tangy-sweet sauce that was a perfect complement to the slightly bitter taste of the greens. Easier still, because I saw that the next table was the one where the Emperor sat, and so my wait would be over soon.

Don't be silly, I told myself, *for the odds are almost one hundred to one that you will be able to sit anywhere close to him. No, you will most likely perch at one end. The most you can hope for is that your stepsisters will take no note of you.*

This course appeared to be more involved than the last, for the dish of field greens was removed promptly and replaced by medallions of chicken in a light, savory sauce. I had been following Gabrinne's lead, so at least I had not made a fool of myself by rising once the salad had been taken away. I also began to see why the girls had been so circumspect about their portions, for truly one could only have a few mouthfuls of each course, or risk being full before the main dish was even served.

"And we are very lucky, for the next course is the largest, and so the one that takes the longest, and it is for that one that we'll be seated at the high table," remarked Gabrinne after she had taken two very delicate bites of chicken, then laid her fork down on her plate. "Plenty of time for you to speak to the Emperor, and for me to renew my acquaintance with Lord Senric."

"So you do know him?" I asked.

"Oh, everybody knows everybody else. That is," she amended, and shot a rather guilty glance in my direction, "the dukes and the earls, mostly. My father has known Lord Senric for many years, and he has visited our estate several times. He never took any particular notice of me, but it has been several years now since he last visited, and most likely he does not know that I am now a young lady ready for the marriage bed."

I choked on my wine at these bold words, and she grinned and shook her head.

"Why so modest, Ashara? That is why we are all here, is it not?"

"I—well, perhaps, but—"

"But nothing." She drank some of her own wine before adding, "I have kissed a young man several times, and I must confess that it was quite pleasant. I can only imagine that it will be even better with Lord Senric, for he will have had much more practice."

What I was supposed to make of any of those pro-nouncements, I was not certain. Of course I had never kissed a young man, much less participated in any of the activi-ties I had accidentally spied Mari and Janks sharing that one notable day. Even so, I thought of the Emperor kissing me, of his arms going around me, and a shiver fluttered its way down my spine.

My voice deliberately prim, I said, "And I imagine that your parents would not like to know that their daughter thought nothing of speaking of such things."

Gabrinne only laughed, and raised her glass of wine toward me in a mock toast. "Ah, you may say that, but I saw the look on your face just before, and it was anything but proper. You were thinking of him, weren't you?"

Since I could not deny it—well, deny it without Gabrinne spotting the lie immediately—I only looked away from her and took another very small bite of a chicken medallion.

"As I thought." She pushed her plate away and dabbed at her mouth with a napkin of linen so fine that in my house-hold it would have been used for a gown, not a bit of cloth to wipe one's hands with. "It looks as if the servants are pre-paring to clear away this course from the high table. We will need to look sharp, for I am not sure exactly how they are going to determine who sits where."

"It is really no matter—"

"It is for *me*. You may sit at the end and stare up at the ceiling and feel put upon, but I must sit close to Lord Senric, and that means sitting close to the Emperor, for the Duke is but two places away."

"Of course," I said at once. I reminded myself that Gabrinne had her own stakes to play here, and it was selfish of me to ignore them. "I will do what I can, but I do draw the line at fisticuffs."

The grin returned. "Then I daresay that makes you better than half the girls here."

I could only shake my head at such a remark, but I did follow her lead in touching my mouth with the napkin and wiping my hands thoroughly before I set it aside. Around me I noticed the other young women were doing the same, then shifting to the edges of their seats, as if they expected to break into a sprint the second the signal was given.

My heart began to pound, and I willed myself to stay calm. There were three more days after this one—three more opportunities to see him, possibly speak with him. I could not act as if everything hinged on this single night.

The chime sounded, and everyone jumped out of their seats as if pinched. No one ran, precisely, but it was certainly an inelegant rush that descended upon the high table. Gabrinne was a pace ahead of me, and I followed in her shadow, hearing the familiar voices of my stepsisters only a few paces behind me.

"Jenaris, move faster! If only you weren't so fat—"

"I am not fat—someone is in my way!"

Somehow I forced myself to not look back, to keep moving forward. And then it was as if we hit some sort of invisible wall, for a distinguished-looking older gentleman stood between us and the table, one hand raised.

"I admire your enthusiasm, ladies, but there are seats for all. Two at a time, please."

As somehow Gabrinne and I had managed to place ourselves more or less at the head of the pack, we were neck and neck with two or three other girls, all of whom shot us venomous glances. I guessed they would not be so ill-disposed toward Gabrinne once they learned she had no designs on the Emperor, whereas I was already the source of a good deal of ill will because of the attention he paid me the day before.

We stood there, irresolute, apparently no one wishing to show poor breeding by stepping forward first. I wondered how long this impasse would last.

But then I heard the scrape of a chair being pushed back, and the Emperor rose from his seat and came toward our group. His dark gaze flickered over all of us, at last coming to rest on me, and he smiled.

"This way, ladies," he said with a nod at Gabrinne and me, and spread his hand toward the empty seats at the table.

Words seemed to fail both of us, but we managed a curtsey, then went to take our seats—I across from the Emperor, and Gabrinne next to me, where she would be on the diagonal from where Lord Senric sat. Not perhaps the most ideal location for conversation, but apparently she deemed it well enough, for she smiled as she allowed a servant to push in her chair. I also took my place, swallowing nervously and praying that my stepsisters were not tall enough to have seen exactly what just transpired.

The Emperor returned to his own chair and smiled at me, expression warm and perhaps almost too familiar, while in the seat next to him his sister appeared to repress a grin of her own, and on his other side the Dowager Empress, a beautiful but forbidding woman of perhaps some fifty years, shot a scowl at me from beneath a pair of perfectly arched eyebrows.

What on *earth* had he been thinking?

CHAPTER EIGHT

Torric

No doubt my mother would have said some imp possessed me, to show such favoritism in front of everyone. After all, for the other two courses, I had been content to let Lord Hein manage the placement of the girls at my table. None of them interested me in the least, although I did my duty by smiling and making conversation with them, even as my eyes continually sought out Ashara where she sat across the chamber. When she turned up at the front of the latest group, it seemed the most natural thing in the world to make sure she had the best spot at the table—she and her friend, who I believed was the youngest daughter of the Earl of Kelsir, although I could not recall her name.

To my surprise, that young lady, though bold enough in other respects, seemed not interested in me in the slightest, and instead turned her attention toward Lord Senric, inquiring as to his grape harvest with a most predatory gleam in her eye. Ah, so that was her game. I wished her luck with it, for in my estimation the Duke had gone long enough without a wife. And I had to confess it was a relief to know that at least one of these young ladies had no desire to be Empress.

The others, though…

I looked across the table to Ashara. Thank the gods that Lord Hein had had the good sense to make sure the center-pieces weren't so tall they obscured my view of my dinner companions. Her gaze met mine for a few seconds before she looked down, a warm flush staining her cheeks.

Yesterday I had thought her lovely, but she seemed even more beautiful now, in a dark green gown that brought forth mysterious copper glints from within her russet hair, and which warmed her ivory skin. Also, as befitted a dinner dress, the bodice of this one was cut lower, and I saw the faintest hint of the shadows between her high, full breasts, a contrast to the slenderness of her neck, the pronounced collarbones beneath the heavy necklace of gold and green tourmalines. Desire stirred within me, and I forced it back. Now was not the time to be indulging such things.

"It is good to see you again, Ashara," I told her, which was certainly no more than the truth.

"And you, Your Majesty," she replied in her low, sweet voice.

How I wished to hear her call me by my name! However, I knew I could not ask such a thing of her—not here in front of my sister and my mother, and the other noble lords who had a place at the high table. Perhaps once we had the opportunity to be alone I could urge that…and possibly other intimacies…from her, but not now.

No, here we could only speak of the commonplaces propriety allowed, but that was better than nothing. "And are you enjoying the dinner, Ashara?"

"Yes, Your Majesty. The food is wonderful, and the flowers are so very beautiful. Someone must have been working from sunup to create so many lovely arrangements."

It seemed rather an odd comment to me—of course someone had been working on the flowers all day; that was what servants were for. Since it was clear that she was sincere, and, truly, the hall did look rather impressive, I only nodded. "Lord Hein said the roses would not last much longer anyway, so best they be put to some good purpose. I confess I do not pay that much attention, save that there are arrangements all over the palace in the warm months, and not so much in the winter."

She smiled at that. "Well, Your Majesty, they are lovely, but his lordship is correct. They will last through the first frost or two, but after that they are gone until the spring."

"Do you have many roses at your home?"

A shadow seemed to pass over her face. "At the—at our townhouse here in Iselfex, we have none. It is all cobbles on the street, and although our cook grows geraniums in her window boxes, it is not quite the same thing. There were— there are lovely gardens at our country estate, but we do not go there often."

There was such a combination of wistfulness and sadness in her tone that I longed to know more, to ask why they should stay here so long in town if she appeared so clearly disinclined to it, but that question seemed somehow too intimate. Instead, I inquired, "But will you ride tomorrow? I know some of the young women will only come to the reception, and not participate in the hunt itself, for they do not count themselves good enough riders. I hope you do not include yourself in that number, even if you spend a good deal of time here in the capital without much opportunity for riding."

She waited until the servant at her elbow had finished filling her wine goblet to the halfway point. When she replied, her voice was soft but firm. "It is true that I have not had the chance to ride as much lately as I would like to, but when I was young—that is, my father and I used to ride all the time, and I think I shall manage well enough. He had me in the saddle before I was barely old enough to walk."

I recalled then that her father had been dead these ten years or so, which could explain the note of quiet sorrow in her tone. Perhaps it was hurtful for her to recall the times they had spent together, when it seemed clear enough to me, even though she had said nothing specific on the topic, that she did not get along very well with her stepmother. A common enough story, but at least she had managed to attend these festivities despite all that. In a way, knowing even this small fact about her heartened me and made me even more anxious for the future, for by making Ashara my bride I could take her away from a life that she apparently did not find all that appealing.

Oh, that's a good tale you've spun for yourself, I thought then. *You know nothing of the kind. Yes, it would please you to be her rescuer, but certainly she has said nothing to indicate that she needs rescuing.*

"That's a relief, then," I told her, and hoped she had not noticed the pause before I spoke. "I know there are some good horsewomen among those assembled here, but I must confess I hoped you would be among them."

"No fear," she said, and smiled. "I am sure my mount cannot rival those from your stables, but I will manage well enough."

"I would offer you the loan of one, but then all the girls would want the same treatment, and that, I fear would require me to borrow horses from my guard…which, if I'm not mistaken, would lead to a great deal of grumbling. I'm sure your mount will do well enough, and I will try not to set too hard a pace."

"Do not make it easy on my account, Your Majesty," she replied, with a glint in her amber-green eyes. "Or you may find it is you who are lagging behind."

Her expression had grown lively, and so I thought she must enjoy riding a good deal, and did not have much opportunity for doing so while living here in town. I was glad my sister and I had decided on a hunt as one of the activities in this week-long carnival in my quest for a bride, even though my mother had thought the idea quite foolish, and even Lord

Hein had expressed his misgivings in hosting a hunt with quite so many participants.

As it turned out, however, a good many of the young ladies had already demurred, and so the gathering would most likely number somewhat under two hundred. Even that might prove to be unwieldy, but those of my guard who were riding with us would have to do their best to keep everyone from mishap.

"I do not think lagging behind will be much of a problem," I told her calmly, although as I spoke I wondered if I would have to rein back Thunderer, my favorite stallion, to keep him from taking too much of a lead.

"And what is your horse's stock, Miss Millende?" my mother put in, deliberately using a form of address that should have been reserved for someone of lesser birth, and not a nobleman's daughter.

To her credit, Ashara did not even blink. "I fear I do not precisely know, Your Majesty. My aunt is loaning me one of hers, as my stepmother does not keep a stable while we are here in town. It is so much more convenient to use a hired carriage when necessary."

My mother sniffed, shot a sideways glance at me, as if to say, *This is the girl attracting all your attention?*, and then pointedly turned to Lord Keldryn, who sat on her right, and began asking him about the prospects of an early frost that year.

The snub was quite obvious, and I sent an apologetic look across the table at Ashara. To my surprise, I thought I saw the faintest lift at the corner of her rosy lips, as if she were more amused by my mother's bad behavior than anything else.

Such a reaction raised the young lady even higher in my estimation, for I thought if Ashara could handle my mother, then she would make quite the estimable Empress, even putting aside my desire for her. "So your aunt is loaning you one of her horses? That is very generous of her."

For some reason Ashara flushed then, and did not quite meet my eyes. "Yes…she does not care for town and lives some ten miles away, in Karthels."

"And is she your father's sister, or your mother's?"

"My mother's."

She seemed disinclined to give any more information than that, and I let the matter go for the moment. Truly, I did not care who her aunt was or who her connections might be. The important thing was that she had offered Ashara the loan of a horse so she might participate in the hunt tomorrow.

By then the servants had filled Ashara's plate, and that of her fellow diners at the table. Indeed, a choice cut of lean roast beef and vegetables and fig compote had appeared on my own plate almost by magic, although I knew that must have been done as I was speaking with Ashara. I picked up my fork and knife and cut a piece of the meat, knowing that I must allow my guests some time to eat, even if I had little stomach for it. Much better to keep speaking with her, to take these few moments we had before once again the seating arrangements changed, and she was hurried along to the final table.

But she seemed slender—almost too slender—and it did not seem chivalrous to keep her from eating. Perhaps her stepmother kept a frugal table, or was one of those given to fads such as not eating red meat, or bread, or eschewing cheese. I did not know how much time we would have to talk on the morrow, but I vowed then that I would do whatever was necessary to make sure she never slipped out of my sight during the hunt. After all, the Forest of Islin was wide, and there was always the chance that we might get lost in it together...

"I truly do not know what you see in her, Torric," my mother said darkly, and set her glass of port down on the spindly-legged table of inlaid ebony next to her. "She seems quite insipid to me. And who are her family? No one, as far as I can tell!"

Somehow I managed to refrain from letting out a sigh. This was no more than I had expected from my mother, after all.

Of course Lyarris was quick to say, "I think she seems perfectly lovely. And her father was a baronet, was he not, Torric?"

"Yes. He passed away some years ago, but to my knowledge Ashara is his heir. That makes her birth gentle enough for me. Surely you can find nothing in her manner that is objectionable?"

A sniff. "Perhaps, but nothing noteworthy, either, besides that hair of hers. The Empress of Sirlende should be a young woman of more spirit, like Baron Aldrenne's daughter, or the daughter of the Earl of Kelsir."

I could not help but laugh then, and remarked, "I get the distinct impression that Lord Hildar's daughter has set her sights elsewhere."

"Oh, you noticed that, too?" Lyarris put in. "Yes, Mother, it seemed to me that Gabrinne Nelandre showed a particular interest in Lord Senric, so I think it is not much use to suggest her to Torric. And if he has settled on this Ashara Millende, what of it? What is wrong with allowing him the choice of his heart?"

"Oh, that is very noble," my mother said. "Would that all of us were allowed 'the choice of our heart'!"

I had had enough. "For all the gods' sake, Mother, are you going to drag that up again?"

"You will not speak to me in such a tone, Torric! You may be the Emperor of Sirlende—"

"In one thing you are right, Mother. I am the Emperor of Sirlende, and so I will make the final decision here, with no one to say me nay. Do you understand?"

Another woman might have resorted to false tears then, or some other attempt at invoking filial guilt. My mother, however, did not stoop to such meager ploys. "I understand that my son is a fool," she retorted in cutting tones, and stalked from the chamber, her attendants falling in around her as soon as she went through the door.

For a second or two my sister and I only gazed at one another. Then she said wearily, "Must you always provoke her?"

"Perhaps you should instead ask her why she always allows herself to be provoked! Indeed, I think she would be dreadfully disappointed if we didn't have at least one argument each day."

"Oh, Torric." Lyarris went to pour a scant measure of port into her glass; I had told the servants to wait outside after they had attended to us when we first entered the small salon, the chamber where my family tended to gather after public affairs such as the dinner this evening. Eavesdrop the attendants would, of course, but I saw no reason why I should make things easier for them.

"Don't 'oh, Torric' me," I said irritably. "I have long since given up trying to make peace with her—I fear I have neither the stomach nor the energy for it. Now, you—you I will listen to. So do you think I am being foolish?"

"Not exactly," she replied, the words coming slowly, as if she were stopping to consider each one before she uttered it. "That is, your acquaintance with this young woman has been exceedingly short, no more than a half hour together all told, but you would have had even less if Princess Lisanne had survived. It was not as if you could have sent her back home to her father if you found she did not suit you."

That was no more than the truth. The late princess, if she had lived, would have come to Iselfex with her own attendants, greeted with all the pomp and majesty such an event required—and then we would have been married that same night, and sent to bed as well, that we might get down to the business of providing Sirlende with an heir. Very likely we would not have exchanged more than twenty words before we became man and wife in every sense of the word.

I could not help but think that my way of selecting an Empress for Sirlende was a fairer one.

"At any rate," Lyarris continued, "Mother will bluster and say horrible, spiteful things, for that is what she does, but she cannot stop you from choosing Ashara Millende, if that is your will. The girl seems lovely to me, and well-spoken, and if her family is not grand, still they are of gentle birth, which is all that matters."

Her words calmed me somewhat, although my mother's reaction still rankled. Perhaps someday I would learn to stop seeking her approval. In the meantime, I wished to turn the conversation to happier topics. "And what of you? I did not see Lord Sorthannic at the dinner this evening."

She lifted her shoulders, attempting to be casual, but I saw the disappointment in her face. "He is not much of one for gatherings such as this, and so he sent his regrets through Lord Senric, but said he would come to the hunt tomorrow."

"Which does you little good, seeing as you are not riding out with the rest of us." My sister, though a good rider, did not care for the bloodthirsty nature of hunting, and so rarely set forth on such outings.

"No, but I will be at the reception afterward with everyone else, and I am sure Lord Sorthannic will attend that, as it would be seen as rude for him not to."

This seemed sensible enough. Besides, it would be far easier to carry on a conversation of any import at the reception after the hunt, rather than while pounding away on horseback in search of an elusive quarry. What that observation boded for any interactions between Ashara and myself, I was not sure, although I vowed that I would find some way to get her alone, to slip away from the endless burden of servants and guards and advisors who seemed to dog me everywhere I went.

I said, "Well, then, you must make sure to corner him as soon as you can, for I fear that as soon as more of the young women become aware that my heart is already settled on Ashara Millende, they will seek to transfer their attentions to some other nobleman, as the Lady Gabrinne has already done."

Rather than take offense at this remark, my sister merely raised an eyebrow and smiled a little. "Do you have so little faith in me that you think I cannot keep Lord Sorthannic's interest when confronted by a pack of rivals?"

"Of course not…you know I was only teasing you." I drained the last of my port and went to refill the glass—that is, fill it partway, for I saw Lyarris watching my actions, and knew she would take me to task if she thought I was overindulging. The gods only knew that a blissful drunk might be just the thing to erase this latest confrontation with my mother from my mind, but nursing a hangover during the hunt the next day did not appeal much, either. So I set the decanter back on the table and allowed myself only a measured sip.

My sister was watching me carefully, brows drawn together as if in thought. "If you truly have settled on this young woman as your choice, then why bother to go through with the next three events? Surely it is not precisely fair to keep up the hopes of all the other candidates if you have no intention of marrying any of them."

Would that it were that simple. "And neither would it be fair, I suppose, to cancel things so suddenly, and to disrupt the plans of everyone who had thought to stay here through the end of the week, or—as you pointed out before—paid for gowns for the events being held on those days. Also, I believe Lord Hein would have a heart spasm if I were to call a halt to the proceedings at this stage, not when he has already ordered the food and the decorations and hired the musicians and so forth. No, we will have to play this charade through to the end. Anyone with two eyes to see will know that I have made my choice, but I will make no announcement until the ball on Friday."

Lyarris gave a reluctant nod. "I suppose that does make sense, even though some part of me wishes you did not have to do such a thing."

"Ah, well, it will not be a complete burden, as I will try my best during the next three days to spend as much time with Ashara as possible. Besides, if I were to send everyone home now, that would include Lord Sorthannic, and I most certainly don't want to deprive you of his company."

"How altruistic of you."

But her tone was amused, rather than irritated, and so I knew she was not put off by my statement. No, it would not be fair to her—or to the Lady Gabrinne, with her pursuit of Lord Senric—to call a halt to things prematurely. Chafe at the delay I might—or rather would—but after all, three days was not so long when measured against the lifetime I envisioned with Ashara once the events planned this week had run their course.

I did know that, whatever else happened, Ashara Millende was destined to be my wife.

CHAPTER NINE

Ashara

O h, gods, what had I been thinking? What demon had possessed my tongue, made me tell the Emperor all those lies? Truly, I did not know what my aunt had planned for the hunt tomorrow; as far as I knew, she might be thinking that I would wish to sit out the ride itself and only attend the reception, as quite a few of the young ladies apparently planned to do. But to say to the Emperor that he would have to work to keep up with me, that I was nearly his equal in the saddle?

Once upon a time I had been an excellent rider. It was true that my father had me on the back of a horse before I could barely walk, and there was no corner of our estate I had not explored—and many beyond its borders I had traveled as well, since I learned to jump low walls and hedges before I was barely six years old. But I had not ridden a horse in nearly ten years. Perhaps my muscles would remember skills that my mind could not. I would have to hope for the best.

If, of course, Aunt Therissa even provided me with a mount. We did not have a chance to speak when I returned after the dinner at the palace, for Janks was already in his room adjoining the stable, and my aunt and I hurriedly exchanged places in the shadows around a corner of the building, afraid to even speak a word lest he overhear us and come to investigate. Afterward I scuttled up the back steps into the kitchen as quickly as I could, heart pounding, sure someone would discover me coming back inside. Luck was with me that much, though, for Claris was in the pantry, taking stock of her supplies for the meals the next day, and I went to the half-washed dishes and set to as if I had been standing there all along.

Even though I had not been caught, sleep did not come to me easily that night. Part of it was worry for what the next day might bring, of course, fear that either my aunt could not locate a horse, or, possibly worse, that she would find a way to provide me with a mount, and then I would have to hope and pray I recalled enough to ride it without giving away the fact that I had not been on horseback for nearly a decade.

Beyond that, though, I could not keep my mind from turning over and over again the words the Emperor and I had exchanged, the warmth in his dark eyes as he looked at me, the rich velvety timbre of his voice. Everything about him seemed designed specifically to set my heart racing, my blood somehow running hotter in my veins. No, I could no longer deny that he had taken a particular interest in me, not with the way he had singled me out, given me the place of honor directly across from him at the high table.

"You may even be the Empress before I'm a duchess, if the way His Majesty looks at you is any indication," Gabrinne had whispered to me before we parted ways for the evening. At the time I had demurred, shaking my head, but inwardly, in some deep, secret place in my soul I barely wanted to acknowledge, I knew she was right.

Why the Emperor had singled me out from all those other young women, I could not say. Could this be another, subtler spell, even though my aunt had denied that her magic could be put to such a use? I wanted to say no, that of course she had been truthful with me, but I barely knew her. I knew nothing of her, save that she had expressed a desire to help me, as the daughter of her long-dead sister.

Very fine motives…if they were her only motives. Perhaps she was only one member of a secret group of magic-users, someone who put herself forward to help me so that she and her fellows might have access to the Emperor for their own nefarious reasons.

No, surely that was only a dark fancy spun from my own tortured thoughts. After all, even if there were such a group, surely they could have found a far more likely candidate than I, a girl who had spent the last ten years of her life washing dishes and sweeping and fetching and carrying for her termagant of a stepmother.

And so my mind played with me, until at last I fell into an uneasy slumber, fretting even then over what the next day might hold. My sleep was filled with nightmares of riding a horse with eyes of fire, a dark stallion that carried me forward over a precipice until I was falling, falling, with no hope of rescue. I slipped into darkness, and it swallowed me whole.

Would that I could say the next day was an improvement, but it certainly did not start out that way. I brought breakfast to my stepmother and stepsisters in the dining room, with a misty golden morning sun pouring in through the tall window on the east side of the house. Naturally she was grilling them as to the goings-on at the palace the night before, and neither of them looked particularly pleased by the news they had to impart.

"Oh, la, the Emperor is very handsome," said Jenaris as she spread a piece of toast thickly with butter and quince jam. "But he pays no attention to any of us."

"I don't think she's even that pretty," Shelynne added with a scowl. She broke a piece of bacon in half and ate one section. "Oh, yes, so she has that red hair, but what of that? She looks like a skinny scared rabbit."

I tensed, but somehow managed to keep my hand from shaking as I poured more tea into my stepmother's cup. The fragrant steam curled upward, and I found myself wishing I might have some as well, to steady my nerves. But tea was far too expensive to be wasted on the likes of me.

"Red hair?" my stepmother said in sharp tones. Her dark gaze flicked toward me for a second, but then she seemed to relax slightly, as if realizing that I had been here all last night, so of course I couldn't possibly have attended the dinner at the palace. "And who is this girl?"

"No one knows," Jenaris replied with a shrug, helping herself to the last of the bacon on the platter. "I think someone said her name was...Aislinn? Sharanne? Something like that."

"Well, which is it?" my stepmother demanded. "Those two names sound nothing alike."

Jenaris mumbled something around a mouthful of bacon, and her mother let out an exasperated breath and turned on Shelynne. "And I suppose you know nothing as well."

A lift of the shoulders. "How could I, Mamma? I sat next to Jenaris the whole night, so I heard the same things she did. Anyway, what does it matter who this girl is? All that matters is that she isn't either of us."

For Shelynne, this was actually some remarkably clear-headed thinking. Indeed, what did it matter who the Emperor had apparently chosen, if it was not you?

All the same, I found my throat and stomach tight with dread. Oh, how I wished I had given the Emperor a false name, although which one I could have chosen, I had no idea. My knowledge of the nobility was scanty at best, so I could not have come up with something plausible, some distant relation of a well-known family. Such a subterfuge would have been easily discovered, and discredited.

"You are both being remarkably silly," my stepmother snapped. "Acting as if the race has already been won, when there are still three days ahead of you in which you might catch the Emperor's eye! And you should do what you can to find out more about this girl, for it's only by studying an enemy that one can defeat them. Do you understand?"

The two sisters exchanged confused glances, then nodded halfheartedly.

My stepmother did not appear mollified, but she said nothing further, and instead only returned to her own neglected breakfast and began to eat, all the while staring at her daughters as if she were not quite sure they were actually a product of her womb.

As for myself, I made my escape as soon as I could, using the excuse of requiring more hot water for the teapot to leave the room. My heart was pounding and my hands trembling.

It had been difficult enough to escape my stepsisters' notice prior to this. What on earth was I to do now that their mother had instructed them to spy on me?

"Not to worry," my aunt told me in soothing tones early that afternoon, after I had escaped to the stables to meet her. "The same magic that tricks their eyes into seeing you in elegant gowns rather than those rags your stepmother deems it seemly for you to wear also tricks their ears. You could tell them your name directly, and they still would not be able to recall it."

"Then how can the Emperor hear it correctly?" I halfwhispered, shooting a worried glance in the direction of the kitchen door. "Or, for that matter, my friend Gabrinne?"

"Because they mean you no ill."

I frowned, and my aunt said,

"Oh, for goodness' sake, what difference does it make *how* it works? It is magic, dear girl, and it is doing all it can to protect you."

"Is it doing anything more than that?"

She shot me a questioning look. "What are you asking, Ashara?"

I smoothed my hands over my skirts. That day's spell had already been cast, and so I wore the semblance of a fine riding suit in closely woven deep brown wool. "I am asking if your spell is doing something else…making the Emperor fall in love with me, perchance."

"Of course not!" Her expression seemed horrified enough that I thought I might believe her. "All I am giving you is the opportunity. Everything else comes from you, dear girl. Have you so little faith in yourself?"

There was a question. I had not had many opportunities for faith, whether in myself or in others. "I do not know," I said simply.

At once her features softened, and she took my hands in hers. "I cannot imagine how difficult things must have been for you. But I am telling you the truth, Ashara. The Emperor is falling in love with you because you are strong and lovely and good. Not because of a spell. Believe that, and believe in yourself."

For some reason her words brought tears to my eyes, and I struggled to keep them from spilling over my cheeks. "I—I will try," I murmured.

"Good girl. Now go." Her dark eyes twinkled then. "I think you will find something a little better than a coach waiting for you this time."

That could mean only one thing. I thanked her hastily and rushed out, glad that my stepsisters had already gone and that Janks would not be about, either, as Claris had sent him out for more firewood for the kitchen hearth.

After I slipped through the gate and went around the corner, I found a young man of about my age standing there, holding the reins of the most beautiful blood-bay mare I had ever seen. Her legs were elegant but powerful, her dark mane and tail meticulously brushed.

"For you, miss," the young man said, and cupped his hands so I might hoist myself into the sidesaddle.

"No need of that," I told him, my voice sounding light and joyous, even to me. "I can manage." And I put one foot in the stirrup and pulled myself into the saddle, disposing my skirts around me as if I had been doing that very same thing every day since I was a child.

He shook his head and grinned, but did not seem offended by my refusal. "Her name is Maelyn, and she will bear you well."

"Thank you," I said. "I will take good care of her."

A small half-bow. "And she of you."

For the first time I noticed a second horse, this one not nearly as eye-catching, standing a few paces past my own.

"Mine," the young man supplied. "Your aunt says I'm to ride with you, act as your groom."

She did appear to have thought of everything. "Your name, sir?"

He flashed a grin at me. "Aldric, my lady. Follow me." In short order he was mounted on his own horse and leading me through the crowded streets.

Although perhaps I should have kept my head down, to prevent anyone from getting a good look at me, I must confess I was too entranced by my surroundings to be so circumspect. For the last ten years—save the past few nights—my world had consisted of my stepmother's house and the small cul-de-sac where it stood. Of course I was never allowed to venture any farther than that, as I might run away. And although I had ridden forth in a carriage along these same streets, I could not see and hear and smell the city in a coach as I did now, on horseback.

All around me were people of all different shapes and sizes and ages, from the young girl on the corner selling clove-scented lemons—a sovereign antidote for the stink of the streets—to the carter behind me, his hands so gnarled with arthritis I wondered that he could hardly hold the reins of his horses, which looked barely younger than he. My ears rang with the noise, for everyone was shouting out their wares, or cursing someone whose wagon had cut them off, or talking loudly to be heard over the din.

I stared and stared, but retained enough of my wits to follow Aldric as he led me to the city's eastern gate, where we emerged into a throng as loud and sizable as the one we had just left, save that they were headed into town to conduct their business. We rode further, and the crowds diminished even as the countryside grew more open and more green. Off to my left I saw a dark blur that gradually resolved itself into a great forest of pine and oak and other trees I did not recognize. Against that dark blur fluttered a number of pennants in colors both bright and somber, and beneath those pennants were more pavilions, and a great mass of people.

My hands must have clenched on the reins, and Maelyn gave a little snort and tossed her head, as if in protest. At once I relaxed, then bent close and murmured, "No fear, my beauty—we will have some fun soon enough."

At least, I hoped so.

Men in the black and silver livery of the Imperial house gestured me toward a group also on horseback, while indicating that Aldric must go in the opposite direction, back where the rest of the grooms and other attendants appeared to be congregating. I shot him an apologetic look, but he only shrugged and said, "'Tis no problem, my lady," before heading off where he'd been directed.

As for myself, I nudged Maelyn forward in a slow walk so that I might take the measure of the group I was approaching. Yes, there were far fewer young ladies on horseback than had attended the dinner the night before; I thought I counted something more than a hundred, not including the noblemen and guards who would also be riding along. It still seemed a goodly number to be engaging in a hunt. At least here I knew I could avoid my stepsisters, since they were not riding, and must be back in one of the pavilions, pretending to have a good time while waiting for His Majesty and the other hunters to return.

Then I saw him, sitting straight in the saddle, his head bare and his dark hair gleaming in the sun. He wore a plain doublet of very dark green, and high brown boots and gloves to match. Even from that distance, I could sense his gaze fastening on me, and he smiled, teeth flashing as he raised his hand.

I gave Maelyn a gentle nudge with my knees, and she picked her way carefully through the crowd, somehow managing to sidle up to the Emperor's great black stallion without actually bumping into any of the other horses. Several of the young women astride those horses shot me annoyed glances, but they knew better to say anything when it had become increasingly clear that His Majesty had extended me some special favor.

"Good afternoon, Ashara," he said, and ran an appraising eye over the blood-bay mare I rode. "Your aunt is obviously a good judge of horseflesh, if that is the mount she chose for you to ride."

"She does have exquisite taste, Your Majesty," I allowed, reaching up to stroke Maelyn's neck. "I daresay my own father had no better horse in his stables."

"Now I see why you were so confident at dinner last night." He smiled at me, and it was as if the sun had doubled in intensity. I felt a rush of heat go over me that had very little to do with the warmth of the afternoon.

Somehow I managed to keep my tone light as I replied, "As to that, I suppose we will just have to see, Your Majesty."

He laughed then and gestured for the same tall, dignified man I had met last night, whom Gabrinne had identified as Lord Hein, to approach. "Are we all more or less assembled?"

"Yes, Your Majesty. All those who said they would ride are accounted for, and so we may commence at your pleasure."

"It pleases me that we start now," the Emperor said, and his gaze slid sideways toward me before he looked back at his seneschal.

Lord Hein bowed. "Of course, Your Majesty."

I heard several shouted commands then, although I could not make out what they were. However, the guards interspersed with the young women and the nobles seemed to fan out and take positions where they were evenly spaced amongst everyone else, and then the conversation died off as a great pack of noisy dogs was brought out, straining at their leashes. A horn sounded, and the hounds were let loose, baying and barking as they charged into the forest.

My father had not been a great hunter—and we did not have the wealth to support a stable of horses and hounds—but I knew enough about the process that what happened next wasn't entirely unexpected. The great throng of horses, which had been standing placidly only a few seconds earlier, now leapt forward, a straining mass of horseflesh following the dogs into the trees.

Thank goodness Maelyn seemed to know exactly what to do, and she surged into the woods with the rest of them, her pace picking up with no signal from me. The Emperor on his black stallion was just a few yards ahead of me, and I signaled my own mount that she should follow them. Without hesitation she shifted the direction in which she was running so we were nearly in a straight line, the space between us closing fast. I had no idea whether any of the other riders' horses were as good as ours, or whether they purposely hung back so they would not be seen besting the Emperor, but for whatever reason, it seemed the gap between the two of us and the rest of the group was slowly but steadily growing.

Even the guards appeared to be falling behind, much to their consternation. I heard one or two desperate cries of

"Your Majesty!", but the Emperor affected not to hear them. Indeed, he turned and looked over his shoulder at me, then grinned, his teeth seeming very white in the relative gloom of the forest. He said nothing, but that glance told me everything.

So you want a race? I thought. *Then you shall have one.*

I flapped the reins against Maelynn's neck and felt the powerful muscles beneath me push forward with a burst of speed that brought us nearly neck and neck with the Emperor's stallion. Odd how it seemed that my muscles recalled exactly what to do—how to balance myself in the sidesaddle, to lean into my horse's stride, becoming one with it.

A stream meandered across our path, and the Emperor's horse sailed directly over it. I felt Maelyn tense for the jump, and I caught my breath, wondering if I could still maintain my seat through it all. It had been a very long time since I had ridden at all, let alone jumped over the low hedgerows on my father's estate.

But then Maelyn's leap was over so quickly I hardly had time to think about it, and we were tearing down a narrow track, so narrow that once or twice I felt a tree branch scrape against my shoulder, or my leg. And all the while the sounds of the other riders and the belling of the hounds grew fainter and fainter, until at last the Emperor and I might have been the only ones riding through these woods.

Because the track was so cramped, I let Maelyn fall behind. It was impossible for two to ride abreast here. After a few more minutes, however, we emerged into a clearing, and I leaned forward and whispered, "Now, Maelyn."

She bolted forward, hooves tearing at the dead leaves and dry grass underfoot, and we shot ahead of the Emperor and his horse, thundering to the other side of the glade, where I pulled her to a stop and patted her heaving sides.

"I believe that makes me the winner, Your Majesty," I called out as he came to a halt a few paces away.

"So it does, Ashara." He did not seem disappointed that I had bested him; indeed, he smiled as he dismounted and came forward, extending a hand to me.

Of course I could not refuse it, so I wrapped my fingers around his and allowed him to help me down from the saddle. "Thank you, Your Majesty."

"Torric," he said.

Those dark eyes seemed to be searing into me, and were far too close. I looked away, instead staring down at the muddy earth. "I could not," I murmured.

"Even if I command it?"

I glanced up then, forced myself to meet his gaze. "So you command me to not address you as my Emperor?"

"If that is what it takes, yes." He still held my hand, and I felt his fingers tighten around mine. "Please."

This request shocked me so—who had ever heard of the Emperor saying "please" to anyone?—that I said, "Very well...Torric."

The smile returned. "Ah, that is better. What use for such formalities, when it is just the two of us here?"

I had to concede that he had a point. "So do you often do things like this?"

"Like what? Run off into the woods with a beautiful woman?"

Heat flared in my cheeks, but somehow I made myself hold his gaze, and not stammer and stare down at my feet as I wished to do. "Well, not precisely that, but a little. That is, do you often go tearing off and leave your guards behind? I must say they sounded quite worried."

Some of the light went out of his eyes, but his tone was casual enough as he said, "Ah, I wish it were so, but no—they dog my steps every minute of my life. This is a blessed respite."

I caught the note of weariness in his voice, and wondered at it. Then again, I had very little idea of what an emperor's life was like. He had just given me a glimpse that perhaps it wasn't quite as rosy as I had thought it might be. "And you have no fear, being out here without their protection? After all, I assume you must have guards for a reason."

He shook his head and chuckled. "I have ridden in these woods since I was a boy. There is nothing here to harm us, for all the bears and wolves were driven to wilder places long ago. And if I have aught to fear from my fellow man, well, then, let them come." His hand strayed to his hip, and for the first time I noticed that he wore a long knife—or perhaps it was a short sword—in a scabbard of finely tooled leather hanging from his belt.

Whether he had meant his words to hearten me, I did not know. I must confess that the sight of that knife was not particularly encouraging, and I hoped he would have no cause to use it. "Do you think they will find us soon?" I asked.

An offhand shrug. "I do not know. If they give my scent to the hounds, in time they will come here. But they will have to divert them from their present quarry for that to work, and that may take some time." His eyebrows lifted, and those dark eyes were intent on my face, as if seeking to read my very thoughts from my expression. "Why? Do you wish for them to find us?"

Oh, I had no good answer to that question! For while some part of me trembled to be alone with him like this, a far greater part was very glad to be here, to stand in this glade with the rustle of the leaves around us, and the gentle touch of the wind on our faces, and the sounds of distant bird song. We might have been the only two people in the world.

"No," I said at last. "I must confess I do not."

There was something very beautiful about his smiles, something more than the way they revealed his straight white teeth and crinkled at the corners of his eyes. For some reason I thought he did not often have occasion to smile like this, joyously and with no care as to what anyone around him might be thinking. "That gladdens me, Ashara. It is so difficult to say what is truly on one's mind when surrounded by so many people, don't you think?"

With that statement I could most heartily agree. "Oh, yes. Indeed, sometimes I wonder how you must bear it, to live so much in the public's eye."

Almost as soon as the words left my mouth, I wished I could take them back. His expression darkened, and the finely sculpted lips compressed somewhat. Then he shook his head and said in a low voice, "Could you bear it, Ashara?"

"Could I—I am not sure what you mean," I faltered, although I thought I did, and the idea thrilled me and frightened me at the same time.

He took my hands in his, and I almost fancied I could feel the heat of his flesh through the thin kidskin that covered both our fingers. "Could you bear that scrutiny, to live your life as the highest lady in Sirlende, knowing all eyes would be upon you at all times? For that is what it means to be Empress."

This was all too sudden. A wave of faintness washed over me, and I pulled my hands from his, stumbling over a tree root as I tried to back away. At once his arm was around my waist, supporting me, strong and sturdy.

"It frightens you," he said flatly.

"No," I protested. "That is—this is all so sudden. We only met the day before last, and have had very little opportunity to speak to one another. And now you are saying—" I broke off and shook my head. At the same time, though, I realized that I had made no attempt to pull away from him, that he held me now more intimately than anyone ever had before.

"I am saying I have chosen you, Ashara. Oh, I will go on with this farce, because the wheels have been set in motion and it will be too difficult to stop them, but know now that I have eyes for no one but you. And I knew this from the first time I saw you." His dark eyes were keen, studying me, and he added, "Tell me now if you do not feel the same way. I can think of no one else I would rather have as my wife, but I am not some tyrant of old, forcing an unwilling woman to his bed."

Unwilling? I let out a quavering sort of laugh and shook my head. "No, Torric, it is not that I do not feel the same way. To be honest, I do not know what I feel. I cannot stop thinking of you, of the way your lashes almost hide your eyes when you smile, the sound of your laugh—everything. I thought these were just the foolish fancies of a young woman, that you could not possibly be thinking of me, that you would of course want someone far grander for Empress, that—"

And I could go no further, for he pulled me to him then, his mouth on mine, the taste and feel and scent of him filling the entire world. I had not thought how real a man could be, how solid and strong, how I would open my mouth to his and feel our bodies press together, how a sudden unexpected heat would flood along every vein so that I could do nothing but cling to him and pray that this bliss would never end.

It did, of course, but long moments afterward. He pulled away just far enough for me to catch my breath. One hand reached up to brush a stray strand of hair away from my face; it must have come loose during our headlong gallop through the woods.

"Does that mean yes?" he asked. The words were soft, spoken barely above a murmur, but I thought I saw a glint of amusement in his eyes.

"Yes," I said. "Oh, yes. But—for you. Because of you. Not because I want to be Empress. The thought rather terrifies me, to be honest. But I would have fallen in love with you if I had seen you on the street, driving a cart of vegetables to market."

At that remark he actually tilted his head back and laughed, a good hearty laugh that seemed to echo through the forest. "Ah, that paints a pretty picture. I can only imagine what my mother would say if she overheard such a comment."

I recalled the icily beautiful woman with the sharp tongue at the dinner table and tried not to shiver. The Dowager Empress was certainly not a very congenial woman. It seemed I would be trading my harpy of a stepmother for a mother-in-law who was equally intimidating, but I would not allow that to deter me. I thought I could put up with a good deal if it meant I would have Torric.

Besides, the palace was very large. How difficult could it be to avoid her whenever possible?

"I would think she'd be happy to know that I want you for you, and not because of the position such a match would give me."

"'Happy' and my mother are not two things that go together very often." His expression sobered. "In fact, I believe she would not even understand such a sentiment, for she has come to believe that the only reason for a marriage is to advance oneself."

"She did—she did not love the late Emperor?" It felt odd to ask such an intimate question, but after all, Torric and I had just shared our own intimacy, and I had agreed to be his wife. Surely there should be no secrets between us.

Well, save the one I must keep, on pain of death.

"Gods, no. It was a match made for politics, as these things always are." Torric frowned and turned away from me slightly, seeming to stare at the horses, who had taken advantage of our wandering attention and had begun to graze on the dry autumn grass. "I think he tried to care for her—my father was a man of great good humor, whatever else one might say about him—and he did not wish for any discord in his household. But she had loved someone else, and had the match denied her, and so she forever closed her heart to him. And to my sister and me as well, I think. She could not look at us without seeing him, you know, and it kept her from forming a mother's attachment."

My heart was wrung upon hearing such revelations. The gods knew my life had not been a happy one these past ten years, but before that I had had my father, had known that he loved me and wished only the best for me. And my mother had loved me as well, in those scant few years we had together before she was taken from us so prematurely. It was hard, but how much harder must it be to have a mother who had never loved you, who only saw you as the offspring of a man she despised?

Silently I went to Torric and put my arms around him. He was no longer the Emperor, but a man who had seen his own share of hurt, a man I hoped to comfort. Almost at once he returned the embrace, folding me against him, his lips brushing against my hair just past the brim of the jaunty little cap I wore.

"I am so sorry," I murmured, and I felt his arms tighten about me.

"No need. I am a grown man, and have long since resigned myself to the situation. But you see now why I wanted to choose my wife, to make my marriage something more than a sham created by politics."

"I do see," I told him. "And glad I am that by some miracle you found me amongst all those other young women."

"That was not hard—you shine forth among them like a diamond in a mountain of coal."

Those words brought a flush to my cheeks, though of course he could not see it with my face buried against his chest as it was. "Ah, well, you must still shine a light on a diamond to see its sparkle, must you not?"

"True enough." He released me then, and took my hands in his. "Ashara, I wish we could return and tell everyone what has passed between us here. But we have two more days to go ere these festivities are done and I can finally name my bride. Can you manage to keep a secret for those two days?"

Oh, I was good enough at keeping secrets. Not trusting myself to speak, I nodded.

"Excellent. And do not be jealous if you see me paying attention to some of those other girls, for I must pretend enough to keep people from guessing. Know that my heart is yours and yours alone."

I understood the reasons for this, and although I did not care for them overmuch, I hoped I could be brave enough to accept them. Two days was not such a span of time after all. We had only met two days ago, and yet now I could barely imagine a world without Torric. "I shall not be jealous," I told him, then shot him a sly smile and added, "As long as you do not mind if perhaps I flirt with other young men?"

He put a hand to his breast and mock-staggered backward. "Ah, Ashara, you wound me! Very well, flirt if you must. It will keep people guessing."

To be sure, I did not think I cared much for the idea of leading on young men in whom I had no real interest.

However, if such subterfuges would help to keep the true nature of my relationship with Torric a secret, then so be it. I opened my mouth to say as much, but then I heard the pounding of approaching hoofbeats, and the baying of the hounds, and I knew that our idyll here in the forest was about to be cut short.

Torric heard them, too, of course—his head went up, and he turned away from me, his mouth tightening. In an undertone he said to me, "I will find a way to be alone with you tomorrow night. Be ready."

"I will," I said, and wondered what he had planned. I supposed I would find out soon enough.

He moved away from me, toward my horse, and made rather a fuss of adjusting the girth on my saddle. I wondered what he was doing...until I realized he was putting on a show for the men who even now burst into the clearing, a harried-looking Lord Hein at their head. No doubt Torric wanted the search party to think my horse had bolted and brought us here, and he was only trying to assist me so that we might rejoin the others. Quickly I leaned up against a tree, and put a hand to my brow as if distressed by what had just occurred.

As I did so, he caught the gesture and winked at me, even as some ten mounted guards burst into the little glade. Despite everything, I felt a little rush of relief.

Whatever happened next, at least I would not have to face it alone.

CHAPTER TEN

Torric

To say Lord Hein was displeased would be a severe under-
statement, and Renwell Blane, the leader of my guards,
was even more incensed.

"Your Majesty, anything could have happened!" he said,
as I helped Ashara back into her saddle and then got back up
on my own horse. "It is not safe—"

"On the contrary, Blane, it is perfectly safe. These woods
are an imperial preserve. There is nothing here more dangerous than a few foxes. Indeed, it is the foxes who should be in
fear of their lives, not I."

Something that sounded suspiciously like a muffled
snort came from Ashara's direction. I dared not look at her,
for I wanted to make sure all attention was centered on me,
and kept away from her. I could imagine her expression,

however—those amber-hazel eyes dancing with mischief, her lovely lips pursed in an attempt to hold in her laughter.

"Your Majesty—"

"Enough. I understand your concern, even though I believe it is entirely unwarranted. Now, Blane, since Lady Ashara's horse has been stopped, and we are all safe and sound, I suggest we go back to the reception before we miss it entirely."

Blane and Hein exchanged knowing looks, but of course they knew better than to pursue the debate any further.

"As you wish, Your Majesty," said the captain of my guard, and wheeled his horse around. Lord Hein fell in behind him, and the rest of the troupe surrounded Ashara and me. No more daring escapes for us; I sensed that the men would ride as close to us as propriety allowed so that we might not have another chance to leave them behind.

Ah, well. I could not ask for anything more, really. I had had my time with Ashara, had tasted her sweet lips and felt her slim form pressed up against mine, and it seemed greedy to wish for more of her. Not yet, anyway. Perhaps the cynical observer would have said it was a foregone conclusion that she would accept my offer of marriage, but I was not so sure. I had spent too much of my life surrounded by those currying favor and saying that which they thought I expected to hear to not perceive the ring of truth when I heard it. Ashara had said she loved me for me, and not my rank, and I believed her.

Truly, it would be difficult to pretend, to make the world think I had not yet made up my mind, but I would do my best. It would be better for Ashara, I thought, if I spread my attentions around somewhat, for I had already seen that many of the other girls had cast malicious glances in her direction when she rode up today. That we had disappeared into the woods together would make tongues wag even more, I wagered, and so I must do what I could to stop their wagging, if only briefly.

I did not look back at her, but I was keenly aware of her presence there, almost fancied I could smell a sweet drift of perfume from her hair. Foolishness, really—there were many scents here in the forest, not all of them pleasant, so to think I could sense the flowery scent of her hair rinse was merely fancy on my part.

It would have been a grand thing for me to slow my horse so I rode parallel with her, so I could reach out and take her in my arms and ride far, far away, someplace where I need not have guards surrounding me everywhere I went, someplace where I would not have to look at Lord Hein's frown or the scowl the captain of my guard still wore. But since I knew such a maneuver would be blocked before it even began, I merely rode on, my head high, a smile born of long practice on my lips.

And so it was that we cantered back to the edge of the forest, to the green field where the pavilions had been set up and a crowd awaited us. It appeared that the other young women who had participated in the hunt had long since dismounted, their horses led away. The murmur of their voices grew louder as we approached, drowning out the sweet strains of a group of musicians in the largest of the pavilions.

I dismounted and handed off the reins to a waiting groom. As much as I wished to go back to Ashara, to help her down from her horse, I knew that would only be showing the sort of regard I was attempting to conceal. So I marched toward the imperial pavilion as if I did not have a care in the world, leaving Ashara to manage on her own—and hoping she would understand the motivations for my actions.

Lyarris greeted me with a rueful smile. "I hear you have had quite the adventure."

"Oh, nothing much. The young lady's horse bolted, and I followed, to make sure she came to no harm."

"Is that what happened?" My sister's dark eyes danced as she gave acknowledged the lie; she knew of my feelings for Ashara, even if she did not realize how serious things had become between us. "Well, I am glad the 'young lady' is all right, and you as well. Mother was furious, as you can imagine."

I could, unfortunately. "Where is she? I must do my best to avoid her."

"Oh, she has gone off to one of the other pavilions, for she thought it too crowded in here. I daresay she will be back soon enough, once she has wearied of a new batch of people bowing and scraping to her."

"Careful, sister—you are beginning to sound a bit too much like me."

Lyarris did not precisely grimace, but I saw her mouth tighten. "Well, it has been one thing after another, you know—first she did not care for what the musicians were playing, and then she complained that her gown was too long to be walking about in this grass, and then the cooks did not make the meat pastries she wanted…even though she told no one of her preference. I expect she thought they should just pick the idea out of her mind, like one of those mages in the old days who were supposed to see your thoughts. Anyway, it has been rather trying, and…" She broke off then, and her gaze strayed to the tall form of Sorthannic Sedassa where he stood on the other side of the pavilion, speaking with Lord Hildar. Yes, I could see why my sister would be put out, when she finally had a chance to steal some time with the Duke of Marric's Rest, only to be thwarted by the incessant complaints of our mother.

I saw no sign of Lord Hildar's daughter, the irrepressible Gabrinne, or of her quarry, Lord Senric. "Is the Duke of Gahm here? I thought he was supposed to attend."

As I had hoped, my question distracted Lyarris from her romantic woes, and she smiled. "Oh, yes, he's here…pursued by a very determined Lady Gabrinne. I believe she led him over to that stand of oak yonder. Something about helping her determine if the leaves are about to turn."

"She couldn't think of anything better than that?"

A shrug. "It seems to have worked, because they went forth a quarter-hour earlier and have not returned. I have to say that he did not seem all that reluctant about going with her."

"No, I somehow doubt he would. There is something in her aspect that tells me she isn't above stealing a kiss or two, as long as no one is looking." Even more than that— the daughter of an earl was watched too closely to be truly wanton, but I had the feeling Gabrinne would have no problem allowing Lord Senric to compromise her just a little, if it meant a speedier trip to the altar.

"And what about you?"

I raised my eyebrows. "I am not sure I understand what you are asking."

She shook her head. "Oh, play the innocent if you must, but I know you better than that. Tell everyone that Lady Ashara's horse bolted and you most chivalrously followed to see that she came to no harm…but I rather think there might have been some kiss-stealing involved there as well."

"And I rather think that perhaps you have been spending too much time writing down people's stories, and so are inventing them when in fact there are none."

Being Lyarris, she did not take offense at my words, but only smiled somewhat. "You may tell yourself that, if it makes you feel better. But now I think you had better make your rounds, or the young ladies will be even more restless than they are already. You should have heard the chatter when news came back that you had disappeared into the woods to the gods only knew where!"

Since I had a good idea of how raucous it must have been, I was very glad I had not been around to hear it. But my sister was right—I needed to walk amongst the young women, smile upon a chosen few, and make it seem as if I had not a care in the world, and specifically no special regard for a certain Ashara Millende.

As I stepped from the pavilion, two guards immediately fell in behind me. It appeared Renwell Blane was taking no chances.

Smothering a grin, I went to the tent where roughly a third of the young women had gathered. At once they fell in around me, filling the air with their babbling: "Your Majesty, is all well with you?" "Your Majesty, you gave us all such a turn!" "Your Majesty, are you going to have another hunt, since this one ended so badly?"

I turned to see who had asked that last question, and looked down into Brinda Aldrenne's glinting dark eyes. It did not surprise me that she should be so forward; I had heard she was quite the horsewoman, and so of course she would be upset that her chance to shine should be set so awry.

Raising a hand, I said, "Ladies, my deepest apologies if the afternoon has not gone quite the way we all expected. I am here now, and am quite well. And Lady Brinda," I added, making sure to catch her gaze and hold it, "I do regret that the hunt did not turn out as planned, but unfortunately we have a strict schedule this week, and I cannot ask my seneschal to set up another hunt."

Her mouth turned down, making what I normally would have considered to be a rather pretty pout...if I did not know how much lovelier Ashara's mouth was, or what a viper Brinda could be. "I understand, Your Majesty," she replied, and although her tone was uncharacteristically meek, I saw a flash of anger in her eyes.

I knew better than to acknowledge that anger, however. Still smiling, I said, "Be of good cheer, Brinda. Perhaps I can assuage your disappointment by asking you to sit by me at the musicale tomorrow evening?"

The anger was gone immediately, replaced by a bright avaricious glint. "Oh, Your Majesty, I would be so honored!"

"Excellent," I told her, and went on to smile and even laugh as best I could as I made my way through the pavilion before moving on to the next. Gods, what a sacrifice I was making. To have to endure Brinda Aldrenne's loathsome company all the next evening! But I could think of no better way to pacify her, and it was only for a few hours. Besides, I had already told Ashara I would find a way to slip off and be alone with her, so I did have something to look forward to. How precisely I was going to manage such a feat, I did not know. Ah, well, I had some hours in which to formulate a plan.

In the meantime, I would just have to suffer the company of all these importunate young women, and hope none of them would notice how weary I already was of all of them.

Truly, the rest of the afternoon proved to be as tedious as I had expected, with two exceptions. As I returned to the royal pavilion after dutifully making my rounds, I spied Lord Senric and Gabrinne Nelandre standing very close to one another, their fingers entwined. Probably no one else noticed, or cared; he was not the prize all those girls sought. Well, save one. But I smiled a little as I entered the pavilion, a smile that only broadened as I saw my sister and Lord Sorthannic apparently deep in conversation, oblivious to the jaundiced stare my mother was sending their way.

"You look displeased," I said casually, signaling one of the servants for a goblet of wine. All that talking to all those young women had dried out my throat most uncomfortably. "I thought you did not disapprove of such a match."

She lifted her shoulders. "My daughter should be marrying a prince. But since there are none to be had, I suppose she must settle for a mere duke. I just wish the duke in question were someone else."

Good thing the two subjects of our discussion were so engrossed in their own conversation that they seemed not to notice my mother's words, for she took no care to keep her voice down. A servant handed me my wine and bowed. I took a sip before saying, "Why? Sorthannic Sedassa seems like a very worthy person."

"Oh, he is handsome enough, I will grant you that. And he does seem to have some skill on the tourney field. I just wish his father had had the sense to marry a good Sirlendian nobleman's daughter instead of some commoner from South Eredor!" She uttered the word "commoner" with such bile she might as well have said "whore."

I did not know why I should be surprised; I had heard much worse from her over the years. Even so, I found myself defending the woman in question, though I had never met her and doubted I ever will. "I have heard that her family is quite prosperous, and in fact owns extensive vineyards in South Eredor. So I do believe there are commoners and commoners, Mother."

She gave me a blank look. "But they are involved in trade, Torric."

At that point I decided to abandon the argument. I knew I would never win, and expending the energy seemed a useless exercise. For all her complaining, she would not openly oppose the match, if it were to happen at all, simply because she knew there were few candidates of acceptable rank and age to take Lyarris' hand in marriage. Lucky for Lyarris, only I as the Emperor had the power to outright forbid her the match, and of course I would do no such thing. If the Dowager Empress envisioned Lord Sorthannic's mother as some common wench not above stomping the grapes from her family's vineyard, well, so be it. I did not know the Duke of Marric's Rest all that well, but I rather imagined he would only laugh if word of such spiteful fancies came to his ears.

Wishing to turn the conversation away from Lord Sorthannic's relations, I asked, "And how is the work progressing on your gown for the ball on Friday evening? Lyarris told me it was going to be quite magnificent. Everyone else will pale beside you."

"I rather doubt that," she said, "seeing as I am far past the prime of my youth. But thank you for distracting me." She cast a disapproving glance toward the Duke of Marric's Rest and my sister, and then at the denizens of the pavilion as a whole. "Since you have done your duty and walked amongst your adoring crowds once again, how much longer must this farce go on? I am becoming weary and wish to lie down and rest before supper."

For once I agreed with her. I had had my stolen time with Ashara, and then done as I must and met the other young women once again, and so there seemed to be little reason to continue the reception. Save one, of course.

I looked toward my sister and the Duke just in time to see him bow low over her hand and smile before exiting the pavilion. Since their little interlude had come to an end, it seemed an appropriate time to signal to Lord Hein.

He came over at once, and bowed. "Yes, Your Majesty?"

"It seems that the event has run its course. You may begin the business of having the young women disperse."

"Of course, Your Majesty."

Watching him perform his duties was always a pleasure—he seemed to manage everything so smoothly that one didn't quite know how things happened, but somehow they always did. Within a few minutes crowds of young women began to flow past, those who had participated in the hunt retrieving their mounts, and those who had not going to the carriages that had been waiting for them all this time. They assembled into a huge moving mass, heading toward the road and back to town, leaving a trail of dust in their wake.

As they passed I searched in vain for Ashara, thinking surely I would see the rich burnished copper of her hair amongst the sea of brown and black, but the crowd was too thick. I tried to keep the disappointment from rising in my breast, for truly I had shared a precious space of time with her, something which could not be taken from me. And I would see her tomorrow evening, whatever it took. I needed some sort of reward for inflicting Brinda Aldrenne upon myself.

In due time the imperial pavilion emptied as well, and I saw my sister and my mother into their carriage before mounting my own horse and riding off after them, accompanied by my guards. There was still a hum of activity around the reception area, activity I guessed would go on until sunset—packing up the uneaten food, breaking down the pavilions and the camp furniture and loading it all onto the great wagons that had been parked some distance away so as not to interfere with the festivities.

Although I enjoyed riding, I almost wished I could be in the carriage with Lyarris, just so I could learn something of what had passed between her and Lord Sorthannic. Then I realized we could not share any confidences, not with our mother there as well. We would have to talk later, after she had retired for the evening. That was one blessing—at least the Dowager Empress did not care to stay up late, and often retreated to her chambers long before the rest of the company would even begin to contemplate repairing to their various domiciles.

It would be good to see Lyarris settled, although I knew I would miss her a good deal. Marric's Rest was some days' ride north, and although the Sedassas had a very fine town-house here in Iselfex, Lord Sorthannic did not appear to have much taste for the capital's entertainments and diversions. This raised him in my estimation rather than the reverse; I knew my sister would have a steady, worthy man as her husband, and not someone given to dissipation and idleness, or hanging about the court and currying favor.

But I was getting ahead of myself. One conversation, no matter how intimate it might look, was certainly not a clear indication of an attachment. Perhaps now that I had my future with Ashara settled, I wished to make sure everyone else around me enjoyed that same happiness. I thought again of her sweet lips, the heat of her body, and wanted to drive my spurs into my mount's sides so I might rush forward and find her, take her to the palace here and now, make her my wife before the night was over so I might taste all of her, not just her lovely mouth.

Somehow I managed to restrain myself. Such headlong action would gain me nothing, save a group of very disgruntled young women—not to mention their parents, who had gone to considerable expense to make sure their daughters would present as well as possible at court. Better to expend my energies on determining the best way to slip out of the musicale and have Ashara meet me someplace hidden, someplace secret and safe.

The musical entertainment was planned for the large audience hall, as we did not need quite as much room as we had the night of the banquet. Besides, Lord Hein had intimated during his planning that preparing the grand ballroom would take more than the space of a day, and so another room was required for the musicale. In the audience chamber was a dais which usually held the throne I used on audience days, but on the night in question would instead host the musicians, with large screens of carved wood set behind them.

I would be seated in the front row of the audience, of course, which was better than sitting on a throne on the dais, but still highly visible. What I needed was a reason to get up and leave the room…but with everyone watching me, how could I do so in a manner which seemed plausible? Well, an Emperor had many claims on his time. It should not be too difficult to have someone appear and summon me away—on urgent matters of state, or a similar emergency.

Lord Keldryn came to mind first, but I knew he would vigorously protest such a subterfuge, especially if he were to learn of the true reason behind it. Lord Hein would be too busy making sure everything was running smoothly for me to make any further demands on his time. But Renwell Blane…yes, the captain of my guard would do as I bade him, and surely no one would think it odd that my captain might need to speak with me, even in the middle of a musicale.

Yes, that would probably work. Now, to get Ashara out of the room as well. I could always send her a note—once I had someone identify exactly where the Millende household was located—but that seemed as if I would be tipping my hand, to send a personal note to her house. I recalled then that she had appeared friendly with Gabrinne Nelandre. That young lady certainly had no interest in being Empress, and so it should not discommode her to carry a note from me to Ashara.

I recalled then that the audience chamber had a secret passage in the southwest wall, opposite of the wall where the dais was located. If I instructed Ashara and Gabrinne to take their seats in the back row, then Ashara should be able to slip away and use the passage, which was hidden behind a tapestry. But how to keep people from noticing? I would have to enlist the Lady Gabrinne's aid in that—surely that enterprising young lady could come up with some way to bring all attention to her, so that no one would be looking in Ashara's direction.

Yes, that should do nicely.

That night I could not avoid company, as the trade ambassador from South Eredor had arrived several days early—an over-zealous wind, he claimed, although I wondered if King Vandor's spies had alerted him to my quest for a bride, and so sent the ambassador ahead of schedule, so he might bear witness to the goings-on and report back when everything was done. Not that I cared one way or the other, for the affair was certainly not a state secret. Besides, Sirlende certainly had nothing to fear from South Eredor. Its location made it an important shipping partner, but it was so small that the least of my provinces could have swallowed it whole.

So I endured the dinner as best I could, and smiled and made the appropriate responses. I had been glad to learn that Lord Hildar and Lady Gabrinne were to attend the function, as were Lord Senric and Lord Sorthannic. No doubt my seneschal had tendered their invitations solely to make sure it was a congenial group at dinner that night. At least he'd had the good sense not to invite the Baron of Kheldane and his gimlet-eyed daughter, although I thought that decision probably had been made based on the gentleman in question's rank and not because of his less than amiable personality.

Once I had learned Gabrinne would be there, I penned a hasty note to Ashara, instructing her on where and when to slip away from the audience the following evening. I did not sign the letter, deeming such a precaution wise in case Gabrinne should somehow let the note out of her sight. Then I folded it up and put it in the pouch on my belt, waiting for the opportunity to speak with her.

I had to hold back until after the dinner had concluded and she and her father were preparing to leave. The ambassador, of course, was staying on at the palace, but the Nelandre family had taken up residence at their townhouse for several weeks.

A touch on her elbow, and I said quietly, "A word, Lady Gabrinne."

She shot me a quick, speculative look but curtsied immediately. "Of course, Your Majesty."

I led her a few paces away from everyone else, noticing as I did so her father's smile of sudden interest, and the frown that passed over Lord Senric's face. He certainly had nothing to fear from me, but a little jealousy might just help to spur him along.

Dropping my voice to barely a whisper, I told Gabrinne, "I need you to do a favor for me."

Questions fairly danced in her eyes, but she said only, "Anything, Your Majesty."

I passed the folded piece of paper to her. "Make sure you get this to Lady Ashara before the musicale begins tomorrow evening. You will see her, won't you?"

"Oh, yes, Your Majesty. We'd already planned to sit together, since you went and told Brinda Aldrenne that she could sit next to you."

At another time I might have taken her to task for such pertness, but I let the remark pass. After all, I could not tell her that I had made such an offer to that wretched girl merely to throw any sharp-eyed observers off the scent. My tone neutral, I said, "Very good. And make sure to sit in the back row tomorrow evening."

"As you wish, Your Majesty." The words were correct, but I caught the lilt in her voice and the glint in her eyes, and knew she was madly speculating as to the contents of the note.

"I will know if that seal is disturbed," I told her, and she tossed her curls.

"As if I would do such a thing, Your Majesty. Don't worry—my friend will get this safely."

"Thank you, my lady. That will be all."

She curtsied again and all but tripped back over to her father, who gave her an indulgent smile. His hopes would be dashed soon enough, I feared. I would just have to hope that a duke would be an adequate replacement as a son-in-law.

As for the rest, everything seemed to be falling in place. Tomorrow evening I would see Ashara again, and we would have a stolen time together once more. After that remained only the ball, the time when we finally would be able to announce our engagement.

I smiled, knowing my plans were set, and that nothing should be able to hinder us further.

CHAPTER ELEVEN

Ashara

Returning home after such a glorious afternoon brought with it an even greater sense of disappointment than on the previous days. For this time he had kissed me, had professed his love, had asked me to be his wife. Bad enough we should part after such shared moments, that he must go among those other young women and pretend his heart was not yet given—that he should offer to have Brinda Aldrenne, of all people, sit next to him at the musicale.

The worst, though, was returning to the house on Stonecross Circle, of hastily trading places with my aunt before I could be discovered missing. It was still light, and Janks was roaming in and out, fetching firewood now that the nights had begun to be chill. There was no time to tell Aunt Therissa of what had passed between Torric and myself, no time for anything save a whispered "thank you" and a quick flight across the courtyard and up the back steps while my aunt hurried through the back gate and shut it quietly behind her. I had had no opportunity to inquire as to where she might be staying, but I thought it must be an inn near enough by that she could come and go here without too much difficulty.

And oh, how wretched to assist with serving dinner and have to listen to my stepmother grill Jenaris and Shelynne on the events of the afternoon, and to get their decidedly skewed perspective on what had occurred.

"The Emperor disappeared with that red-haired girl whilst on the hunt, but then they came back and went their separate ways, so I doubt he has any great desire for her company after all," declared Jenaris, after putting not one, but two rolls on her plate.

My stepmother sent her a scorching glare. "*One* roll, Jenaris."

"But Mamma, I've already touched it. I cannot put it *back*."

"Ashara, take the roll and put it in the dust bin," my stepmother commanded.

Knowing I could not possibly gainsay her, I stepped forward and took the roll between my thumb and forefinger, then marched it into the kitchen and dropped it in the refuse container. My heart panged as I did so, for there was a time I would have been very covetous of that discarded roll. Today I had eaten my fill at the reception, knowing my dinner would be sparse at best, but there had been many days before this one when I had had no such largesse to supplement my diet.

Claris raised her eyebrows at me as I disposed of the roll, and I could only lift my shoulders.

"Well, here is the soup," she said, without further comment, and I took it back to the dining room.

"...and the Emperor is going to sit with Brinda Aldrenne tomorrow evening, so you see, he really cannot be *that* interested in that one girl," Shelynne was saying as I set the soup tureen on the table and then retreated to a corner in case I should be called upon for some other task.

"I would say that is good news, except he is sitting with Lady Brinda and not you, and so you are in no better a position than you were yesterday," her mother replied tartly before helping herself to several ladlefuls of soup. Thank goodness our house was not quite so grand that I was expected to actually serve the food instead of simply bringing it to the table.

"Oh, Mamma," Shelynne said, sounding quite exasperated. "He has not given either Jenaris or me so much as a second glance, so I very much doubt anything is going to change between now and tomorrow evening."

I was surprised to hear such common sense coming out of Shelynne's mouth. Perhaps I had misjudged her.

"There is always a chance," my stepmother said darkly. "But if he is not going to choose either of you, then at least better that it be a baron's daughter rather than some redheaded chit whose name no one can seem to recall."

At these words she cast a baleful look in my direction, and I stared down at the floor, not daring to meet her eyes. Of course she could not suspect—not with my aunt here every day to stand in my place and hide my absences—but even so such scrutiny unnerved me.

"How is your hand, Ashara?" she asked abruptly, and I started.

"My—my hand?" I repeated.

"Claris said you cut your hand this morning whilst peeling potatoes. May I see it?"

Oh, good gods. Of course my own hands, although covered in a fairly notable collection of healed and half-healed scars, had no fresh wounds upon them. I gave a nervous laugh and said, "Oh, it was nothing, ma'am. It looked ill enough at the time, for it bled freely, but it is really only a trifle."

"I will be the judge of that. Come and show me," she commanded, "for I do not want you getting an infection when I will have so much need of you tomorrow to get the girls ready for the musicale."

There being nothing else I could do, I went with reluctant steps to stand by her, and extended my right hand. I had cut it earlier in the week, but it was already healing, showing a thin red streak along the forefinger. All I could do was hope that in the flickering candlelight she wouldn't notice the wound was no longer fresh.

My stepmother frowned as she looked down at it. "Oh, that is nothing. From the way Claris was talking, I thought it was far worse. Well enough. Go on—take the empty soup bowls and bring the next course."

Feeling limp with relief, I did as she bade me, for once not even caring about her peremptory tone of command. Claris watched as I came into the kitchen and took up the platter of roast beef, and asked, "Are you sure you can manage that with your hand?"

Now *she is inquiring as to my hand? Would that she had asked earlier so I might have been more prepared.* "It is fine. Really, I hardly notice it."

Well, that wasn't even a lie.

I returned to the dining room with the main course and was glad to hear that the conversation had turned away from me—the mysterious redheaded girl, that is—and gone on to a discussion of their preparations for tomorrow evening, of whether to bathe first thing, or wait so that they might be fresh for the festivities, which were not to begin until after sunset. Not that it really mattered, for even if they were to have their baths the moment they rose from their beds, my stepsisters would of course not exert themselves that day, but would instead lounge about as much as possible, wishing to conserve their energy for their all-important assignation at the palace.

Whereas I would be run ragged once again, and would have to do my best to present a good appearance when I was finally able to tear myself away from this wretched house.

No matter, I told myself, *for Torric already loves you, and if you appear a trifle weary, he will certainly not hold such a thing against you.*

That thought buoyed me a little, and gave me the strength to endure the rest of the evening—the inevitable dishwashing and scrubbing and putting the dishes and pots and pans away, the wiping down of the dining room table. Tomorrow would be tomorrow, and I would live through that as well, for I knew that I would see Torric that evening.

And that was all which mattered.

Truly, there was a good deal of hubbub the next day, which I had expected, but at least both my stepsisters' gowns passed muster, and so I was not drafted for any last-minute hemming or other repairs. They had decided to bathe later in the afternoon, and so spent most of their time in their room, Shelynne working at her embroidery, which she actually did excel at, and Jenaris not doing much of anything save lying abed and getting up from time to time to try the effect of a different set of jewels against her gown of celadon-green damask.

My stepmother's sister, the baroness, had offered the loan of some pieces from her own collection, and so the jewelry in question was quite magnificent—a set of emeralds in heavy gold, or creamy sea pearls in silver with sapphire accents. Jenaris decided on the emeralds, then spent a good deal of time sitting in front of the mirror and trying the heavy necklace about her throat, turning this way and that so the light would catch in the facets of the stones and flash with purest green.

I will admit that I quite envied her those jewels, but tried to console myself that, whatever my aunt had planned for my wardrobe tonight, it promised to be equally magnificent.

But it will not be real, I thought then. No, it wouldn't, but I knew if I wished for emeralds after I was Empress, Torric would be only too glad to oblige me. Let Jenaris have her peacock moment—her jewels would be borrowed as well, after all.

At last, after a light supper at around half past five, it was time to draw my stepsisters' baths, and to lay out their gowns and underthings, and their fans and cloaks and the pretty little embroidered pouches made to match their dresses. As usual, Mari attended to their hair, and even brushed powdered stain from a jar onto their cheeks and lips. When she was done, they did look rather lovely, although Jenaris wore a somewhat pinched expression, possibly because her new gown had been constructed with a good deal of whalebone built into the bodice to help slim her down somewhat.

The carriage rattled up to the door, and they sailed off into the night. Several blocks away, the watchman rang the hour. Seven o'clock. I had only half an hour to effect my own transformation and get to the palace.

I gathered up my stepsisters' discarded towels and made for the door, planning to use a trip to the laundry room off the kitchen as an excuse to get out to the stables, where no doubt my aunt already awaited me. However, I had not gone three paces before my stepmother said, "Ashara, when you go downstairs, fetch me a glass of port. I am feeling quite fatigued after all this tumult."

"Yes, ma'am," I said obediently, but inside I repeated a few choice curses I'd heard Janks utter over the years. If my stepmother was expecting me to come back upstairs directly, how could I possibly slip out to the stables? She'd be sure to notice if I were gone for more than a few minutes.

I fairly flew down the stairs and to the kitchen, where I told Claris that her ladyship requested port. As she went to pour it, I hastened to the laundry room and dropped the towels in the basket reserved for soiled linens and such, then hesitated. Did I dare slip outside and take my chances?

"It's ready," Claris called, and I knew I had no choice.

Holding back a sigh, I took up the little tray with the blown-glass goblet of port, as well as the sweet little wafers my stepmother liked to take with it. She had retired to the sitting room off her bedchamber, and I went there and deposited the tray on the table next to her favorite chair.

While my first instinct was to flee the room as soon as I had completed my errand, I knew that would only raise her suspicions. So I made myself pause a few steps away from the door, and asked, "Do you require anything else, ma'am?"

She had been standing at the table with the mirror hung above it where she usually performed her toilette; she did not give me an answer at once, but instead continued with taking the jewels from her ears and around her throat, and then placed them inside a small box of inlaid wood. After that she began to pull out the pins which held her hair in place, until finally a thick rope of unnaturally dark hair hung down her back.

Through all this I waited, all too conscious of the minutes ticking by, knowing I could do nothing about it. Finally she sat down and lifted her glass of port. "Is everything all right, Ashara? I must confess that you seem rather...anxious."

"Oh, no, ma'am," I said immediately. "Only that Claris is expecting me in the kitchen to help with the dishes, and if you did not need anything else..."

"Well," and she tilted her head to one side, as if considering, "that will be all for now, I suppose. I shall ring if I need anything else. Go on, if Claris is needing you."

I sketched the hastiest of curtseys and all but ran down the stairs, wondering as I did so what excuse I could use to slip out back to the stables. My stepmother had already had her port, so no need for me to go the wine cellar. And Janks had already laid all the fires, which meant I did not have any excuse to fetch more wood.

But Claris, bless her, called out to me as soon as I entered the kitchen, and told me to fetch Janks from his room off the stable, because she needed him to get a combination of dried herbs down from the highest shelf in the pantry.

"Nothing for it, except herself expects me to compound all new hair rinses for the girls, and this is this first chance I have to do it. Go get Janks for me, there's a love."

I murmured a breathless "of course" and rushed outside—not to Janks's quarters, but to the stables themselves. I would have to let Aunt Therissa fetch him while I hastened away.

She shot me an alarmed glance as I burst into the stables. "Ashara, it is so very late—"

"I know," I said, "but my stepmother would keep me at the most foolish tasks, and this is the first chance I've had to get away. Even now I am supposed to be fetching Janks, but you can do that after I've gone."

Comprehension lit her features. "Of course, my dear. Then here we are." She murmured the words of her spell, and at once I was resplendent in a gown of a deep blue green, against which my hair shone like pure copper.

"Thank you," I said. "I have so much to tell you, but no time in which to do it!"

"Don't fret about that. We can talk later. Just go, and show the Emperor how beautiful you are." And she murmured a few words again, and transformed herself.

At that I could only nod, now a little more used to seeing my own face staring back at me and smiling. There was time for nothing else besides that, and I hastened out the door, glad that my gown was a dark color so I might have a better chance of hiding amongst the shadows as I made my way to the gate. No sooner had I lifted the latch than I heard my aunt's voice—my voice—calling for Janks. Using the distraction, I slipped out onto the street and into the waiting carriage.

I couldn't even think what the time must be. They rang the bell only on the full hour, and so it could be only seven-twenty...or seven forty-five, in which case I was dreadfully late.

True, they had never started precisely on time at any of the other events. I prayed that would be the case this evening, for a late arrival at a musicale would be so much more obvious than at an open-air reception.

There were no carriages in the great courtyard before the palace, and my heart sank. Still, there was nothing I could do but press on and hope that I could slip into a seat in the back row without anyone noticing. For the first time I was glad that Torric had planned to sit with Brinda Aldrenne; it would have been too dreadful if I had had to make my way up to the front row with everyone watching.

An impassive-looking footman directed me to the chamber where the musicale was being held. The plaintive, sweet tones of a harp, viol, and flute drifted out into the corridor, and I swallowed. So they already had begun.

I tiptoed into the room and surveyed the back row. Yes, there was an empty seat on the end—and in the chair next to it sat Gabrinne. That is, I thought it must be she, judging by the riot of dark curls hanging down her back. Thank the gods that the empty seat was in an inconspicuous location.

Moving as silently as I could, I approached the vacant chair and sat down. Gabrinne started, then leaned over and whispered, "I was beginning to think you weren't coming!"

"I was delayed," I whispered back.

"A delay that could have cost you dearly," she replied, prompting a "shh!" from the pinch-faced girl sitting on her right side. Gabrinne grimaced, lowered her voice, and said, "I was supposed to give you this."

I felt her shove a piece of heavy folded paper into my hand. Puzzled, I stared down at it, saw that it had been sealed with a blob of crimson wax, although the wax had no crest or other identifying mark. Even so, I thought I could guess who it was from.

Wincing at every crackle of the thick paper, I carefully broke the seal and unfolded it. I had never seen his handwriting before, of course, but it seemed uniquely his—heavy and slanting, every stroke strong and sure.

Beloved, I must see you alone. At the midpoint of the musicale, the captain of the guard will come in to call me away. When you see me leave, slip away as well. There is a hidden door behind the tapestry on the south wall; use that, and follow the corridor behind it. You will come to a secret place known only to the imperial household. Your friend has said she will cause a distraction so you may leave unnoticed. Be ready.

This astonishing missive caused me to raise my head and cast a questioning look at Gabrinne. She glanced down at it and grinned, then nodded, as if to indicate she was ready to do her part when the time came.

I hastily refolded the paper and placed it in the pouch my aunt had provided, then folded my hands on my lap and willed myself to be calm. The musicians played on, but I feared I did not pay them much mind, even though I enjoyed music very much and often wished I could hear more of it.

It was nerve-wracking, to say the least, to sit there and maintain a placid expression on my face, to pretend I had nothing more on my mind than the music filling the chamber. Some time later—it felt like hours, although I knew it could not have been that long—a severe-looking man wearing a steel breastplate over his black and silver doublet entered the room, bowed, and went straight to Torric where he sat in the front row. The two of them had some sort of whispered exchange, and then he rose from his seat, appeared to offer some sort of apology to Brinda and the other young women in the row, and went out.

A murmur of voices swept over the room, no doubt of everyone attempting to determine what on earth could have taken the Emperor away from such an important event. I sat rooted in my chair, knowing I should go, but also knowing

I could do nothing until Gabrinne began her distraction, whatever that might be.

I was to find out soon enough.

"A mouse!" she screeched, and gathered up her heavy silk skirts and climbed onto her chair. "A mouse! Right there!" And she pointed a little farther down the row.

At once all the young women began crying out as well, either attempting to get on their own chairs so they would be out of harm's way, or scrambling to exit the row altogether. While the commotion grew and the music lurched on, the musicians clearly unsure what to do, Gabrinne whispered sharply, "Go on! What are you waiting for?"

I needed no further prompting. As young women began to scatter in all directions and footmen began to converge to seek out the offending rodent, I ran for the tapestry hanging on the south wall and lifted it, then felt along the paneling until my fingers found a small recess. I pressed on it, and a door swung inward. At once I slipped behind the tapestry and went through the door, then closed it behind me.

The corridor was dim, but I thought I saw the faint glow of candlelight some yards ahead. Moving carefully, I made way toward the light and prayed this was the "secret place" Torric had written of.

And so it proved to be, as I emerged into a small chamber some fifteen feet square, with a table and chairs in a heavier, more antique style than how the palace was currently furnished. Torric stood there, holding two silver goblets, while a flask of wine sat on the table itself.

"You were late," he said, and held out one of the goblets to me. "I began to fear all my plans would be for naught."

I took the goblet from him. "A thousand apologies. I was...delayed."

"Apparently."

Luckily, I saw no anger in his features. "I came as quickly as I could, once I had the chance to get away."

"'To get away'?" he repeated, looking more closely at my face. What precisely he saw there, I did not know, but it must not have been good, for I saw his eyes narrow before he asked, "What are you not telling me?"

Too much, I fear. I swallowed, then said, "It is nothing. Only—only my stepmother and I do not precisely see eye to eye on things. Of course I have said nothing to her of what has passed between the two of us, but I fear she has her suspicions. She wants everything for her own daughters, and as little as possible for me, and so she can be...difficult."

Torric took a grim swallow of wine. "Difficult, you say? I can teach her true difficulty, if she is causing you any sorrow."

His tone and expression told me he would be all too happy to intercede on my behalf, but of course I could not allow such a thing. "Oh, no, Torric, there is no need for that. After tomorrow night it will not matter, for we will have announced our engagement, and she will realize that I will soon be free of her control."

"I do not like it," he said flatly.

"I must confess that I do not like it much, either, but if I can endure her for another twenty-four hours or so, then surely it is not asking too much that you do the same?"

For a brief span of time he said nothing, and I worried that he would attempt to press the issue. Then something in his visage seemed to relax, and he gestured to the neglected goblet in my hand. "As you wish, my love. But drink with me—you have a look about you that says you are in need of some wine."

"That much is true," I confessed, and allowed myself a sip. I had had very little to eat that afternoon, what with all the hubbub in the household getting my stepsisters ready, and so I knew I could not have too much, or it would surely upset my head.

Torric was silent, watching me. I feared he would comment on my less than healthy swallow of wine, but he did not. Instead he inquired, his tone casual although his expression was not, "And which ones are your stepsisters? Have I paid any particular notice to them?"

"No, you have not—much to their chagrin." I had to quell a smile. Perhaps it was cruel of me, but some part of my soul was very glad that Torric had taken no notice of them at all. It was the only victory I had had over them. "Their names are Jenaris and Shelynne. Jenaris is rather, well...rounded, and—"

"Fat, you mean," Torric said with a grin.

"I do not mean fat. She is rather plump, however, and Shelynne has an unfortunate tendency to squint, as her eyesight is not very good."

That revelation prompted a chuckle from Torric. I raised an inquiring eyebrow at him, and he explained, "I do recall one girl who was always peering at me with the most peculiar expression. I thought perhaps she was touched in the head, and so kept my distance, but now I realize it was only extreme near-sightedness. That explains much."

"At any rate, my stepmother is perhaps not the most impartial judge of their charms—"

"I can see why."

"—and so she is not pleased when my stepsisters come home with tales of some red-haired girl who has charmed the Emperor. Luckily, they have not clearly seen me with you, and so there is always the possibility that it is some other young woman with red hair, and not me, but even so—"

"I understand." A certain glint entered his dark eyes, one that I did not entirely comprehend but which somehow made a flush rise to my cheeks. "Are you not glad that I am being so circumspect?" He waved a hand to indicate the hidden chamber where we now stood.

"'Circumspect' probably would have involved trying to stay away from one another until tomorrow night, but I suppose this will have to do," I said primly.

"Oh, come, Ashara, are you not glad you are here with me? Could you really have waited until tomorrow night for this?"

And before I could even think of a reply, he had set down his goblet and plucked mine from my hand, and pulled me into his arms. Oh, how strong he felt, how impossibly tall and solid and real! Of course I did not protest, but let him touch his mouth to mine, let his tongue caress my lips before moving to taste me even more fully.

A searing wave of heat moved through my body, seeming to throb through my veins, warming me everywhere—yes, even there, at the very center of my womanhood. I could not protest, did not even wish to. This was what I wanted, the feel and scent and taste of him, his hands moving over my body, his mouth moving down my neck to elicit a gasp from me even as a delicious shiver rocked me to my core.

Oh, what I wanton I was! For I knew in that moment I wanted all of him, wanted him in the same way Mari must have wanted Janks. For a second I had a flash of memory, of her legs wrapped around him, of his body on top of hers, and I wanted Torric to do that to me, to push me down onto his bed and fill the emptiness inside me. If he had told me then and there that the secret passageway went farther, led all the way to his own chambers, I would have gone with him willingly. Not just willingly—eagerly.

But sanity took hold, and after a moment I pulled away from Torric. Not abruptly, but gently, so I could look up at him and smile. His own face was flushed, and I saw the need in his eyes...but then he nodded, as if reminding himself that I was a lady, and his affianced bride, and that to push things much further would not be wise.

"Truly your blood runs hot, Ashara," he said in ragged tones, and then reached up to remove the golden circlet that contained his heavy dark hair so he might push it back off his forehead, as if he was in need of cooling.

I well understood how he felt, for though the neckline of my gown was fairly low, as befitted an evening dress, it still seemed suddenly stifling in the small chamber. "Yours as well, Your Majesty."

He sent me a slanted look at the honorific, and then smiled and shook his head. "It is perhaps better that we stop there, for I have no intention of compromising you."

Was it wrong that I felt a stab of disappointment at his words? In that moment I thought I rather wanted to be compromised. Ah, no, that would not be wise at all. I reached for my goblet and took a very unladylike gulp. "Then I hope it will be a very short engagement."

"Extremely short," he said at once. "Days. Hours, if I have anything to say about it."

I stifled a laugh and went to him, this time slipping my arm around his waist so I might be close, although I did not attempt to initiate another kiss. That was far too dangerous. "I rather think your seneschal might have a word or two to say about that. He does seem to be quite concerned with following the forms."

"Bother that." Torric pulled me closer against him, and placed a gentle kiss on the top of my head.

Something about the touch of his lips against my hair sent another thrill through me, although this wasn't quite desire. Perhaps it was just the tenderness of the gesture. After all, I had had very little tenderness in my life.

"If I could, I would have a priest marry us five minutes after we make the announcement at the ball," he added, and something in the fierce, quiet tone of his voice told me he really would do exactly that, if allowed.

Odd how less than a week ago I would have been sure that the Emperor of Sirlende could order everything exactly as he willed. Now, after knowing Torric for only a few short days, I knew that things did not precisely work that way.

"Ah, well," I said, making sure I did not sound overly concerned, "you would not want to deprive me of the joy of having a wedding gown designed, would you? Although I'm sure once you see my ball gown you will think I couldn't possibly have anything finer made."

This was, of course, another prevarication. Since I had had so little time to speak with my aunt, I really did not know what she had planned. However, judging by what she had managed to conjure for me so far this week, I had no doubt that my gown for the ball would turn out to be something truly magnificent.

He shook his head, and spun me to face him. His eyes, framed in those amazing thick lashes, seemed to bore into me. "My love, trust me when I say I am not particularly looking at your gowns. I am looking at *you*."

Again heat rose to my cheeks, but I did not look away from that intent dark stare. "Well, if we are making confessions here, I have to admit that if someone asked me what you had worn any particular day this week, I am not sure I could have answered. I spent all my attention on your face."

"Only my face?" he inquired, clearly amused.

"That, and other things," I replied, and let my gaze wander from the perfect symmetry of his face to the broad, strong shoulders and chest.

"And here I thought you were so innocent and pure?"

"I am, in body," I said frankly. "In mind, however…"

"Ah, I have had a taste of that. In fact, I think I am sufficiently recovered to try another."

Once more he took me in his arms, and I tasted the wine on his tongue and breathed in the warm, woodsy scent of his hair, and felt my body flare with heat again. And so we stayed for a long while, until we broke apart, gasping, and Torric murmured that he must return, for he had already been away too long.

I wondered how I might steal away back into the chamber where the musicale was being held, but he interrupted that thought, saying, "If you do not mind, my love, I think it would be more discreet for you to go directly to your carriage. If Gabrinne did her work sufficiently, then I doubt anyone is looking for you, and it would be safer if you did not try to sneak back in the way you got out."

That seemed sensible enough, although I wished I would not have to miss the reception. However, it would give Torric another opportunity to lavish his attention on some other young woman—Brinda Aldrenne, most likely and most unfortunately—and therefore deflect any inquiries away from me.

I nodded, and he continued, "I will lead you farther down the passageway. It comes out into the courtyard, and the footmen can then call for your carriage."

"Of course, Torric."

We kissed again, and then he took me by the hand and let me out into the dimly lit corridor, down past several narrow passages that broke off from the main one. I wanted to ask why these secret hallways were here at all, but we moved so quickly that I did not have the opportunity. Quite soon, we emerged into the damp, cool evening air—or rather, I did. Torric hung back so he might not be seen, and pressed his lips to my hand one last time before disappearing inside.

His absence felt like a hole in my heart, but I told myself not to be silly, that I would be seeing him tomorrow night, and then we would never be separated again.

The footman blinked in confusion as I approached him and inquired for my carriage. I was sure the poor man must have thought I materialized out of nowhere. Even so, he hurried off to do my bidding, and in a very brief amount of time my own driver was helping me up into the coach.

We rattled off into the darkness, and I lay my head against the cushions and shut my eyes, thinking of Torric's mouth on mine, his arms around me. And that was enough for now, because this was the last time we would have to say goodbye.

After the ball tomorrow, all of Sirlende would know I was to be their Empress.

CHAPTER TWELVE

Torric

Oh, it was hard to let her go, to watch her square her shoulders and walk away from me. The expression on her face told me all I needed to know. She had no more wish for this parting than I did.

But I had learned to master the travails of hard duty, even though I cared little for them. This would be our last separation. After we announced our engagement, I would make sure that Ashara was installed in an apartment here in the palace until our wedding day. Her recent revelations were enough to convince me that she should spend no more days under her stepmother's roof.

I felt my features harden into a mask of cold anger, thinking of the callous way that shrew had apparently treated the woman I loved. Ashara was perfection; she should not have to suffer a single harsh word, let alone see her unworthy stepsisters favored over her. I wished I could show this step-mother exactly what I thought of her behavior, but as Ashara wished me to let it go, I would...if reluctantly.

One of the branches from the hidden passageway emerged in a storeroom, and that was where I had already planned to come out, deeming it the least likely place for anyone to see me, appearing as I would from a doorway hidden behind a stack of unused furniture and outdated paintings. I slipped out and closed the door behind me, then brushed some dust from my velvet doublet. Blane had set two of his guards to await me in the corridor outside, for of course he would not allow me to return unescorted to the chamber where the musicale was being held.

If those two men thought there was anything strange about the Emperor of Sirlende exiting an unused storeroom while hundreds of prospective brides waited for him on the other side of the palace, their impassive faces did not reveal such musings. No real surprise; after all, it was not their place to judge my doings.

I set a brisk pace as I returned to the audience chamber and my expectant guests. Everyone turned to face me as I entered the room, and the musicians faltered briefly but then found their rhythm once again. Face composed in pleasant lines, I took my seat once again next to Brinda Aldrenne, whose sly eyes were full of questions she did not quite dare to ask.

Mercifully, the music did not last too much longer—not that I do not enjoy music, but if the musicians were ending their set, it meant we were that much closer to the conclusion of the evening, and therefore that much closer to tomorrow. The ball. Ashara.

My loins tightened as I recalled the feel of her mouth, her sweet scent, the taste of wine on those soft, full lips. I was not used to denying myself, but I had to stop her—stop us, for if we had pressed on, I would have abandoned all caution and slipped away with her to my bedchamber.

No, I could not think of that. Soon enough she would be my wife, would be mine in every way possible, but until then I had a role to play.

The musicians stood, and everyone clapped dutifully, but I could tell the mind of every young woman there was occupied far more with the reception that was about to follow, their penultimate chance to catch my eye. I must confess that I did feel a pang of guilt then, for most of them were honorable enough, here because they hoped to advance their family's name, and I knew I was deceiving them. Then again, they had all gone into this knowing that only one woman could be my wife. Was there anything so terribly wrong about realizing who that woman was before the five days ended?

I guessed that the women around me would think there might be, but I could do little about that now.

"...some air, Your Majesty?"

"I beg your pardon?" I inquired, realizing that Brinda Aldrenne had been speaking to me and that I hadn't heard half of what she'd said.

Those narrow dark eyes of hers narrowed further. "I was just saying that they were opening the doors to the courtyard, and asking if you wanted some air?"

A transparent ploy. While I had to give her some credit for attempting to keep me to herself, I knew I would never allow myself to be alone with her.

"Ah, I think it better that I take a turn around the reception chamber. But you are certainly welcome to accompany me."

Her expression, which had begun to cloud over, suddenly cleared, and a triumphant little smile played about her mouth. Now, this was one young woman I would feel no guilt over disappointing.

The audience chamber had an adjoining room that was sometimes used when the crowds expected were deemed to be of greater than average size. Now the servants were swinging open the large doors that connected the two spaces, and I saw in the chamber beyond tables heaped with sweets and the sort of small savory dishes so popular for evening functions, along with many bottles of wine that gleamed like dark jewels amongst the autumn leaves and warm-toned flowers.

Already people were flowing into that room, their hunger enhanced by having to sit and listen to music quietly for the greater part of two hours. As I rose from my seat, Brinda got up as well. She seemed determined to stick by my side like a cocklebur, and I made myself repress an exasperated sigh.

We had just entered the reception hall when two more young women approached us—or rather, they seemed acquainted with the Aldrenne girl, and sidled up to her in an obvious attempt to get closer to me. I recognized them at once, for they were a perfect fit to Ashara's description of them: one overly plump, the bodice of her pale green gown obviously more fortified than a castle's walls in a vain attempt to contain her generous bosom and rounded stomach, the other one passably pretty, but with an odd strained look to her dark eyes that belied their myopic tendencies.

The stepsisters.

I believe I managed to smile, and if the expression was somewhat strained around the edges, I do not think they noticed, for they were too busy curtseying and saying, "Good evening, Your Majesty."

"Lady Jenaris and Lady Shelynne Millende, Your Majesty," Brinda told me. Her tone seemed to indicate that she did not mind making the introduction, for she saw neither of them as a threat.

No, it is the sister who is not here who is the true threat...

"Ladies," I said, and bowed. How I wished I could say something cutting to them, a few carefully chosen words to let them know that I did not approve of them or their stepmother. But I had promised Ashara, and I did not make promises lightly.

"And what did you think of the music, Your Majesty?" inquired Shelynne, squinting as she attempted to focus on my face.

"I thought it was most excellent, my lady. And you?"

"Oh, it was quite the thing. Jenaris and I both adore music, although we have little opportunity to hear it. We—" And she broke off, for her sister had quite obviously jabbed her in the ribs to prevent her from saying anything else.

"What she means, Your Majesty," Jenaris cut in, "is that while we have music all the time, at dinner, or when we have our own dances at our house, we do not have quite so many musicians. So it was a treat to hear six of them playing at once."

At this revelation Brinda rolled her eyes, clearly not fooled by this pretense to a level of wealth I was sure they did not have. Yes, their mother had married a baronet who had passed away and left behind some wealth—Ashara's jewels were a testament to that if nothing else, although I supposed they could have been heirlooms of her own mother—but from what I had heard, most households of their rank did not employ regular musicians, but only hired them in for special occasions.

There did not seem to be much point in calling the sisters out for their lies, however. If it made them feel better to pretend to a wealth they did not possess, so be it. Their company was clearly tedious, but at least it prevented me from being alone with the predatory Aldrenne girl.

"Some refreshments?" I suggested, and spread a hand toward the glorious feast before us. Truly, it did look quite enticing. The heat of those kisses with Ashara seemed to have consumed my own supper, and I was hungry again.

"Oh, yes," said Jenaris. "I fear I am quite famished after all that music."

"But Jenaris, Mamma said you were not to eat anything—"

Another elbow to the ribs, and Shelynne went silent as she shot a glare at her sister and rubbed her side.

Brinda sniggered, then said, "I fear I am not that hungry, but perhaps some wine?"

The last thing I wanted was to share a cup of wine with her, but to refuse would be churlish. Worse, it would prove that I was only spending time with her to make it seem as if I had not yet made my final choice.

So I nodded and headed toward the refreshment tables. A servant hurried up to me, and I said, "Some wine for the lady. And you, Shelynne, Jenaris?"

They both curtseyed and blushed and said yes, of course, that would be lovely. The manservant fetched them all goblets of wine, then asked, "And for you, Your Majesty?"

"Yes, I think so." A goblet or two of wine would help get me through the evening, no doubt.

He brought it to me, then bowed and asked if there would be anything else. I surveyed the group of young woman and said, "Ah, put together a few plates of some delicacies. I trust your judgment."

A stammered thank-you and another bow, and he went to fulfill his duties. As he did so, I could see Brinda's brow lowering; no doubt she had not thought she would be saddled with the stepsisters for more than a few minutes. Then again, perhaps they were doing her a service. With the three of them clustering around me, there was not much room for any other, prettier supplicants to approach.

The servant came back with several plates of food, one of which he handed off to the young women to share amongst them, and the other to me. I took it and thanked him, then turned back to my three hangers-on, amused to see that Brinda declined any of the savories or sweets, while Jenaris promptly grabbed a plump pastry with a fig filling, over her sister's protests. Yes, I would definitely be doing Ashara a service by removing her permanently from their company.

"So, Your Majesty," Brinda said after taking a large swallow of wine, "what do you have planned for tomorrow evening? Is it going to be truly spectacular?"

You have no idea. But I only shook my head and took a bite of cinnamon-spiced meat pie. After I was finished chewing, I replied, "Ah, you know I cannot reveal such things ahead of time. Lord Hein wants the evening to be a true surprise."

She pouted. I had the feeling she used that pout often on her father, to good effect, and therefore thought it must be equally compelling for all men. Now I merely found it tedious, especially since I knew it was just as calculated as the rest of her expressions and utterances. "Not even the tiniest bit?"

I shook my head. "State secret, my lady."

Shelynne had been squinting around the room, as apparently she had abandoned her attempts to prevent her sister from eating the rich food provided. "I do not see her—is she not here tonight, Your Majesty?"

"Is who here?" I inquired, even as Jenaris rewarded her sister with a third, especially vehement elbow to the rib cage.

"You know. The girl with the red hair. What is her name? Sharanne? Aislinn?"

It was on my lips to say that I thought it odd she did not even know her own stepsister's name, but somehow I found myself unable to reply, as if the words had caught in my throat. Perhaps it was only the memory of my promise to Ashara that I would not speak of her to them, even in such an innocuous context, but I did find it passing strange. At any rate, I did not answer immediately, but drank some wine first, as if that could somehow clear the odd blockage in my throat.

"Oh," I said casually. "I have not seen her here this evening, but that is of little matter, since I have all you charming ladies for company."

And of course they simpered and smiled and curtseyed, even while I looked past them, my eyes seeming to search through the very palace walls to find my Ashara, whose name I somehow seemed unable to speak.

"What on earth was that business with you leaving the musicale tonight?" my sister asked, crossing her arms and fixing me with the sort of pointed stare that told me she would not allow any prevarication.

"Affairs of state," I said breezily. "I noticed you seemed very chatty with Lord Sorthannic."

"We are not discussing that." But her cheeks did turn pink.

"*You* may not be, but I am."

"Torric—"

"It is of no matter. I came back, didn't I? I did my duty by entertaining some of the most tedious young women it has ever been my displeasure to meet."

Lyarris shook her head. "Yes, I fear they seemed rather common, from what I could see. And Brinda Aldrenne? What was the point of that? Did you not refer to her as a 'viper' only a few days ago?"

"I did. All the more reason to spend some time with her. Now she has gone home happy and satisfied, sure that she has caught the Emperor's attention at last. She will be quiescent and less likely to scheme when in such a state, so all in all I believe the evening was a success."

"You are incorrigible."

"Am I?" I smiled at her, perversely pleased by the small frown she wore. "I would think you would be glad that I was showing favor to other young ladies, and not lavishing it all on Ashara Millende."

The frown deepened. "I did not see her at all, actually. Did you tell her to stay away, so you might put Lady Brinda and some of the other young women off the scent?"

"Oh, she was there, but she left early."

"And that disturbance with Gabrinne Nelandre and the mouse?"

I said nothing, but something in my expression must have given me away, for Lyarris set down her small goblet of port and fixed me with a very set stare.

"Tell me you did not plan that!"

"No, I confess the mouse was all Gabrinne's idea. Rather brilliant, don't you think?"

She laughed then, as if to show that she had quite given up on me. "If you intended for it to cause a most unseemly disruption, then yes, it was quite brilliant. You had left before that, but oh, the screaming and the fighting over who would get out first. Then there were the stalwarts who would not leave, but stood on their chairs, and all through the commotion those poor musicians had to soldier on as if nothing untoward was happening. Truly, you did them a great disservice with your plans. I can only hope you gave them a little extra compensation for their trouble."

As a matter of fact, I had; as I left the hall, I gestured for Lord Hein to come speak with me, and told him to double the musicians' fee, as they had had quite a trying time of it that evening. I explained as much to Lyarris, and she nodded in approval.

"Well, that is something, I suppose."

It seemed she would not pursue the matter further, thank the gods. True, it had been something of a fiasco for Lord Hein and those poor musicians, but at least I had gotten my time alone with Ashara. A fair enough trade, I thought. I said, "Did you know that those two awkward girls are Ashara's stepsisters?"

"Are they? Oh, dear. I can see why you're so eager to steal her away as soon as possible."

"That much is true. And the oddest thing happened—" I had intended to tell Lyarris the story of how they somehow didn't know it was their own stepsister in whom I had such a particular interest. Once again, though, the words seemed to lodge in my throat, and I coughed.

My sister frowned once again, although this time in concern. "Are you quite well, Torric?"

I swallowed some of my port to get rid of that odd dryness, then replied, "Yes, I am fine. Too much talking this evening, that is all."

She did not appear entirely convinced, but she shrugged and seemed to let it go. "Well, you must be relieved that there is only one more event to get through."

"More than I can say. Truly, I was beginning to think I would never see the end of it all." It did boggle me somewhat to contemplate that, at this same time tomorrow night, I would have announced to everyone my intention to marry Ashara Millende.

"It has been rather a process, but it seems you are happy with your choice. More than happy, really. I am glad for you, Torric." Lyarris came to me then and gave me a quick hug.

I was somewhat surprised, for as a rule we were not an openly demonstrative family. She must have seen something of my happiness in my face, realized that I was truly pleased with my choice and looking forward to making her my wife.

My arms tightened around my sister, and then I let her go. "I will admit that when I set forth on this venture, I was perhaps a little worried I might not find anyone who caught my fancy. But it seems those fears were for naught."

"That is true. And while there will be many disappointed young women in Iselfex tomorrow night, I know of at least one who will be nearly as happy as you and Ashara."

I sent her a pointed look, thinking of Sorthannic Sedassa, and she shook her head with a rueful smile.

"No, Torric, I am speaking of the Lady Gabrinne. She seemed to stick to Lord Senric's side all night like a cocklebur, and if he does not ask for her by the end of the weekend, I am sure she will be asking the reason why."

No doubt of that. The young lady's determination was a little fearsome, but the Duke did not seem to mind overmuch. For myself, I preferred someone a little less forward. Such behavior might be charming in the young daughter of an earl…not nearly as much in an Empress, who must consider the implications of everything she said. Ashara seemed far more thoughtful, soft-spoken but sure of herself, a fortuitous combination. Yes, she would make a fine consort, in every manner possible.

"A fine example of deciding upon what one desires and then using every means possible to achieve it," I agreed, and lifted my goblet of port, as if to make a toast. "May all the disappointed young ladies make equally fortuitous matches!"

"That is a worthy wish. I drink to that as well." Lyarris finished the last of her fortified wine, then set down her goblet, even as she stifled a yawn. "It is very late. I should have been abed hours ago."

"I am glad you stayed up to talk to me."

She darted over and gave me a quick kiss on the cheek. "I could see you wished to talk. But tomorrow is going to be quite a long day, and I know I need my rest, even if you do not."

"Sleep will be difficult, I think."

Her dark eyes glinted. "No doubt you will be tossing and turning like a child dreaming of his Midwinter presents, but I beg of you, brother, do at least try. You don't want to frighten off your intended bride with a pale face and black shadows under your eyes, do you?"

"I most decidedly do not. The port will help, I think."

"Then good night, Torric. After tomorrow night, everything will be very different."

She sent me a brilliant smile and then went out, her lady's maid, who had probably been drooping and yawning outside the door the entire time, following dutifully after her. I saw a brief shadow as one of my guards leaned over to shut the door behind them, and I was alone.

Not for much longer, however. I had meant what I said when I told Ashara that ours would be a speedy engagement. Damn Lord Hein's preparations and Keldryn's hand-wringing and my mother's complaints that no proper imperial wedding could be planned in less than three months. I cared for none of that. All I wanted was Ashara. I would take her in her chemise if I had to.

Yes, my sister was right. After tomorrow, the whole world would be different.

CHAPTER THIRTEEN

Ashara

Although leaving Torric in such a manner wrenched my heart, in a way it was good that I came home so much earlier than my stepsisters. Once again I had little opportunity to speak with my aunt, for the early hour meant that Janks was not yet abed, and so we had to settle for a few whispers setting the time for our meeting the following night before she departed and I scurried into the kitchen. But at least coming home at that hour meant I should get a fair amount of sleep...as long as my stepmother didn't have me up before the sun preparing Jenaris and Shelynne for the ball.

After I had said goodnight to Claris and laid myself down, glad that it was Mari's job to undo the sisters' gowns and hair and glad as well that Janks had already laid the fires, I found it more difficult to sleep than I had thought. Every time I closed my eyes I fancied I could feel Torric's mouth against mine, his arms around me, taste the wine on his lips and smell the woodsy scent that came from his hair. The more I told myself not to dwell on such things, that I needed my rest to prepare for tomorrow, the more it seemed I recalled every detail of that kiss, of our conversation, every plane and angle of his wonderful face.

Oh, yes, I was wildly in love...and in want, if the responses of my body were any indication. *You will be with him soon enough*, I told myself firmly. *Now, let yourself sleep, or you will regret this obsession tomorrow when you must face him with puffy, red eyes from lack of rest.*

This advice seemed eminently sound, and finally I drifted into slumber, secure in the knowledge that the Emperor of Sirlende loved me, and that this would be the last time I would ever have to sleep on this wretched pallet.

"Ashara, did I not tell you that the curling rods must be placed in the fire immediately?"

I already knew that nothing I did or said would please my stepmother, so I merely replied, "You did, ma'am, but then you sent me downstairs to see if that was where Shelynne had dropped her comb—"

"Don't be stupid, girl. You could have set the rods in the fire before you went downstairs to look for the comb. Now you've wasted a good quarter-hour!"

How I managed to not roll my eyes, I wasn't sure. Perhaps because I was so close now—only a few more hours of this, and then the stepsisters would be gone, and I would allow my aunt to cast her spell one last time. Then I would ride off to the palace, and I would be done with all of my stepmother's insults and cajoling. Torric had made it clear that he intended me to stay there once the engagement was announced, and of course I had no argument with that plan.

Since any sort of reply would only earn me a further rebuke, I merely gave a brief, apologetic curtsey and laid the comb on the dresser. At least I had found it. The gods only knew what kind of reprimand I would have gotten if I had "wasted" all that time and still not found the missing hair ornament.

After that I went immediately to the hearth and laid the long rods in the fire. It was Mari's task to wind the girls' long hair around each iron cylinder to achieve the beautiful hanging curls fashion dictated, so at least I would not be burdened with that tedious chore.

However, that did not mean I didn't have a long list of duties to attend to, starting with making sure their slippers were properly polished, and all their gowns and underthings and purses and fans laid out, all separated correctly so there would be no mix-ups. And although I knew my aunt had to have something truly splendid planned for me, I did not see how it could rival the lovely and costly gowns my stepmother had ordered—cut velvet in a deep wine shade embroidered with gold and pearls for Jenaris, and figured silk in an exquisite dark turquoise edged with silver and crystals for Shelynne.

I knew I dared not touch the trim, or run a hand over the fine fabric in admiration. To do so would only bring down the wrath of my stepmother, who no doubt would accuse me of soiling those beautiful gowns. No, I could only lay them out while wearing the white kid gloves she had instructed me to put on before beginning the task, and set the thin silk chemises and stockings next to them, being careful not to snag the fine material.

While I was doing this, both Mari and my stepmother were brushing the girls' hair as they stood in front of the fire in their dressing gowns. Each lock had to be perfectly dry, or it risked getting scorched by the curling rods. When at last my stepmother was satisfied, Mari began curling Jenaris' hair first.

Not that Shelynne was given a chance to rest, however. While her sister was being attended to, she was surveyed carefully by her mother, then given a careful coating of cosmetics—reddish stain on her lips and cheeks, a smudge of charcoal along her upper lids, and a dusting of pale, pearlescent powder over everything. From a corner I watched this entire procedure in some fascination, looking on as my half-pretty stepsister was transformed into quite a bewitching creature. Yes, I had heard that the ladies in the court resorted to such subterfuges, but this was the first time I had ever seen these same devices used on an ordinary person, as the procedure was far more intricate than the simple brush of a bit of stain on one's lips.

"Stop gaping, Ashara!" my stepmother snapped. "Surely you can think of something more useful to do than stand there and stare at us like a fish on a line. Go downstairs and fetch more firewood, for we must keep the fire hot until we are done."

"Yes, ma'am," I said promptly, and hurried down the stairs. Normally this would have been Janks's job, but of course he was forbidden the girls' chamber while they were dressed only in their robes.

"Gods, what a hullabaloo," Claris declared as I entered the kitchen. "They can't be off soon enough, as far as I'm concerned. I wanted to bake a new batch of bread today, but no, herself wouldn't have it. Said she didn't want me using up the firewood."

"That's what she went me for," I explained.

"She'll set the chimney on fire if she's not careful," the cook said darkly. "All to fancy up those two, who haven't a chance in the world of catching His Majesty's eye."

I gave a noncommittal shrug, as I knew she was right but didn't dare admit such a thing out loud. "I'd best get the wood and go back upstairs, for she's sure to let me know if I've taken too long."

"That's no more than the truth." A sigh, and she went back to swirling the broth she was making.

At least I did not have to go outside to fetch the firewood, as Janks had brought in a substantial load earlier that day. I bent and gathered as much into my arms as I could, being careful not to give myself a splinter in the process, then dashed back upstairs. Mari was still winding Jenaris' long hair around the rods, but she appeared to be almost done. Good thing, too, as Shelynne appeared to be fairly dancing with impatience as she waited her turn.

"Go on, put some more on the fire," my stepmother instructed me with narrowed eyes. "You've practically let it go out."

As the fire appeared to be more or less dancing away happily, I knew this was simply more hyperbole on her part.

However, long years of these sorts of reprimands had taught me that the best thing to do was give an apologetic nod and then attend to the matter at hand forthwith.

Let her upbraid you as much as she wishes, I told myself. *Indeed, consider it a gift to her, since after tonight she will no longer have the opportunity to do so.*

This pleasant thought brought a small smile to my lips—one that my stepmother noted at once.

"What are you grinning at, you foolish girl?" she demanded. "I see nothing funny in the situation!"

"Oh, no, ma'am, it isn't that," I said quickly. "I suppose I was just smiling because of how lovely the gowns are and how pretty Jenaris and Shelynne look."

This lie seemed to mollify her, and she let out a "humph" before crossing around to Jenaris' other side to see how her hair was progressing. "I swear, Mari, you are slower than the Silth in Janver," she snapped, and the maid started a bit and then bit her lip as she unwound the curl she had been working on from the rod.

If it had been anyone else, I might have felt a bit sorry for her, but I had been on the receiving end of far too many of Mari's slights and petty cruelties to summon up much sympathy. As it was, I retreated once more to my corner, standing ready in case I should be called upon for any further trivialities.

For the nonce it seemed my stepmother had forgotten me, for she watched as Mari finished off Jenaris' hair, inspected it closely, and at last gave a grudging nod. "It will do. Come, Shelynne, it is your turn. I suppose I should be grateful your hair isn't quite as thick as your sister's."

At this remark Shelynne stuck out a mutinous lower lip, but she appeared to realize that arguing the point would get her nowhere. Still pouting, she settled herself on the stool beside the fire while Mari set to.

It was Jenaris' turn to receive a careful application of cosmetics, only in her case they did not create nearly as much of a metamorphosis as they had with her sister. No, I reflected, she still looked something like a pig, with her upturned nose and round chin, only a pig with lip color and darkened eyelids.

That thought made me visualize an actual pig wearing lip stain, and I had to stifle a giggle. No, it would never do to appear too high-spirited, or my stepmother was sure to guess that something was going on.

But she appeared to be preoccupied, finishing off the final touches on Jenaris' plump cheeks before she called me over to help with her eldest daughter's ensemble. First the silk stockings and their silk garters, and then the gossamer-fine chemise, and finally the glory of the gown itself, with all those tiny seed pearls glowing from the heavy gold trim that wove its away around the neckline and embellished the separate sleeves, which tied on to the main gown with lengths of golden ribbon.

Once she was arrayed in her finery, Jenaris appeared as resplendent as she ever would. The gown was very fine, as was the tiny cap of embroidered gold brocade that topped her dark curls.

Yes, she looks lovely...until you gaze at her face, I thought with some spite, and then was ashamed. Truly, it was not

Jenaris' fault that she was not as handsome as her mother or her sister. Then again, she made no attempt to ensure that her character was attractive, even if her face was not, so certainly some blame for that must rest on her shoulders.

By then Mari had finished with Shelynne's hair, and the dressing process began all over again with her. She truly did look lovely when we were all done, so much so that I actually clapped my hands together and exclaimed, "Oh, Shelynne, you look so beautiful!"

She beamed at that, even as her sister scowled, for of course I had offered no such compliment to her. "Am I? Truly?"

"Yes, you'll do very well," her mother cut in. "I think His Majesty will truly notice you this evening."

"Oh, he spoke with me last night, and Jenaris, too, but gave no indication of being in love." A shrug, the silver trim of her gown glinting in the candlelight. "But that is all right, for I am beginning to think that Lady Gabrinne had the better plan by seeking out a nobleman for herself instead of trying to catch His Majesty's eye. If I truly look as pretty as you say, then perhaps I should try to catch the notice of an earl's son, or a widowed baron, rather than chasing after the Emperor."

"Fine," scoffed Jenaris. "I think it an excellent plan, for that will make one fewer in contention for the throne."

"Do not talk such nonsense, Shelynne," her mother said. "In one thing Ashara is right—you are looking very beautiful this evening, and it would be foolish to waste that on some piddling nobleman rather than the Emperor himself. I'll hear no more of it."

Upon hearing this, Shelynne subsided; she knew as well as any of us the folly of defying her mother. Instead, she let out a little sigh, and began to gather up her fan and her bag. Jenaris did the same, and I hurried to slip her cloak onto her shoulders, taking care that I did not disarrange her careful curls in the process. A moment later I did the same for Shelynne, and then it was time for them to descend the stairs to the carriage that waited for them outside.

I hoped then that my stepmother would dismiss me, for I knew time was wasting, and I had my own preparations to make. But after a few final admonitions to her daughters to smile their brightest and save all their wittiest banter for the Emperor, she turned to me, gave me a look of some suspicion, and said, "Ashara, go to Claris and have her fix me a light supper, for all this tumult has me quite famished."

My heart sank at those words, even as I wondered precisely what that slanting glance of hers had meant. Oh, I was eager to be away, but I thought I had done very well in pretending I had nothing to look forward to, that this evening was no different for me than any other. I also knew she would expect me to wait until the meal was prepared and then bring it up to her in her chambers, and I most certainly did not have time for that. The ball was set to start at eight in the evening, and if I were lucky I had barely a half hour for my aunt to transform my ragged clothing into an elegant gown and for me to get to the palace.

Protests would be useless, however, so I merely curtseyed and said, "Of course, ma'am. I'll see to it directly."

I went then to Claris and delivered my stepmother's request. She nodded. "Well, I've got this nice broth already made up, although she'll have to make do with yesterday's bread. Be a love and get me those quince preserves from the pantry, will you?"

As I carried out this request, a sudden idea struck me. Just as I was handing over the jar of preserves to the cook, I grabbed at my stomach with my free hand and made what I hoped was a grimace of agony.

"What is it, Ashara?" she asked. "Are you quite well?"

"I—don't—know," I panted, putting on my best imitation of someone forcing their words out past a good deal of pain. "I have—the most grinding cramp—oh! I have to go!"

And I fled out the back door, heading for the noisome little outhouse that Janks and I shared. The other ladies of the house used chamber pots, but of course such niceties were too good for the likes of me. However, I did not go to the outhouse, but instead hurried into the stable and shut the door behind me as quickly as I could.

"I would give your stepmother a piece of my mind about how she is always delaying you, but after tonight I suppose it will not matter," said my aunt as she emerged from her normal hiding place in one of the far stalls.

"Oh, no, and we must be quick, for the only way I could think of to escape was to pretend a griping of my belly. I do not think anyone will pursue me to the outhouse—at least, not right away, but—"

"I understand," she said, and her eyes twinkled a bit. "But thank you for that piece of intelligence, for now I can make sure to be wan and dragging and look thoroughly ill when I am pretending to be you. But in the meantime—" She broke off, smiling, and then uttered the words of her spell, the syllables this time sounding even deeper and richer, as if the enchantment she was casting was far greater than any she had done before.

The air seemed to shiver around me, and it was as though I felt thousands of glimmers of light pass over me, somehow *through* me. And when I looked down, I saw I wore a gown so magnificent I was sure its like had never been seen before, not here in the courts of Sirlende or anywhere else on the continent.

For it seemed almost as if I had been clothed in a dress of molten copper, the fabric glinting every time I moved, and yet somehow also light and airy. I was sure it would swirl most beautifully around me as I danced. And the sleeves were worked with copper bullion and topaz and golden pearls in designs so intricate I could hardly guess at their patterns, with that same pattern repeated around the low neckline of my gown. Echoing the color of the dress itself, only a shade or two darker, my hair spilled over my shoulders in heavy curls, gleaming like a new and rare metal.

"Gods..." I breathed, and my aunt clapped her hands together in delight.

"Oh, good. I hoped you would like it. I've been dreaming it up the past two days."

"Like it?" I repeated, and shook my head. "I could never have imagined anything so beautiful ever existed."

"Well, to be fair, it doesn't *really* exist, you know. Now, turn around so I can make sure everything is perfect."

Dutifully I spun for her, the gleaming copper skirts swirling around me with a whisper. As I had thought, the fabric moved beautifully.

"Yes, that should do," she said after she made a careful inspection. "I don't see how the Emperor will be able to look at anyone else once he catches a glimpse of you in this."

"But that's just it—he won't be looking at anyone else. We've already promised ourselves to one another. We were merely waiting until tonight to make the announcement."

At that revelation she beamed and pulled me close so she could crush me in a fierce hug. I began to open my mouth to protest, but then realized of course she could do no damage to my hair or gown, so I shut my mouth just as quickly and returned the hug.

"Ah, then, I suppose the dress does not matter so much. Still," she added, looking me over once more, "I am glad that you will be this magnificent when the Emperor reveals to everyone that you are the choice of his heart, for I cannot see how anyone could not believe the right of such a decision. You do look like an Empress."

Her eyes teared up then, and I made some sort of concerned sound. Aunt Therissa waved a hand and shook her head, saying,

"Oh, I am happy. I just wish—I wish my poor sister could have seen the lovely young woman you've grown up to be. She would be so very proud."

Those words brought on a tightness in my own throat, but I swallowed and told myself this was no time to weep. After all, I did not want to go to Torric with reddened eyes and a swollen nose. "I am glad you think she would be pleased. I will do my best to make her proud."

"I know you will. Now go! It is one thing to be just late enough that you make a fine entrance, but after that it is just rudeness."

Didn't I know, after having to sneak into the musicale the night before. So I kissed my aunt once again and gathered up the gossamer glinting fabric of my skirts, then hurried out into the night. This time I did not take any great care at concealment, but ran to the back gate and let myself out. Janks was nowhere to be seen, and so I was safe, this last time I must escape my stepmother's house.

All during the carriage ride I made myself breathe deeply, to calm myself as best I could. This was the last event of five; I should be an old hand at appearing in front of so many people by now. I had survived unscathed so far, and only a few hours now separated me from my engagement to Torric and the start of a new life. Yes, that was exciting and nerve-wracking in its own way, but at least I could at last banish the fear that had been dogging me for the greater part of a week, the worry that sooner or later I would be revealed for the fraud I was.

Yes, it was late, but not horribly so. As the carriage slowed to a stop inside the palace gates, I saw that mine was the last coach to arrive, but several still lingered there as well, indicating their passengers had only just alighted a moment or two before. Heartened by that observation, I waited with a heavily beating heart as the coachman came around and handed me down, then bowed.

"Truly, you do look like a princess, miss," he said.

"Thank you," I replied, realizing I had never asked his name, as I had always been in such a hurry when coming and going from my aunt's house. "I think tonight you will not need to wait for me."

"Ah," he replied, and nodded knowingly toward the palace and its myriad windows gleaming like gold in the darkness. "Have high hopes, I suppose. Well, I've been paid to stay here until needed, so I think I'll do that. You can always send word at the end of the evening if things should turn out otherwise."

He seemed determined, so I nodded my agreement and then hurried off toward the looming front doors of the palace, which now stood open and let out a flood of light and the distant sounds of music and the murmur of many people's voices. It was still difficult for me to believe that this imposing edifice would soon be my home.

With that thought to propel me, I made my way down the seemingly endless main corridor, past the ranks of men who stood guard there, and on to the ballroom. There I paused just on the threshold so I might peer inside and gain my bearings, and it took everything within me not to gasp out loud in delight.

For while I had noted how sumptuous the decorations had been for the previous four events, they were as nothing compared to the fairyland I saw before me now. If there were any roses left in the gardens of Iselfex and the surrounding towns, I would have been very surprised, for it seemed there must be thousands upon thousands of them gathered in the ballroom, swagged on every wrought-iron chandelier, hanging from every sconce, festooning the dais where the musicians played, gathered into sumptuous arrangements on the tables that held the food and drink. The scent of all those massed flowers was almost overwhelming, and I blinked, attempting to get my bearings.

But everywhere I looked there was something else to catch my attention, from the cunning little candles set amongst the roses, making them almost seem as if they glowed from within, to the bewildering color and variety of the attendees. Everyone had turned out in their finest, and it seemed the Emperor must have put out the call for all noble gentlemen between twenty and forty to be here as well, so that no one should have to lack for a partner.

Girls in scarlet and azure and coral gowns moved in the slow, stately steps of the *linotte*, while their partners, dressed in soberer hues of black and gray and deep blue and green, kept the pace with them. Jewels glistened from ears and necks and wrists, and shoes spangled with discs of silver and gold peeped out from beneath gleaming silk and luxurious velvet.

I stopped just inside the door, scanning the crowd for Torric, but I did not see him. Perhaps he was on the dance floor, continuing the charade for just a while longer.

"Good gods, what a gown!" came Gabrinne's voice from over my right shoulder, and I turned toward her, glad beyond measure that she was there to greet me.

"Oh, Gabrinne," I breathed. "Isn't it all wonderful?"

"Yes, it is," she replied at once, staring at me in amazement. "Where on earth did you get that fabric? I have never seen its like!"

Luckily, I had anticipated a question such as this, and had concocted a story during the drive to the palace. "It was a gift from my aunt. She has traveled extensively, and bought it in Keshiaar many years ago. They do wonderful things with textiles there."

"I wish I had your aunt!" Gabrinne exclaimed, eyeing the dress with some envy. "Then again, I am not sure I could carry off that color, whereas it suits you most astonishingly. A lucky purchase!"

I lifted my shoulders. "Well, my mother—her sister—had hair the same color as mine, so my aunt already knew it should work quite well one day. Besides," I added, casting my own admiring glance over her gown of deep emerald damask, with trim of silver and peacock-hued pearls, "your dress is very beautiful, and looks wonderful on you."

She dipped a mischievous curtsey, a dimple showing in the corner of her mouth. "Thank you for the compliment, Ashara! I will admit that Lord Senric did praise it quite excessively when he first saw it."

"And where is he?" I inquired. "For I would have thought you'd keep him close by your side, what with all these predatory ladies looking for dance partners."

"As to that, I sent him off for a cup of wine, but then I saw you come in, looking like every princess from every tale I'd ever read, and I quite forgot about the wine!"

"But luckily I did not," a deep voice cut in, and I looked over to see Lord Senric standing a few paces away, a silver goblet of wine in either hand.

Seeing him up close, I had to say that he was quite the fine figure of a man, although he was a good deal older than either Gabrinne or I, or even Torric. But the Duke of Gahm stood tall and straight, and had a fine hawkish nose and determined chin. There was something, too, about those hooded dark eyes, something compelling, and I began to see why Gabrinne had made him the particular object of her quest for a husband.

He extended one of the goblets to her and the other to me, even though I was sure he must have intended it for himself. I began to demur, and he only shook his head.

"No, my lady, I am not churlish enough to drink in front of you when you have none. It is an easy enough thing for me to fetch another. But I think I will wait, for I have heard the next dance is a *verdralle*, and Gabrinne has promised it to me."

"Yes, I have," she said, "and you would hear something of it if you went off and left me alone while everyone else was enjoying themselves. But despair not, my lord, for you and I can share my cup, and we shall do quite well that way."

He smiled at her, and something in his expression reminded me of the way Torric would gaze at me, and so I saw then that the Duke did have a true regard for Gabrinne. This realization warmed my heart, for I had not yet been able to observe them together, and I had wondered how much of a connection they actually shared.

"This is most generous of you, Your Grace," I said, and sipped from the wine, for to refuse it now would be quite rude. Besides, a bit of wine might help to settle my nerves.

"You are quite welcome," he told me, and it sounded as if he actually meant it. "That is a very stunning gown, my lady. You should not linger here by the door, but should go further into the ballroom, so that more might admire it."

Gabrinne laughed, and her dark curls—which I could tell needed no coaxing from a curling rod—bounced with the movement. "What he really means is that the Emperor is out there now, doing his duty by dancing with the pock-marked daughter of the Earl of Treglende, and if you stay over here, you will not catch his eye in time for him to dance the *verdralle* with you."

Her merriment was contagious. I smiled and said, "Well, then, I guess we had better move a little closer, for I suppose if I am not hasty, then he will be stuck with the Lady Brinda, or someone even worse."

"There is no one worse," Gabrinne said darkly. "Senric, darling, hold the cup for me, will you? The floor here is so dreadfully crowded."

I did not miss the fact that she did not precede his name with "lord," nor that she had called him "darling." That familiar? Had he already asked for her hand? I supposed it was possible, although I would have thought she'd tell me such important news as soon as she saw me.

He did not comment on her familiarity, but took the goblet from her as we wove our way through the crowd so that we might be closer to the dancers. For truly, although the ballroom was enormous and could easily accommodate a hundred couples, there were far more than that milling about: talking, eating, drinking, or watching the dancers. I kept a firm grip on my goblet and was glad that I had drunk from it somewhat, so at least it wasn't quite so full. Even so, I was glad when we more or less made it to the edge of the crowd, and therefore had a better view of those actually dancing.

They moved past, the steps of the *linotte* slow enough that I could make out the intricacies of the ladies' gowns, or the fine cut of the men's doublets. And then at last *he* came by, wearing the severe silver and black of his house, but so exquisitely tailored that it seemed to outshine the most elaborate garb there. Diamonds glittered from the white gold circlet on his brow, and he was so perfect in every way that my breath caught at the sight of him, and I wondered how he could be a mortal man and not a god, when he so surpassed everyone there.

His eyes widened as he appeared to see me, and it seemed he almost lost his step but recovered, moving on smoothly as if nothing untoward had happened.

"I have no doubt who the Emperor will be dancing the *verdralle* with," Gabrinne whispered in my ear, and this time I did not bother to contradict her. Why tell more lies, when in such a short time everyone would know of Torric's and my true feelings for one another?

A quick swallow of wine seemed my best recourse then, and I remained silent, tasting the rich, heavy savor of the unknown grape. With a shake of her curls, she leaned over and murmured something to Lord Senric, but I could not make it what it was. No matter. My entire attention was consumed by watching Torric make his circuit of the dance floor, those agonizing moments of waiting until the dance was finally done and he came straight toward me, ignoring all the women who attempted to approach him as if they were not even there.

"My Lady Ashara," he said, stopping a foot or two away and bowing from the waist.

I curtseyed at once, as did Gabrinne, while the Duke bowed as well. "Your Majesty," I replied formally, all too aware of their watching eyes.

Torric seemed to perceive my diffidence, for he said, "My lady, if no one has claimed you yet, I would be honored to have you as my partner for the *verdralle*."

"No, I am newly arrived, and so have no partners as of yet."

"Then consider yourself claimed…for this dance."

I curtseyed again, and he waved to a passing servant for his own goblet of wine. The man rushed over at once and handed off the last vessel on his platter. Torric drank deeply, then gave the goblet back to the servant.

"And if you are done, my lady? I think you will find it difficult to dance whilst holding on to that goblet."

"Oh, of course," I said, even though I had not drunk even half the vessel's contents. But I gave it over as well. If I had need of more later, I had no doubt Torric would procure it for me immediately.

I could not help but feel Gabrinne's eyes upon us during this exchange, as if she were attempting to see something between us beyond the polite, empty words. But then the musicians played a chord, signaling that it was time for those who wished to dance to take their place upon the floor, and she and Lord Senric also handed off their shared goblet to the serving man, so they would have their hands properly free as well.

Torric wrapped his warm fingers around mine and led me out of the crowd and into the center of the room so we might begin to form the circle of dancers required for the *verdralle*. As we stood there, waiting for the music to begin, he bent toward me.

"You are the most beautiful thing I have ever seen," he murmured.

"So are you," I replied frankly, and he laughed.

"Well, then, I suppose that makes us well-matched. Are you ready?"

"Why, yes. I have been practicing my steps."

Those amazing sooty lashes swept down over his eyes, concealing them. "That is not what I meant."

"Then yes, I believe I am ready for that, too." In that moment, I knew I could face anything, as long as I could do it by his side.

And then the music began, and he pulled me into his arms, and I let myself be swept away, knowing we were moving toward our future, and all was beautiful and right and perfect.

CHAPTER FOURTEEN

Torric

By the gods, I did not know what I had done to deserve her, but I would not question their wisdom in putting such a woman in my arms. When my gaze first fell upon her this evening, I could not quite believe it was my Ashara. True, it was her sweet face, that fall of russet hair I admired so much, but she was garbed more elegantly than either my mother or my sister. I had not even stopped to wonder how a baronet's daughter could possibly have afforded such finery. My only thought was, *There is a true Empress.*

And now she was here, moving about the polished floor as if it were no great thing to be dancing in the heart of the palace, to be the center of all eyes, for all her deprecating comments about practicing her steps. She smiled up at me, those beautiful lips curving as if in pure pleasure, and I fell in love with her a little more, when I had not thought it was possible to love her any more than I already did.

"You were late again," I told her, after we had taken a few steps.

Her amber-green eyes laughed up into mine, reminding me of the autumn wood where we had shared our first kiss. "It does seem to have become rather a habit of mine. I assure you that in general I am quite prompt...when my stepmother isn't delaying me."

"Well, she shall delay you no longer. I hope you prepared for this night by packing your things, for as soon as I make the announcement, I will send men over to fetch them so you need not spend another night under her roof."

An unreadable expression passed over her lovely features. "Oh, I have not that much to pack, I fear."

I let out an unbelieving chuckle. "I find that difficult to believe, if your wardrobe of this week is any indication."

For a few seconds she said nothing, although her pretty white teeth caught on her lower lip, as if she were not sure of the best way to respond. Then, "I would say that this week has been an exception, Your Majesty. Most of the time I am not nearly so grand."

Had her family done the thing I had feared, and gone into debt to ensure that she made a fitting impression on me? But no, that did not jibe with her remarks about her stepmother not showing her much favor. Frowning, I tried to work at the puzzle, and then decided to abandon it. After all, it did not matter one way or another. If they had gone into debt, I would make sure those debts were cleared, and if not, well, I would soon have a wardrobe fit for an empress constructed for her.

"You are quiet," she said, and I caught a trace of worry in her tone.

"Only thinking of our future together, my love," I told her.

Her face brightened. "That is something which has been much in my thoughts as well." She cast a quick glance around the crowded ballroom and added, "How I wish this evening were over!"

"Indeed?" I inquired dryly. "I will admit that I am not the empire's best dancer, but I did not think I was that bad."

"Oh!" A quick flush stained her cheeks. "Oh, you know that is not what I meant. You are a very fine dancer. It is just the thought of you dancing with all those other women for the next few hours..."

"Believe me, I am not looking forward to it all that much, either. But it is only for a few hours, my dearest, and then I promise you I will never dance with another woman again, even if it causes a huge scandal."

She smiled a little then. "Now you are teasing me, I think. I realize that I cannot always keep you all to myself. Perhaps it is just that I feel as if I am bursting with our secret, and holding on to it for even a few more hours seems so very difficult."

Ah, I well knew that sensation. At the moment I wanted nothing more than to tell the musicians to stop, and to take Ashara up to the dais where they were playing so I could announce to everyone that she was the woman I had chosen for my wife. Or, failing that, at least steal her away to a quiet corridor so I might kiss her again, taste her sweet mouth, this time go further and touch my lips to her perfect white neck, follow a trail to her collarbone and then onto the enticing curve of her breasts where they showed above the neckline of her gown.

My groin tightened, and I immediately forced my thoughts in other directions, ones not quite so arousing. Yes, I would make her mine in every way possible, and as soon as was feasible, but in the meantime I did not want to frighten her with my desire. She was an innocent, I could tell; a passionate one, that was clear enough, but I knew that mine was the first kiss she had ever tasted. There would be many more firsts, each more pleasurable than the last.

But that was certainly not the best way to get my mind running in more innocuous paths. "Not so long now, my love," I said, then went on, "Do you know, that is the third time in a row that Lady Gabrinne has danced with Lord Senric? I was going to ask her, as she is your friend and seems like a lively dance partner, but I fear she is not going to give me the opportunity."

Ashara laughed then and shook her head. "You are probably right. And I am wondering if the Duke has asked for her hand already, for earlier she addressed him by his first name alone, and called him 'darling' right in front of me. Now, because it is Gabrinne, perhaps that was just her way of trying to shock me, but since he took it in stride, it seems there could be more to it than I first thought."

High time his lordship got himself another wife, although I couldn't help thinking he would have quite the handful in Gabrinne Nelandre. Perhaps that was what he needed. A good man, and one of the steadiest in all of Sirlende, but sober and quiet. He might appreciate the shaking-up she was sure to provide.

"Look at us," I said, and grinned, even as I turned Ashara under my arm and spun her around before drawing her close to me once more, so I might smell the perfume of roses that seemed to rise from her masses of copper curls, so close in color to the astonishing gown she wore. "We sound like a pair of matchmaking grannies—although I will freely admit that I am probably the worst of us two, as I have also been doing what I can to encourage the connection between my sister and the Duke of Marric's Rest."

"Oh, yes, I think I saw him speaking with her earlier. He is very handsome."

"Are you trying to make me jealous?" I growled.

"Certainly not. But Lord Sorthannic is very handsome, and your sister is very beautiful, so if they admire one another, then it sounds like it should be a good match." She stared up into my face, one eyebrow lifted. "I am rather surprised you are not marrying her off to some foreign prince, though. Is that not what usually happens with princesses?"

"It is," I admitted. "And if there were anyone suitable, then perhaps that would be her fate. But as there is no one suitable, she is safe to follow her heart and stay close to home, which I must confess I find a far more attractive proposition. For you must know that I am a selfish man, Ashara, and it suits me better to have my sister here in Sirlende than off in Purth or Farendon or even South Eredor."

"I don't think you are selfish," Ashara replied. "I think you love your sister very much, and so of course it is natural that you would not want her to be thousands of miles away."

"Do you always see the good in people?"

I had asked the question in a joking manner, but she appeared to consider it quite seriously, her lashes half concealing her eyes as she thought it over. "I would like to see the good in people—and in general I think most people are quite good, or at least try to be. But there are some who seem to have very little good in them, who seem to enjoy hurting others, or belittling them, or taking advantage of them. So I am not sure I am quite as naïve as you think I am."

This remark had to be about her stepmother...or at least I could not think of who else it might be applied to. Perhaps Brinda Aldrenne, for I was not so blind or deaf that I had not overheard some of her spiteful remarks about Ashara, or seen the way she was so quick to cut down anyone she saw as a possible rival.

While some part of me wanted to press the issue, I decided that was not a good use of the last few moments of our dance. I knew this was the only one we would share, as I had to make the effort to partner as many of the ladies as I could over the course of the evening. "I think you a very perceptive young woman...and a lovely one, and a strong one. And I think you will make a very great Empress."

Her eyes seemed almost suspiciously bright, and she nodded and tightened her fingers around mine, as if she could not find the words to reply. And so we finished the rest of the dance in silence, concentrating only on the feel of being in one another's arms, the sweep of the music and the sensation of knowing that this was so much more than merely a dance, but a chance to reaffirm our need for one another.

When the music ended, we paused and performed the customary honors—I bowed to her, and she curtseyed to me, then thanked me in a somewhat breathless voice for the dance. I had to force myself to remain where I stood, to allow her to walk away and disappear into the crowd. How much better it would have been if I could have kept her by my side, said to hell with convention and let her be my only companion for the rest of the night.

But it would be foolish to cause such an uproar this late in the game. My gaze flicked to the enormous carved clock mounted on the far wall. Only a few more hours to go. Surely I could survive that long.

I began to ponder the wisdom of that decision, though, after I spent the next three dances with young women whose names and faces I could not have even recalled, for they left my memory as soon as we had done the honors at the end of the dance and also melted away into the crowd. One good thing about having to make the rounds, as it were—at least that way I did not have to suffer any of them for more than a single dance.

This fact was brought home to me more than ever when I found myself partnered with Brinda Aldrenne very late in the evening, after she all but elbowed another girl out of the way so she might claim me for a dance. My only consolation was that at least it was for "Grey Mare," a lively piece that did not require the close contact of a *verdralle*. I feared I could not have stomached having to hold that nasty young woman in my arms for such an extended period of time.

Even so, she looked as smug as if she had just been crowned Empress herself, and made quite a show of curtseying as low as she could, so that I might get an eyeful of the bosom exposed by her low-cut gown of scarlet silk. Never in my life had I possessed less of an inclination to gaze on a woman's body, but I summoned a smile from somewhere and then was heartily glad when the music began so she was forced to concentrate on the quick-paced steps of the dance.

Despite that, she commented, "Surely you must have made up your mind by now, Your Majesty? Why, I think it is most unkind of you to keep us all waiting until the last moment!"

This remark was delivered in a teasing tone, one she probably thought was flirtatious. Underneath it, though, I could hear her criticism. My first instinct was to rebuke her for being so forward with her Emperor, but I knew that was the wrong approach. So I merely lifted my shoulders and replied, "My Lady Brinda, the announcement will be made at midnight—less than an hour from now. Surely you can contain your anticipation until then."

"If I must." She pouted, but could not maintain the expression for very long, for the dance's exertions required her to open her mouth to take a breath. "But you cannot give me one hint? Not a single one?"

"That would not be fair, as I have said nothing to any of my partners this evening." *And even if I had, I would not extend you the same courtesy.* "But at least you know that soon the waiting will be over."

She did not reply, but frowned and said nothing for the remainder of the dance, which I found to be a welcome relief. Surely if she possessed an ounce of perception she would have recognized the distaste I felt for her, but as was often the case with self-absorbed people, she had very little awareness of the sensibilities of others.

It was with a great sense of liberation that I bowed to her at the end of the dance and went my own way, glad that I would not be burdened with her company again. And it was then that I encountered my sister, who had just danced once more with Lord Sorthannic. She smiled at me, but ruefully, and said,

"You might want to wipe that sour expression off your face, my lord, for it's a little too obvious how happy you are to be relieved of the lady's company."

"I did not know I was being so transparent." I signaled to one of the servants to bring us some wine, and almost at once the man was handing me a full goblet, and then another to my sister. He bowed and left, and I added, "Truly it seems as if the hours are lasting longer and longer as the evening wears on. Surely it must be midnight already."

"Soon enough." A corner of her mouth quirked. "It is not only wearing on you, Torric—Mother cornered me a while ago and demanded that I tell her who your choice was. I said that I did not know, that you were being very secretive about the whole thing, but I fear she did not believe me."

"It does not matter much whether she believes you or not. The important thing is that she does not know for sure, although of course she must have her suspicions. I did not hide my regard for Ashara soon enough, although since then I think I have done fairly well at not showing her any particular favor."

"Very well for how besotted you are." Lyarris sipped her wine and gazed around the ballroom, as if looking for Ashara, although I could not spy her myself. "She does look rather astonishing this evening, does she not? And her father was a baronet? They must have some other wealth in the family for her to have the means to procure such a gown, and such jewels."

"She mentioned an aunt once. It sounded as if she might be a wealthy woman in her own right, and so perhaps she is the one who has been assisting Ashara with her wardrobe."

"Ah, that would make sense." A small pause, and then she asked, "Are you nervous?"

"Of course not," I replied immediately. Fine words. An Emperor could not admit to nerves…not even to his sister. But there was an odd sensation somewhere in the pit of my stomach, one which, if not precisely nervousness, was something closely related. Anticipation? Perhaps. And while I wanted to announce to everyone that Ashara Millende was the choice of my heart, I knew there would be many disappointed young women surrounding me, and that would be difficult to bear in its own way. True, I did not much worry about breaking the heart of someone such as Brinda Allende—if she even possessed such an organ, which I somehow doubted—but there were many fine girls here who had nothing wrong with them…save that they were not Ashara.

"Of course not," my sister echoed, and took another sip of wine. "I would put you out of your misery and dance with you next, but I know that would only make me a source of bitter rebuke for taking you out of circulation so close to the fateful hour."

"And are you going to dance yet again with the Duke of Marric's Rest? For it seems you have been keeping him rather to yourself this evening."

Her lashes dropped low, and she paused before replying, the teasing note back in her voice, "No, I think we have danced enough to set tongues wagging. For you know that was my sole aim—to draw as much attention as I could from you."

"I thank you for that, although I am not sure it was as efficacious as you had hoped. Still, I appreciate your sacrifice."

"Beast," she said, and let out a small laugh as she tapped me on the arm with her fan. "But no, I am going to dance the last dance with Lord Hildar, and see if I can distract him from fretting that his daughter is making a spectacle of herself with Lord Senric."

"A good plan. In fact, you have given me an idea. I shall have the Lady Gabrinne dance the last dance with me. Since I know her heart is bestowed elsewhere, I will not have to worry about giving her false hope about her chances for the crown. It is an excellent solution, don't you think?"

"Quite excellent," Lyarris agreed. "In fact, I see the musicians preparing themselves once again, so you had best find the lady in question before Lord Senric quite spirits her away."

I bowed to my sister—and winked at the same time, to which she gave me a quite unladylike grin and turned away, no doubt to make herself available to Lord Hildar. And might she have joy of him as a partner. A good man, and a trifle enthusiastic on the dance floor. I could only hope he wouldn't step on all ten of my sister's toes.

The brilliant emerald green of Lady Gabrinne's gown made her easy enough to find. I paused next to her, noting that she stood with Ashara and Lord Senric, and tried my best to appear as noncommittal as possible. "My Lady Gabrinne."

She turned to me in some surprise, but curtseyed immediately. "Your Majesty."

"If you would honor me with the last dance?"

Instead of flushing, as most girls in a similar situation would do, her dark eyes danced, and she sent a mischievous look over her shoulder at Ashara, as if she had guessed my game at once. "Of course, Your Majesty."

I inclined my head toward Ashara and Lord Senric, then led Gabrinne away, seeing that the Duke had bowed to Ashara, and was obviously asking her to be his companion for the dance. Excellent. She would be in good hands with him. And after that...

After that, she would be mine.

Once the music had started and Gabrinne and I made the customary honors to one another, she tilted her head up at me, eyes twinkling. "A good play, Your Majesty. For of course you could not dance this last *verdralle* with Ashara, much as you would have liked to...and I was a safe substitute, for of course I do not wish to marry you."

I had known this already, but to hear her speak it so baldly did take me aback somewhat. "Oh, you don't?"

"Not at all," she said airily. "I expect Lord Senric and I will announce our betrothal to my father this very night, to cheer him up after he hears that you have chosen Ashara Millende and not me."

"And did she tell you this?" I asked, trying to keep the amusement out of my voice.

"Oh, no. Ashara is far too well-mannered for that. But I am not stupid—I have seen how you look at one another, and when you gave me that note at the musicale to pass to her? Well, I knew that clinched the whole thing."

"You are a very observant young woman," I remarked, before turning her under one arm and drawing her back to me. "Perhaps I should give you a post in the foreign service office. No doubt you could pass all sorts of intelligence back to me."

"Oh, yes, I could," she said, eyes shining. Then her expression fell a bit. "But I do not think Lord Senric would be all that excited about such a proposition. He is such a homebody, you know. He's always going on about Gahm and how much I'm going to love it there. I'm sure it is very fine… but I think I will do what I can to encourage him to stay in town whenever possible."

"I wish you luck with that," I told her. I knew the Duke quite well, and also knew he did not share Gabrinne's love of the capital city and its diversions. But that was for them to work out as they could.

She raised an eyebrow. "I believe you might be laughing at me, Your Majesty…just the smallest bit. I do not mind. You'll learn soon enough that the best thing a man can do in this world is keep his wife happy."

"Is that so?"

"Oh, yes. Papa does everything as Mamma wishes, and the household runs quite smoothly. Or at least as smoothly as a household can that has five boys in it."

I began to see where the Lady Gabrinne had gotten her temperament. No doubt her mother was a force of nature as well. My tone neutral, I said, "Then I'm sure you and Lord Senric will sort it out soon enough."

"Of that I have no doubt."

The music began to slow and soften to its closing chords, so I said nothing else, but only led her through the final steps until the song was ended, and we made our bows and curtseys to one another. My muscles seemed to tense, for the moment was now upon us. Somehow, though, I managed to thank Gabrinne in quite normal tones.

"No, thank *you*, Your Majesty," she replied. Then, in a whisper, "And best of luck with your announcement."

I nodded and made my way through the crowd, which now had quieted and was watching the dais, expecting my arrival there at any moment. The musicians had already gathered up their instruments and moved off to one side, leaving the platform empty for me and my family. My mother was even now ascending the steps, with my sister a few feet behind her. The guards had taken up their posts to either side, and the stage was set.

The young women pushed forward, leaving their dance partners behind. Perhaps there had been shared jokes and laughter, even flirtation, but one would not know that now. All of those faces were now tense, mouths tight, as they watched me mount the shallow set of three steps to the dais and take my position in its center.

I paused for a few seconds, then cleared my throat, wishing I had thought to steal a few sips of wine before I had to make the announcement. "My lords and ladies, I thank you all for your attendance tonight, and indeed, at all the events this week. It has been a very great pleasure for me to meet so many lovely and accomplished young women, but as you all know, only one of you can be my wife." Another pause, as my gaze swept the crowd, searching for Ashara in her gleaming copper gown. There she was, nearly in the center and only one row back, with Gabrinne and Lord Senric at her side. Good. I would not have to wait for her to push her way from the very back of the throng.

"As you can imagine," I continued, "this was a very difficult decision, one which required a good deal of deliberation." To my right, I heard something that sounded suspiciously like a snort coming from my sister, but when I cast a quick sidelong glance at her, she looked serene and calm enough. "In the end, however, I knew I must go with the choice of my heart...and that is the Lady Ashara Millende. Ashara?" I asked, and extended a hand to her.

A wave of pink spread over her cheeks, a flush I could see even at this distance, but she bit her lip and moved forward, leaving the crowd behind, and beginning to mount the steps of the dais. At the same time I heard a murmur spread through the crowd, which was only to be expected. However, the murmur did not subside, but grew louder, eventually resolving itself into a single woman's voice crying out, "No, no! You cannot choose her! She is an impostor!"

Ashara stopped on the middle step, the pretty pink disappearing from her cheeks, leaving her pale as death. One hand went to her mouth, and I thought I heard her murmur, "Oh, no…"

The crowd parted to reveal a tall burly-looking young man in the plain dark clothes of a servant and a pair of women, one of an age with my mother, dressed well enough, but with a tight, cruel set to her mouth. And the other—the other—

I blinked, but that did nothing to change the sight before me. For it seemed that I looked on Ashara, but an Ashara dressed in rags, her threadbare chemise hanging off one slender shoulder, her gown of brown linen patched in multiple places. The servingman held her tightly by one arm, as if to prevent her escape.

"What is this?" I demanded, and turned to look at the woman I had thought to call my bride. "Do you—is this your twin?"

She shook her head, her eyes brimming with unshed tears.

"No twin, Your Majesty," the hard-faced woman said, "but a very she-devil, using unholy magic to deceive you! Show them!"

For a few seconds the false Ashara hesitated. She said, looking straight at me, and appearing to ignore the young man who held her, "The only deception here was in the gowns and jewels the Lady Ashara wore. She is no impostor—she is the daughter of a baronet, just as she told you, a young woman whose birthright has been usurped by the very woman who accuses me…her stepmother."

"And who are you, then?" I asked, and would not allow myself to feel any relief at her words.

She stood up straighter, and it was as if the air shimmered and danced around her, before it fell away to reveal a woman of middle years, well-dressed and prosperous-looking. "I am Therissa Larrin, Ashara's aunt."

At once the crowd began to shift and murmur, even as the blood seemed to chill in my veins. So the stepmother's accusations of unholy magic were true. And that meant—

That meant the woman before me had just condemned herself to death. And not just herself, but the woman I loved.

Something in my face must have shifted, revealing my thoughts, for the woman stared at me with a horror equal to that which I felt, and she cried out, "Run, Ashara! Run, or your life is forfeit!"

Just the briefest hesitation, as Ashara raised despairing eyes to me. She mouthed something—it could have been *I love you*, or perhaps only *I'm sorry*—and then she bolted down the steps, past the startled guards, through the crowds. And as I watched, she seemed to *shift*—her gleaming red hair went dark, and the gown of brilliant copper changed to dull blue—making her much more difficult to distinguish.

But that was not the end of her aunt's trickery, for even with that disguise, the guards still converged upon her. She changed again, to the semblance of an older nobleman, and then one of my men-at-arms themselves, as all collapsed in confusion, with everyone accusing those around them of being the young woman in disguise.

"Stop this!" I bellowed. "Seize her!"

I saw a faint smile play around the lips of the accursed sorceress who had caused the destruction of my dreams, and knew that Ashara had somehow gotten away. Perhaps some corner of my soul was relieved, but I could not let myself feel that now. Everything was done and gone to dust.

"Take the sorceress to the dungeon," I said dully, then turned away as the guards converged upon this Therissa.

And pulling the heavy crown from my head, I stepped down from the dais and made my way out of the chamber as the crowd parted around me, silent and shocked. For once, even the chattering nobles of my court had nothing to say.

I left the ballroom, and did not look back.

CHAPTER FIFTEEN

Ashara

Not knowing what else to do, I ran. Somehow my aunt had shielded me, kept me from capture, although she was not so lucky herself. I ran from the palace, out into the dark streets, noting dully that my appearance kept changing, that sometimes the skirts I held were blue, or green, or not even skirts at all, but the breeches and boots of a man. And then at last they were my own skirts of patched brown linen, and I knew she had stopped casting the spell.

What that meant, I did not know. Was she dead, given the sort of summary justice meted out to those found guilty of practicing magic? I could not let myself stop to think about that. I could not think about anything...especially the look of dawning horror in Torric's eyes as he gazed upon me and realized the trick which had been played upon him.

I tore through the streets, glad I had watched from the windows of the carriage as it had taken me to and from my house to the palace, so I more or less knew the route. Once or twice I made a wrong turn and had to stop, gasping for a breath, on some unfamiliar street, praying a night watchman would not see me and demand to know my business. And one time I felt drunken hands grasping at me in the darkness, thinking a woman out alone at this hour must be there for one thing only. In terror I recoiled, feeling the sleeve of my chemise tear as I pulled away from his clutching hands.

Finally, though, I reached the house, which stood empty and quiet. Everyone must still be at the palace, facing the aftermath of my unmasking. Even Mari seemed to be gone; perhaps she, too, had accompanied my stepmother and Janks to the palace with their captive, although I had not noticed her. Whatever the reason for her absence, I knew I did not have much time. I would have to disappear, and that meant taking those things which might secure my survival.

Is it stealing, to take the property that rightfully should have been yours? I did not have time to split such legal hairs, but only seized a satchel from the downstairs closet and emptied a good deal of the silverware into it. Then it was upstairs to take a gown of Shelynne's, and a pair of slippers, and one of her spare chemises. That truly was stealing, but I knew I had to look halfway respectable to sell any of the silver I had just stuffed into the satchel, and I could not do that wearing a threadbare workaday gown and a torn chemise.

No time to change here—I would have to find a safe place to do that elsewhere. I had just slipped back down the stairs when I saw Claris poking her head out of the kitchen door. Our gazes met, and her eyes widened.

"Ashara? What on earth?"

"I can't explain," I said, pushing past her to the back door. I knew I daren't go out the front.

One hand reached out and took me by the arm. "Are you running away?"

"No—yes, well, I suppose you could call it that. Just please know that I never meant anyone any harm. I never—" The tears welled up in my eyes, splintering the pleasant gloom of the candlelit hallway into a thousand shimmering pieces before me. No. I could not cry now. Later, perhaps, when I thought I was safe, I could weep enough to fill the very River Silth, but not now. "I have to go. *Please*, Claris!"

She let go of my arm. "You should have gone long before this, miss. Just don't go hungry." And she followed me into the kitchen, seized two of the fresh-baked loaves from the counter, and shoved them into my satchel. "Now, off with you! I will say I never saw you, if anyone asks."

"Thank you, Claris," I told her. There was so much more I wanted to say, so many thanks I wanted to give her for all her little stolen kindnesses over the years, but I knew there was not time enough for that.

So I ran again, this time down the back stairs and out into the courtyard, past the stables, and through the gate where I had stolen away every day so far this week. Only this time I wore no magical finery, and I looked forward to nothing more than a life on the run.

Oh, gods, Torric, I thought then. *I am so sorry. I did not deceive you, not truly. My love for you was real, even if nothing else was.*

Sometime later I found a disreputable little inn where they grudgingly agreed to take a single silver spoon in exchange for a night's stay. Even I knew that was an extortionate price, but I did not have the will to argue with them, not when they probably guessed the spoon was stolen and they could have turned me in to the city guard had they so wished. Most likely they deemed it not worth the trouble. In any event, I made my way without further incident to a cramped little room on the third floor, huddled up on the thin mattress, which was not much better than my pallet back in the kitchen at home, and made myself go to sleep.

I would like to say that I felt better when I awoke. Unfortunately, I did not. There seemed to be little for me to do except put on my stolen clothing—at least I had taken one of Shelynne's plainest gowns, a dress she only wore while at home, when not expecting company—and eat some bread, and decide what I should do next.

Iselfex was a very great city, and I could expect to hide there more or less safely. However, I knew I would have to do something to hide my hair, for its color was far too distinctive, and would be the one thing about my appearance that was sure to give me away. So after I washed my face and hands in the dingy water in the basin provided for me, I braided my hair tightly and coiled it around my head, then pulled my kerchief over that, making sure it was set far enough forward that none of the fine coppery strands around my forehead could be seen.

From the inn I first went to a silversmith's, and concocted a story of how my parents had passed away and my relations had turned me out in the street, giving me nothing but some silver knives and spoons as my inheritance. Whether he believed this story or not, I could not tell, although my voice did have a fairly convincing quaver to it. But at least he did not cheat me like the people at the inn, and gave me a fair enough price for the pieces, enough ready coin that I knew I would not immediately starve, or find myself sleeping in the street.

I inquired of him as to the nearest apothecary, saying I needed a tincture of herbs to calm my nerves, and he directed me to a shop only a few doors down. While it was true that I could use some calming, that was not my reason for seeking out an apothecary. Several years ago my stepmother had begun to show streaks of iron-grey in her heavy dark hair, and had immediately begun to apply a dye an apothecary gave her. Ever since then her hair had been as raven-black as it was in her younger days, although she did have to use the concoction frequently, since the color began to wear away after several weeks.

It seemed the best way to disguise myself, as it was not the fashion for women to wear kerchiefs on their heads, save when performing menial tasks around the house. I purchased the dye, saying it was for my mother, and hurried out. From there I went back to the inn, paid some of my precious coin for several more basins of water, and effected my transformation, making sure to dye my eyebrows as well so they would not give me away. Luckily my eyelashes had always been much darker than my hair, and so the contrast was not too great.

Some hours later I descended the stairs and left the place. No one seemed to have paid me much mind, but I thought it wiser to move on to a more respectable inn in a better district. As I moved through the streets, I saw guards in the Imperial livery tacking up posters everywhere—much as they had when the Emperor first announced his quest for a bride, although their purpose this time was not quite so benign. No, these sheets had a not very good likeness of me on them, with my red hair taking a prominent place in the description beneath, along with the words "Wanted for Sorcery."

Despite my new disguise, I kept my eyes downcast as I walked, fearful that at any moment one of them would see through my fragile concealment and call me out for the fugitive I was. But though I walked with my heart in my throat and my hands trembling, none of them seemed to notice me.

An hour or so later, I walked shakily into a hostel reserved for young women only, the sort of place where those looking for employment stayed whilst between situations. I had known such establishments existed, as Mari had spoken of them once or twice, and I thought this a far safer place than an inn where all types would come and go, and drink far too much. A young woman on her own was only a target in such a place, whereas here I thought I might be left alone.

The proprietress of the hostel, a stern-looking woman in her fifties named Madam Isling, inspected me from head to toe, and I all but quaked in my stolen slippers, thinking that surely she must notice a spot of dye I had not wiped away, or that my gown did not quite fit—Shelynne, while far more slender than her sister, was still of a more robust build than I. But after a long moment she gave a brisk nod and said, "Very well. And you said your name was…?"

"Mari," I supplied. It was a common enough name, and my wits at the moment were too addled to come up with anything better. "Mari Gelsandre."

"Well, Mari, you look and sound like a respectable enough girl. You may have a room here until you find your next situation, but you are expected to pitch in and help with the upkeep and the cooking. That is how I keep my rates low enough for you girls to have a place to stay."

"Of course, ma'am," I said at once. Truly, I did not think my duties could be any more onerous than they had been at my stepmother's home, and I was so grateful to have found a haven that I believed I would have cheerfully doubled the labor required as long as it meant I could stay here without detection.

From there she directed me upstairs, saying I would be sharing a room with a girl called Lindry, who had to leave her last situation rather unexpectedly, but who had been given a small sum so that she would not find herself on the streets. And I nodded and hurried away, clutching my satchel, glad that Madam Isling did not seem inclined to ask any more questions of me.

Once I entered the upstairs hall, I found a small knot of four or five girls gathered there, talking in excited half-whispers.

"…And they are looking *everywhere* for her!" one girl, small and round, with eyes equally round, but quite large, said. "The Emperor has said he will scour the kingdom until he finds her!"

I realized who the "her" of this pronouncement must be and schooled my features to a more or less neutral expression, even as I sidled closer, hoping to hear more.

"But how did she even get away?" a second girl, this one tall and thin, inquired.

"Oh, it was the most amazing thing!" the round girl exclaimed. "All the guards crowded around her, and it seemed there was no chance of escape, when suddenly there was the most blinding flash of blue light, and she was gone! The sorceress had sent her away—miles and miles away!"

Despite everything, I had to fight to keep a smile from my lips. Apparently the tale had already grown in the scant hours since I had made my escape from the palace. Would that my aunt had truly possessed such skills! But no, all her sorcery lay in illusion and disguise, and I murmured a quiet thanks that she had been able to summon those powers to protect me even as the guards seized her.

My heart wrenched within me then, for I still did not know whether she even yet lived. And Torric—was he searching for me so that I might meet my own punishment? Did he hate me now, hate me for what I had done?

I must have made some small sound, for the little group of girls paused and looked over at me. Summoning a smile, I took a few steps forward and said, "Do not let me interrupt you. It sounds like quite the tale."

"It is not a *tale!*" the round girl replied in indignation. "It is true, and what actually happened at the palace last night, just as His Majesty was about to announce his new bride. Have you not heard anything of it?"

"I confess I haven't," I said. "Or rather, I saw some of His Majesty's guards posting notices about the city as I made my way here, but I thought the girl on them must be some sort of common criminal."

"Well, it is the most astonishing thing, for she is the woman he fell in love with, but it was all sorcery, a spell cast by the girl's aunt to bind him to her, and when the plot was revealed, she was spirited away before she could be captured."

"And—and did the sorceress get away as well?" Thank goodness, my voice did not shake at all as I asked the question.

"No, she did not. She is now in the dungeon, and people are wondering why the Emperor has not already cut off her head, but perhaps he wants to question her first, or some such thing. At any rate, she will not be casting spells again."

The words "cut off her head" caused another lump to form in the pit of my stomach, but I forced myself to remain calm. Yes, Aunt Therissa had been captured, and things were certainly very dire. However, Torric had not yet ordered her execution, apparently. What that meant, I was not sure. Perhaps it was as the strange girl said, and he only wished to question her more. Or perhaps he could not bring himself to execute a woman, even one who had brought death upon herself by using forbidden magic.

"I'm Lindry," the round girl said. "You're new—are you to share my room?"

"Yes," I replied. "I am Mari Gelsandre."

"Well, Mari," she said frankly. "You're very pretty, so I doubt you will have too much trouble finding a situation soon enough, unless the lady of the house is the jealous type, or there is a son with roving hands, which happened at my last house, only they were good enough to recognize it was not my fault, and so they gave me a letter of reference and a month's pay, and so I think I shall do well enough."

This was all said in one breath, and I began to realize I most likely would not have to offer too much in the way of conversation. Well enough, as I feared I would soon run out of lies to tell.

"Thank you, Lindry," I said. "Would you be so kind as to show me our room, as I have walked very far today, and am quite tired."

"Of course," she replied, and grinned at her companions, as if promising to finish the story as soon as she had seen me settled. "It's a good room, as it's on the corner, and so we don't have to share two walls. And even better, it looks out on the kitchen garden and not the street, so it's quiet enough. Here it is."

I looked into the room she indicated and felt a wave of quiet relief wash over me. No, it was not grand, but it was clean and neat, with two narrow beds and a small table between them, and a wash basin in one corner with a cracked mirror over it.

Definitely not the palace, my mind seemed to whisper at me, and I forced the thought away. I could not think of the palace, for if I did I would think of him, think of his eyes and the sound of his voice and the way his lips had once touched mine. And if I thought of that, then I would recall the horror in his face as he stared at me, regarding me as if I were some alien creature he had never seen before.

"It is most pleasant," I told Lindry, and blinked away the tears that had begun to form before they could be anything but small, stinging pinpricks. "And how long have you been here?"

"Only a fortnight. I have been looking for a situation, but I can afford to be somewhat choosy, and so I have not made a decision yet. Tomorrow I will show you where the notice board is, so you can see if there's anything that suits you."

I had heard of these boards; it was how Mari had come to us, after my stepmother had advertised for a new girl when the previous maid had been caught pilfering. Well, I supposed I was a pilferer, too, although oddly I felt little guilt over my petty thefts.

"Thank you," I said. "That will be most helpful, as I would like to find someplace as quickly as possible."

"They turned you off with nothing?" Lindry inquired, and although there was nothing but friendly curiosity in her expression, I knew she would not be put off by any evasion on my part.

Luckily, I had already concocted a story in my mind, knowing I would have to offer something to any prospective employers. "Oh, no, not at all, but I like to be kept busy. I was in the household of Lady Gabrinne Nelandre, but she is just engaged to the Duke of Gahm, and I did not wish to be removed to the country. So she paid me well and gave me a letter of reference, and took very good care of me." I had to hope that Gabrinne would not mind too much that I had borrowed her name; somehow I had the feeling she would not.

Lindry's eyes widened a bit. "That will put you in good stead, to have a reference such as that. I am sure you will have a new position in no time. It is too bad that you do not care for the country, but I suppose it is not for everyone. I, on the other hand, would like it very much." She started, as if a sudden thought had seized her, and asked, "Do you—do you think you could put in a word for me with her?"

Oh, dear. Thinking furiously, I replied, "I wish I could, but I believe her household is already set, and she is not looking for anyone else."

A little sigh. "I suppose it was too much to ask for."

"It is fine," I said quickly, for I didn't want to Lindry to think I would not recommend her because of some failing on her part. "If I can think of any other possibilities for you, I will be sure to let you know."

She nodded at that, and must have realized I was not inclined to further conversation, for she offered a quick smile before saying, "Supper is at five, and Madam Isling always rings a bell, so it is difficult to miss!"

And then she ducked out and left me alone. I let out a sigh of my own at the sudden quiet, then set the satchel down on the bed that was to be mine. Tomorrow I would have to see about purchasing another gown, as I had only the one, and, and...

My mind rebelled at these orderly plans, and my legs seemed to lose their strength as I collapsed on the bed next to the bag containing my precious store of coins. I did not want to think about gowns and situations. I only wanted to think of him, and how I would never hear his voice again, never feel his arms around me, never see the sudden, shocking brilliance of his smile or the richness of his laughter.

Grief overcame me then, and I buried my face in my hands and wept, wondering what on earth was to become of me now.

CHAPTER SIXTEEN

Torric

"I do not understand what you are waiting for!" my mother snapped, and I saw Lyarris wince and give a small shake of her head. "Execute that woman at once and have done with it!"

So easy for her to say. Yes, this Therissa Larrin had admitted to using magic, a thing that had been outlawed for centuries everywhere in the civilized world, but for some reason I had a difficult time seeing her as a foul mage, rotten to the core through the use of forbidden sorcery. She did not look like an evil user of magic. She looked—well, she looked just as a prosperous wife of a knight or baronet might, probably very pretty in her youth, and still handsome enough. Her face was not one that belonged to a person rotten to the core.

However, I knew attempting to explain any of that to my mother would be worse than useless, for she would no doubt see it as weakness on my part that I hadn't had the Larrin woman dragged out to the courtyard and her head struck off with a sword. Never mind that the Crown hadn't meted out that sort of punishment in years, not since the usurper had lost his head once my father's forces were victorious. I would have to order an executioner's platform built, and that would take time.

My voice more even than I had expected it to be, I replied, "I will not have her killed while there is a chance she has information regarding what happened to Ashara. By all accounts she has disappeared into the city without a trace, despite all my guards' best efforts. So executing the one person who might be able to help—whatever her crimes—is not the wisest thing to do, I think."

A scowl, which meant my argument had some persuasion to it, and my mother did not want to admit the fact. "Very well," she said irritably. "But it will not look good, you know, for you to keep her alive indefinitely. The people must see that punishment awaits anyone who uses the forbidden magics."

I did not bother to point out that this was the first time anyone had been caught using magic in more than a century, and therefore the number of possible future transgressors was most likely quite low. "I will take that under advisement."

She sniffed. "Which means you will do as you please. Very well, Torric, but do not come complaining to me when our rule of law begins to completely fall apart."

"No worries on that score, Mother, for you know I do not come complaining to you about anything, as I am aware that I am not likely to meet with any support or understanding."

Despite the myriad ways in which she aggravated me, this was the first time I had been bold enough to say such a thing out loud. Her spine stiffened, and she flashed me a look of such outrage I wondered if she were about to reach out and slap me for my impertinence. But then she seemed to recall that although I was her son, I was also the Emperor, and she stilled.

"I have said everything I have to say. Do as you will, however foolish that may be." And she turned and stalked from the chamber, leaving a palpable cloud of fury in her wake.

"That could have gone better," Lyarris remarked, speaking for the first time as she rose from her chair and came to stand by me at the window.

"I suppose, but I am tired of guarding my tongue around her." Pausing, I ran a hand through my hair and then shook my head. "To be honest, I am weary of everything right now."

"I know," my sister said, and put a comforting hand on my arm. "I cannot imagine how difficult this must all be."

"No, you can't," I replied abruptly, and stopped, somewhat ashamed of myself. Lyarris was the last person in the world I should be snapping at. But somehow I could not find the words for an apology, and so I shifted away from her and stared out the window instead. The day was grey and lowering, a dull mist-like rain blanketing the city. A fitting accompaniment to my mood, I supposed.

"You will find her."

I was not so sure of that. As distinctive as Ashara was in appearance, she seemed to have vanished into thin air—another sorcery, I would have said, although Lord Keldryn had told me that Therissa Larrin asserted over and over that her magic was not of that sort—"illusions only, and nothing that lasts," had been her words.

Of course I had not been to see her. No, she was locked up securely in the deepest vaults of the dungeon, in one of several cells constructed long ago in the age of magic, cells barred with cold iron that had their own sigils protecting them, so that no one contained within could use their own powers. Whether those sigils still worked, my advisors could not say, as there were none among them with magical powers. Still, it seemed the most logical place to put a known sorceress.

"How will I find her?" I asked. "My guards have fanned out through the city and have found no trace of her. Granted, in a city of some two hundred thousand souls, finding a single woman might be difficult. Even so, no one has seen or heard of her, not even at her home."

I hesitated, and despite the grimness of the situation, I had a difficult time repressing a grin. For although the cook claimed she had seen nothing, it seemed Ashara had gone home whilst all the other members of her household were still here at the palace, and had made off with a good deal of the silver, much to her stepmother's dismay. No doubt she intended to pawn it and further finance her disappearance… which led me to believe that the aunt was telling the truth, and that she had no knowledge of her niece after she made her initial escape from the palace grounds.

Lyarris gazed out the window as well, as if somehow she could spy Ashara within the city's teeming masses of humanity. For a long moment she said nothing. Then she turned back toward me and said, "Perhaps you should speak with Therissa Larrin yourself."

"I?" I asked, staring at my sister and wondering if she taken leave of her senses. "The Emperor of Sirlende does not stoop to questioning prisoners."

For the first time an expression of irritation flitted across her normally serene features. "Then perhaps you should stop thinking like the Emperor of Sirlende and more like a man who has lost the woman he loves."

I made an exasperated sound. How dare she stand there and say such a thing! Yes, I had lost Ashara, but more than that, I had lost everything that had passed between us, for now I knew it had all been a lie, all illusions, shifting and formless as mist evaporating in the harsh light of day.

What she saw in my face, I did not know, but Lyarris said calmly, "You are the Emperor, true, but you are also a man, and I saw how you cared for Ashara. It was new and uncertain, true. I just want to make sure that you are not allowing pride to dictate your actions. You have sent Lord Keldryn and Renwell Blane to question Mistress Larrin, and it seems she has been forthcoming enough, but I do not know if they are asking the right questions. Only you can know that for sure, Torric."

This last was said with such a pleading note in her voice that I looked at my sister in some surprise. "You really think it could make a difference?"

"I do not know that it will not." She knotted her fingers together and stared down at them for the space of a few heartbeats before saying quietly, "I cannot imagine that you wish to spend the rest of your life wondering what might have happened if you had had the courage to seek answers for yourself, rather than relying upon your advisors and such to do it for you."

At first I did not reply, but instead pondered her words. Would I be content with letting Ashara go, with letting my mother and those who thought like her have their way, and allow Therissa Larrin to be executed while she still possessed knowledge that might give me the peace of mind I so desperately desired?

Put that way...

"Very well," I told my sister. "I am off to the dungeons."

It had been many years since I had last descended to the dark regions hidden beneath the palace's splendid public rooms. Once when I was a child, the son of the Earl of Landishorne had dared me to play hide-and-seek down there, and we had spent a stolen hour wandering around the dank, unused corridors and jumping out from empty cells and shouting "boo!" before my father's guards found us and dragged us quite unceremoniously back to the upper floors. As I recalled, I was sent to bed without any supper, but that seemed a fair enough exchange for such an adventure.

Now, however, I did not find the place quite so amusing. The upper floors still contained a few prisoners of the worst sort, although most transgressors these days were housed in the new modern gaol built near the city wall. As I approached the entrance to the lowest level, the guards snapped to attention, clearly startled to see the Emperor in their domain, and even more surprised to see him here alone. I had told the two men-at-arms who followed me everywhere to wait at the top of the stairs to the dungeons, and they had followed my orders, though they were clearly most unhappy at letting me descend into the lower levels unaccompanied. For myself, I did not see the need for their worry, as every level of the dungeon had its own contingent of guards, and no doubt they could protect me if anything untoward should happen.

"I wish to speak with Therissa Larrin," I said.

There were four guards present, all them looking rather surly and low-browed, though that could have been a trick of the flickering torchlight. But they straightened in shock at my words, then bowed low. One of them, presumably the senior of the quartet, stepped forward, saying, "Y-yes, Your Majesty. At once, Your Majesty. This way."

Their discomfiture rather amused me, but I maintained a stern expression as the one guard led me down a narrow little corridor, the ceiling so low I felt certain my head was going to scrape against it at any moment. The hallway ended at a single cell, its bars seeming thicker than those of any of the chambers we had yet passed. Strange runes were scratched into the rock at the lintel—the guardian sigils set there centuries before by mages now long dead. I repressed a shiver.

"You may go," I told the guard, and he seemed to pale in the chancy light.

"Your Majesty—"

"I will speak with the prisoner alone."

Whatever courage had prompted him to speak up had apparently fled, for he bowed and left with some haste, not even sparing me a backward glance over his shoulder.

There was a rustle within the cell, and I turned to see Therissa Larrin rise from a mean stone cot with a thin mattress of straw and approach the bars, although I noticed she did not touch them. "So the Emperor himself deigns to enter his dungeon and question the prisoner."

She did not look nearly as downtrodden as I had thought she would. True, her hair was somewhat disheveled, and there were stains on her gown of fine blue wool, but her dark eyes seemed bright enough as she regarded me, her hands planted on her hips.

Under that lively gaze I found myself somewhat discomfited, as if somehow I were the one about to be questioned, and not she. Setting my expression in what I hoped were grim lines, I said, "As I have had no satisfaction from either my chancellor or the captain of my guard, yes, I thought I would speak to you myself. Perhaps you will be more forthcoming with me."

At that remark she actually chuckled. "And here I thought I was being so honest with them. Truly, Your Majesty, I have withheld no information, but if you wish to hear it for yourself, I have no quibble with that."

Surely a woman locked up in the lowest levels of the palace dungeons and awaiting a certain sentence of death should not be quite so light-hearted in countenance or tone. Stepping closer to the bars, I demanded, "Tell me where Ashara Millende is."

"Why?" she asked frankly. "So you can send her down here to share a cell with me?"

"No!" I retorted, then went on, fumbling with my words, "That is, I have every right, as Emperor and as the man who intended to marry her, to know of her location."

"Indeed? For I would say that the Emperor and the man who wished to marry her are two very different people, and I wish to know which of them I am speaking with at the moment."

What an impossible woman. "I assure you, they are one and the same."

She shook her head, and slanted me a little sidelong look. In that moment I could tell she must have been quite beautiful when she was younger, although I did not see much of Ashara in her—something in the half-dimple at the corner of her mouth, perhaps, or in the tilt of her dark eyes. "I find I do not possess that same assurance. For you have come stomping down here, quite high-handed, with such a stern brow, and I fear I do not see much of the lover in you."

For a full moment I could do nothing but stare at her, astounded by her impertinence. I noted the lack of an honorific, but it was far more than that, for it seemed she thought herself well positioned to rebuke me, as if I were the miscreant here. "Do you know who you are speaking to, woman?"

The light went out of her eyes then, and she replied in sad tones, "It seems as if I am speaking to the Emperor of Sirlende, and not the man who loved my niece, and so I fear I have nothing more to say to you." After delivering that remark, she returned to her makeshift seat on the lumpy pallet, and turned her head away from me.

Of all the—I moved closer to the bars and wrapped my fingers around them. As I did so, I felt an odd tingle move through my hands and up my arms. Perhaps I was feeling something of the old charms laid within the metal. That was not enough to keep me from exclaiming, "Have you no heart at all? Your niece is lost somewhere within this city, and I do not think I have to remind you of what may befall a young woman on her own on its streets. Let me help her!"

She shifted, and watched me for a second or two, then seemed to nod. "Ah, that sounds more like the man who loves her, and not the Emperor. You do love her, do you not?"

"I—" My breath seemed to strangle in my throat. Hoarsely, I said, "I believed that I did. But how do I know what I really fell in love with, when it was all an illusion?"

My question only made her sigh, and give a small shake of the head, as if she were impatient with my stupidity. She rose and came to pause a foot or so beyond the bars. From that distance I could see the smudges of weariness under her eyes, the etchings of worry lines between her brows. "The only illusion was her gowns and jewels, you foolish boy. Oh, and I suppose her hairstyles, as I fear her stepmother would not have allowed her to spend an hour curling her hair to make herself beautiful for you. Everything else, though— that was all Ashara, and no doing of mine. How different was it, really, from the artifices those other fine-born women used to catch your eye, the rouge, the powder, the charcoal liner? The stays, and the padding in the bodices of their gowns?

All these things would melt away as well, at the end of the evening. The only difference here is that I used magic to give Ashara the trappings required to enter your little contest. But that is merely a difference of means, and not intention."

I reflected then that this woman had missed her calling, for truly she could twist words as well as any politician or reader of the law. There had to be something fundamentally wrong with her argument, but damn me if I could find it. "That is not the same thing," I said at length, "for paint is not outlawed, nor are overly tight stays, but magic has been forbidden in this land for nigh on five hundred years."

The glint returned to her eyes. "Ah, you have me there. 'Tis true, but it is a foolish law, especially with something so harmless as the kind of magic I can conjure."

"I do not think it harmless at all. Perhaps on this occasion you used it merely to give your niece the semblance of fine gowns and jewels, but I saw for myself how you could make it so your own face was altered, and Ashara herself was changed so she could safely escape. That could be a very evil power, in the wrong hands."

To my surprise, she did not naysay me, but nodded soberly. "There is some truth to that argument. I have seen—" She stopped herself then, and seemed to shiver. "My lord, my only intention was to help my niece. I swear on my own life and hers that no other spells were cast. It was always possible that you would never notice her at all. I did not think that was likely, not as lovely as she is, but still, I did nothing but put her in a position to cross your path. Everything else after that was between the two of you."

Oh, how I wanted to believe that. It would be easy enough to wave away a few conjured gowns and necklaces and rings. I did not want my mother and Lord Keldryn to have the truth of it, that beyond her illusions Therissa Nelandre had cast some sort of spell to make me fall in love with her niece, as no other explanation for the sudden violence of my affections could possibly exist.

"And what was in it for you?" I demanded suddenly. "Did you hope to gain some influence by making your niece Empress of Sirlende?"

At that question she actually laughed out loud. "Oh, my, they have trained you to be the suspicious sort, haven't they?"

"I am the Emperor." Even I heard the stiffness in my tone.

"True, to your misfortune. I cannot say the crown has done all that well for you." Her expression sobered, and she continued, "I have been gone from Sirlende these twenty years, for as soon as my powers began to be too difficult to conceal any longer, I knew I had no place here. So I packed what I could and left, although it hurt greatly to leave my younger sister behind. I have seen many things in those twenty years, my lord, and learned a great deal. But I had never planned to return to my homeland, as I knew one such as I could make no real life for herself here.

"However, in one of those odd twists of fate, I retraced my steps some months ago, and visited a town I had not seen for some ten years, and there it seemed a letter had been held all that time for me by a kindly innkeeper, in case I might return one day. That letter was from the steward of my late brother-in-law's estate, who was let go upon his death, as his second wife wished to rent the country house and make her home in town. Until then I had no idea my dear sister was even dead, let alone her husband, and once I learned that my only niece was all by herself in the world, I hastened back to Sirlende, to make sure all was well with her."

"I assume it was not," I said dryly, for I had not forgotten the things Ashara had said of her stepmother.

"No, it was as bad for her as could possibly be, for that wretched woman who married my late brother-in-law after my sister's death was the very worst sort—vain, and cold-hearted, and concerned only with her own two daughters. She made Ashara a servant in her own household, worse than a servant, really, because at least a servant earns some modest wage in addition to the roof over her head and a bed to sleep in."

At these revelations a cold anger began to burn in me. Yes, I had gotten the impression that things were worse in the Millende household than Ashara had ever let on, but never had I imagined that the poor girl was escaping a life of utter drudgery in those few stolen hours we shared together. No wonder she seemed to find something to marvel at in even the simplest niceties. She had no frame of reference.

I do not know what shifted in my countenance, but something of my thoughts must have shown in my expression, for Mistress Nelandre nodded and said, "You begin to see something of my desperation. I will confess that when I first came to Sirlende, my only thought was of removing her from her stepmother's household and taking her with me, or at least setting her up in a better situation far outside Iselfex. But my arrival here coincided with your announcement of a search for a bride, and I thought that would be far better. I had caught glimpses of her before I met her, saw her going out and fetching water for the household, or running small errands for her stepmother. It was enough to show me that she had grown up as lovely as my younger sister, and I knew that if I could only put her in your path, she would almost certainly catch your eye."

That she had, without a doubt. "So you formed a plan, and somehow got Ashara to go along with it."

"Not without some convincing, I assure you. She understood the consequences, but her desperation to escape her stepmother's household proved to be greater than her fear of punishment."

And could I blame her? After meeting the woman in question—and her two tedious daughters—I could only imagine how terrible serving in such a house might be, even without knowing the entire time that it should have been hers. Yes, I began to understand why Ashara would be willing to risk so much.

"I believe you," I said slowly. "For truly, if your only desire was for power, then it would have been far simpler for you yourself to take on the guise of a young noblewoman, and attempt to trap me that way, rather than drag your niece into the affair."

Mistress Larrin nodded approvingly. "I am glad to see that you are beginning to think for yourself, my lord, and not as your advisors believe you should. And I will tell you that I wish I knew where my niece has gone, but I do not possess the power of far-seeing. I can only tell you what I think."

"And what is that?" I inquired, half-consciously moving even closer to the bars so I might not miss a single word of her reply.

"When we are hurt, when our world has been turned upside down, we often seek out those things that are familiar to us. What Ashara has known for the past ten years is a life of service, even though it is not a life she chose for herself." Mistress Larrin glanced up and away from me, as if her gaze could somehow pierce the layers of rock and earth that separated her from the world above. "I cannot say this with any certainty, for I do not know for sure, but it seems to me that she would have taken her refuge in some household where she could work to earn her keep. Perhaps I am wrong—perhaps she fled the city altogether, and is even now on her way to South Eredor or farther still. But I do not believe that is what she has done."

It could have been that I only needed something—anything—to hold on to. Somehow, though, I heard the ring of truth in the woman's words, heard something that gave me a purpose, a direction in which to go.

"Thank you, Mistress Larrin," I said. "I will find her."

She smiled. "I believe you will."

Lord Keldryn looked up at me in some exasperation. "You want me to do to *what*, Your Majesty?"

"I want you to gather a census of all the households in the city who are seeking to hire a maid or who have hired one in the last few days."

My chancellor directed a quick glance heavenward, as if imploring the gods to return my sanity to me. Then he said, in the overly mild tone that generally signaled his displeasure, "And are you requesting this information because of something that Larrin woman told you?"

"What of it? I have an idea as to where I might find Ashara Millende. That is all you need to know, Keldryn."

"And what will you do when—*if*—you find her?"

A good question. If it had been asked of me only a day earlier, I would have responded bitterly that I planned to have her locked up in the cell next to her aunt as punishment for her duplicity. Now, however...

I missed her. Foolish as it might sound after such a short acquaintance, I longed to hear her voice and her light, sweet laugh, to see her beautiful amber-green eyes and the pretty little purse she made with her mouth when something amused her. I could no more put her in a dungeon cell than I could place my own sister there.

Despite everything, I still wanted Ashara Millende to be my wife. The mere thought of anyone else sitting in the throne beside me, or sharing my bed, was anathema. How exactly I was to manage such a thing, when the taint of magic clung so closely to her, I was not sure. But I was the Emperor of Sirlende, and if I had to change every law that existed regarding the use of magic in order to make Ashara my wife, then I would do so gladly.

"That is my business," I said stiffly. "For now, I need to concentrate on locating her. What happens afterward can be decided then."

Lord Keldryn merely nodded, but I thought I saw in the weary resignation of his features the realization that I did not intend to punish Ashara at all. Rather, the opposite.

"Anything else, Your Majesty?" he said, in the most neutral of tones.

"That will be all, Keldryn. Just make sure the survey is begun at once. We have already wasted too much time."

He bowed and left, passing my sister and giving her another bow as she came into my study. She closed the door behind her and fixed me with an expectant gaze.

"Oh, yes, you were right," I said with some irritation, because I could see the faint smile on her lips, and the subtle air of *I told you so* which seemed to attend her. "Mistress Larrin did have some valuable insights, and so I am following up on that now."

"I am very glad to hear that." After pausing a foot or so away from my desk and regarding me for a moment, she said, "I get the impression that you are not pursuing Ashara merely to give her a cell next to her aunt."

"No, I am not." Some days I was not sure whether I should be pleased or annoyed that my sister could read me so well. Luckily, she was the only person who seemed to possess that ability. "It is clear enough to me now that Mistress Larrin did not intend any true mischief, but only used her powers as a means to give her niece an advantage she would otherwise not have. Do you know that Ashara was treated like a servant in her own home, a house that should have been hers but which her stepmother all but stole from her?"

Lyarris' eyes widened. "How cruel of her! How on earth did she manage such a thing?"

"I do not know," I said, and felt my mouth compress to a tight line. "But I assure you, I intend to find out."

Of course no one could ignore a summons from the Emperor to appear for a private conference, and Bethynne Millende was no exception. She arrived promptly at eleven the next morning, alone, for I had told her to leave her daughters at home. Tedious they might be, but I could not believe they had had a hand in their mother's plotting. True, they had benefited from her duplicity, and I disliked them enough for that. But they had been very young when Allyn Millende passed away, so I had to believe that they were innocent at least of the original plot.

"Your Majesty," she said in unctuous tones, and curtseyed so low I wondered whether she might topple over.

"Lady Bethynne," I replied.

She straightened and shot me what I assumed she thought was an ingratiating smile. Most likely she assumed I had called her here to give her some sort of reward or other honor for uncovering Mistress Larrin's use of magic.

I only regarded her coldly, my face a stiff mask. In doing so, I noticed the gown of fine wool she wore, the rings of gold and garnet, the heavy matching earrings and necklace. Such an ensemble had to have cost a good deal, and, judging by the finery her daughters had worn earlier in the week, she spared no expense to outfit them as well.

My anger flared at the thought of all that money being spent when Ashara had nothing. It was Ashara's inheritance, not theirs.

"Tell me, Lady Bethynne, did you begin planning how to steal your stepdaughter's estate while her father was on his deathbed, or did you at least wait until he was in the ground?"

At my words her smile faltered and she went pale, making the rouge stand out like two livid spots on her cheeks. "Did I"—a titter that did not fool me in the slightest— "*what*, Your Majesty?"

"You heard me." I stood up then, wishing to intimidate her with my height as well as my position as Emperor. "It has come to my attention that you did willfully take away the Lady Ashara's inheritance when she was a child and could do nothing to fight back, and that in addition to such an act of wickedness, you also made her a servant in her own home. Be advised that I have my own solicitors looking into the matter. Your days of living well at Ashara's expense are over."

"Your—Your Majesty—I—" One hand went to her throat, and she looked as if she were about to faint.

Not that I would have cared if she did, save that if she swooned, I would have to call the guards to have her carried away.

"I am advising you now to set your affairs in order, Lady Bethynne, for if—*when*—the Lady Ashara is located, she will have her rightful holdings restored to her." Not that it really mattered if Ashara got her house and estate back, for as Empress she would have no need of those things. However, it seemed a fitting punishment for the woman who had wrongly possessed them for all these years. "Now go, for the sight of you disgusts me."

She hesitated, opened her mouth as if to plea for clemency, and then seemed to see my expression more clearly. No words, but a quick curtsey, far less elaborate than the one she had given me upon her entrance, and then she fled, leaving behind her the cloying scent of the perfume she wore.

The smell made me want to gag, and I unlatched the window and opened it, letting in a cool, damp breeze. The mists of autumn were truly upon us now, and the air outside was grey and moist. I stared down at the city far below me, seeing the movement of people in its streets, although from this height I could not make out any distinguishing features.

"Ah, Ashara," I murmured. "You are there somewhere. And I will find you."

CHAPTER SEVENTEEN

Ashara

Mistress Cholmond lifted the sheet of paper closer to her nose, squinting at the words on it. She must be very near-sighted, which I thought was all the better. There was no way she would ever be able to connect the face on all those notice boards with the new serving girl she had just hired.

"An excellent reference," she said, although I wondered if she were even able to read the forged letter I had given her. "The Lady Gabrinne Nelandre! Well, then, you are very used to working in a fine household. I hope you do not think mine will be too much of a come-down."

"Oh, not at all, Mistress Cholmond. I am very grateful for the opportunity to serve here."

She nodded, as if satisfied, and set the letter aside. I had purchased the paper and ink the day after I arrived at Mistress Isling's boardinghouse, at the same time I went out to procure another change of clothing and certain other necessities. Thank goodness my penmanship had not deserted me, and the letter seemed to pass muster...not that the woman inspecting it appeared all that discriminating.

"You can start immediately?" Mistress Cholmond inquired.

"Yes, ma'am. I only need to go back to Mistress Isling's to gather my things."

"Excellent. Do that, and return here this afternoon. I am having a supper party this evening, and it will be a good opportunity for you to see how things are done here."

At that I bobbed a quick curtsey, retrieved my false letter of reference, and hurried back to the boardinghouse. Luckily, it was only a brisk ten-minute walk away, and so I was able to conduct my business without too much difficulty.

"You were not with us long, Mari," Mistress Isling said to me as I packed my few belongings in my satchel and gave her the coins I owed her for the three days I had stayed there.

"No, ma'am. I have found a very good situation with Mistress Cholmond." And it was a good situation, I told myself; the lady in question was a widow, but one of some means. I guessed her late husband had been in trade, although she had not mentioned such a thing. But there was no title I could see, and so it seemed logical that he must have been a wealthy merchant of some sort. She had no children, but seemed to be fairly active socially, which meant I should be kept busy.

Not that I minded. I wanted to be busy. If my day was filled with mindless tasks, then perhaps I could keep my thoughts away from Torric, from the deep ache at the center of my being that felt as if some part of my soul had been plucked out.

"Best of luck to you, Mari," Mistress Isling told me. "I would that all my girls could find a situation as quickly as you have."

I gave her a smile and then turned to go. Lindry had gone out earlier, and that made me a little sad, for I wished I could have said goodbye to her before I left. But I told myself that perhaps I could return in a few days to make a proper farewell. In the meantime, Mistress Cholmond was waiting for me.

It was certainly very different working for Mistress Cholmond rather than my stepmother. For one thing, I had a real room with a proper bed to sleep in, and I did not even have to share it with another girl. She kept a small staff—myself, two footmen, the cook, and her lady's maid—and the house was large enough that we all had our own quarters. It was quite the luxury to sleep on a real bed each night, and to have my own wash basin and wardrobe. And yes, she kept me busy with cleaning and assisting the cook, but the work was not much different from what I had done before, save that I did not have two fractious stepsisters to run me ragged in addition to all my other duties.

I could not say I was exactly content, but the simple order of the household did a little to soothe my soul. Of course I listened as intently as I could whenever the conversation among Mistress Cholmond's guests turned to the goings-on at the court. As far as I could tell, Torric still had my aunt locked up in the dungeon, and he seemed to have turned in on himself, canceling many of the events that should have been held in the palace on those days following my disappearance—feasts and balls and musicales. What that meant precisely, no one could say, although there was speculation a-plenty…especially in the safety of a house located far from the palace, where no one of any importance could overhear their gossip.

"I've heard he's locked himself in his suite and won't come out at all," declared a stout lady of an age with Mistress Cholmond, although far sturdier. "Not any way to be ruling an empire, if you ask *me*."

I set down a tureen of squash soup and retreated to a corner in case anyone should have further need of me. In truth, that was not strictly why I paused there; I wished to be able to eavesdrop further, for I had been yearning for news of Torric.

If Mistress Cholmond noticed my loitering, she said nothing of it. She waited while the senior footman gave everyone a precise measure of soup, then remarked, "Oh, that is being somewhat dramatic, don't you think? For I heard he met with the ambassador from South Eredor, and had his usual open audience for the fortnight, and I do not think he would have done either of those things if he had truly retreated from the world."

"Well, *perhaps*," her guest said. "Even so, it is clear he is not himself, at least according to those I have spoken with who have gone to court."

"He has been disappointed in love, and it must be a trying thing for His Majesty, to have his lady chosen, and then to discover it was all through some horrible spell," said a thin older lady with beautiful snow-white hair.

"Oh, the spell in question does not seem that horrible to *me*," the stout woman commented. "Indeed, I somewhat wish magic were not outlawed, for then perhaps I could find a mage to cast a spell that would make me appear young and beautiful."

Mistress Cholmond, instead of being shocked, only chuckled and shook her head, while the white-haired woman looked wistful and said, "You may have a point there. But it is quite against the law to use such things, and the young woman and her mage—I heard it was some sort of relation—did break the law."

"There are far worse laws broken every day, and no one is locked up for them," declared the stout woman. "Have you seen the thievery at the marketplace lately? The cheesemonger had his finger on the scale plain as day, and yet denied any wrongdoing when I confronted him about it!"

And so the dialogue wended away from Torric and the goings-on at the palace, and moved on to more commonplace topics. Yet somehow their conversation warmed me a little, for I did not sense any true outrage over my aunt's use of magic, but rather a simple tut-tutting over what had transpired. If that was how these comfortable, respectable women viewed the matter, then perhaps there was hope for my aunt.

I would not allow myself to consider the possibility that there might be hope for me.

Two days after that, there was a knock at the front door. Now, it was not my place to open the house to visitors or tradesmen—that task fell to the senior footman, a very elegant young man in his mid-twenties named Jennis. But I happened to be in the foyer, rubbing down the paneling with beeswax, and so I experienced a moment of sheer terror when Jennis responded to the knock, only to reveal a hard-faced man wearing the livery of the Imperial house standing on the doorstep.

Somehow I managed to stay in place, to keep wiping away at the age-darkened wood as if having one of the Emperor's guards show up at the house was something that happened every day.

"Yes, m'lord?" Jennis asked uncertainly. Usually he seemed quite stiff and proper, although I thought he was only a few years older than myself, but in this case he seemed quite as flummoxed as I.

"We have heard that your mistress hired a new maid recently. Is this true?"

Looking even more baffled, the footman shot a look over his shoulder at me. "Yes, m'lord."

The guard pushed past Jennis without so much as a by-your-leave and paused a few feet away from me. "Is this true? Are you newly come to this household?"

Oh, how I wished I could deny the fact. But of course I could do no such thing, not with the footman watching our exchange with equal parts bemusement and curiosity. "Yes, m'lord," I said, and somehow forced myself not to reach up and touch my dyed hair, even though I could not help but wonder if its very falseness might not somehow give me away.

"Your name, girl?"

"M-Mari Gelsandre."

"Is it true that you hired on to his household within the last week?"

Not looking at him, I nodded. "Yes, m'lord."

"And before that?"

Although I knew precisely what he was asking, I had no choice but to pretend I did not understand. "Before that, m'lord?"

A frown creased his heavy brow. "Where were you employed before you came here?" He spoke slowly, carefully enunciating each word, as if he were talking to an idiot or a very small child.

For a second or two I hesitated, turning the dust cloth I held over and over in my hands. I could not think of the best way to reply. Jennis and everyone else in the household thought I had come from the employ of Lady Gabrinne, and if I said anything otherwise, I would be exposed as having come here under false pretenses. On the other hand, if I gave this hard-faced guardsman her name, would he report my words to the palace, thus exposing me as a fraud? It seemed I was doomed no matter what I said.

Then, quietly, "In the household of Lady Gabrinne Nelandre."

He nodded. "Very good." A glance back at Jennis, and the guard said, "That is all I needed. A good day to you." He gave the briefest of nods, then left, the sound of his booted feet very loud on the steps as he went back outside.

Still with a perplexed frown tugging at his brow, Jennis shut the door and shot a quizzical look in my direction. "What was that all about, Mari?"

"I have no idea," I lied.

Unfortunately, I thought I knew exactly what it was about…and I wondered if the time to run had come again.

But fate conspired to keep me where I was—or rather, Madame Cholmond's busy social calendar did. She had another supper party scheduled for that evening, and between cleaning and helping the cook and making sure all the silver was spotless, I had no time to even attempt to slip away. All I could hope was that the guardsman had taken my explanation at face value, and since I did not resemble the missing Ashara Millende overmuch, he had dismissed the whole exchange.

Even so, I could feel my hands shaking as I set out the last of the silver, sense a twisting unease in the pit of my stomach. It was a good thing that I had had so many years of practice in keeping my face from betraying anything of what I felt inwardly, or no doubt Mistress Cholmond would have inquired as to my state of mind.

That good lady, however, while kind-hearted enough, was not overly perceptive, and since she was expecting a party of eight that evening, she had far more important things to occupy her thoughts than her serving girl's megrims. And indeed, as the hours passed and no one appeared to haul me off to the palace dungeons, I began to think my worry had been for naught. Perhaps the guardsman truly had believed my story, and had not followed up on it at all.

Her guests appeared at six o'clock, for my mistress was elderly enough that she did not care much to follow fashion, which in the city dictated that supper must never occur before seven-thirty. As the group invited to dine this evening were all more or less of an age with Mistress Cholmond, prosperous older men and their wives, and a widower so that the men and women would come out even, I doubted they were overly concerned with fashion, either.

They were all seated, sharing commonplaces about the weather or the rising prices of linen, what with the state of affairs in Seldd following the plague, when a smart rap sounded on the door. Hearing it, I felt my heart sink, and wondered if I would have enough time to bolt from the room before Jennis went to see who was there.

"Positively ill-mannered for anyone to be calling at this hour," Mistress Cholmond said in some irritation. "Jennis, go tell whoever it is that I have company, and that they may return tomorrow at a more civilized time."

"Of course, ma'am," he said, and went out of the dining chamber and down the hall to the door.

"Mari," she said, and I jumped.

"Ma'am?" I quavered.

"Stop your woolgathering, and bring in the soup. You will have to serve, as Jennis is otherwise occupied."

I nodded and hurried into the kitchen. No hope of escape there, for the cook immediately handed me a tureen of a shellfish soup, and so perforce I must return to the dining chamber to serve it. Hands shaking, I made my way back to where all Mistress Cholmond's guests were waiting—only to see them all rise to their feet and make a series of panicked bows and curtseys. My gaze made its way across the room and over their bent backs, and met Torric's piercing dark eyes.

The tureen fell from my nerveless fingers and shattered on the floor, sending broth and chunks of crab and bits of onion everywhere, including over the toes of my slippers.

"Ashara," he said calmly enough, although the intensity of his gaze told me there was a great deal going on behind the mask of impassivity he now wore. "You've changed your hair."

"I—" The word seemed to get caught in my throat, and I took a breath. "How did you find me?"

He cast a quick glance at the supper guests, who had now more or less straightened up and were looking back and forth between the Emperor and the serving girl as if they could not quite believe the evidence of their own eyes. His attention seemed to settle on Mistress Cholmond, and he said, "Good lady, do you have a chamber where the Lady Ashara and I might converse in private?"

She nodded, her myopic eyes wide as she strained to get a better look at her Emperor. "Th-there is my library down the hallway, Your Majesty."

"Excellent." His attention shifted back to me. "Ashara."

As there was no way to refuse him, I moved silently past the pop-eyed assemblage, acutely aware of the bits of seafood broth still clinging to the toes of my shoes. I could only hope that I would not track it all over the house.

I was also all too aware of Torric's presence, of how he seemed to loom so tall as he followed me in silence to the library. The chamber must have been a relic of Mistress Cholmond's late husband, for her eyesight was far too poor to allow her to read any of the volumes contained therein. Perhaps it was mostly for show, a rich woman's casual display of wealth.

Torric shut the door behind us. Now that we were alone, the mask dropped away, and he came to me, taking my hands in his and covering them in kisses. At length he pulled back a few inches and said, "Oh, Ashara, I feared I would never see you again."

I stared up at him, certain I must be dreaming. All my fears, all my worries that I would be found and imprisoned for my duplicity—and now Torric was saying he had thought he would never see me again? "I-I don't understand. My aunt is imprisoned, and I thought—"

"She will be released," he replied at once. "At least, as soon as I can think of a way to do so without making it seem as if magic is now allowed in Sirlende. I have spoken with her, my love, and I know why you felt as if you had no choice but to do as you did."

"You are...not angry?" I asked. "For I did deceive you—"

"Only in outward things, petty things. You were no one but you, Ashara, and that is who I fell in love with, not the gowns you wore or the jewels around your neck."

My legs began to quiver. "I believe I need to sit down," I said faintly, then made my way over to the divan, which was situated near the hearth, and sank down on it. Torric followed me there, and took my hands in his. Oh, how warm and strong his fingers were, how welcome their pressure against my own cold and fragile hands! "So…you have forgiven me?"

He gave a small laugh. "What is there to forgive?" A pause, and then I noticed a familiar glint in his dark eyes as he reached out and touched a strand of my unnaturally dark hair. "Well, except what you've done to your hair. I hope to the gods that it is not permanent!"

A flood of relief washed over me, and I found myself chuckling as well. "No, it is not. My stepmother had to treat her hair every three weeks or so, as it began to fade, and so it will be with me. Perhaps it will go faster if I wash it more— she only did so once a week, to preserve the color for as long as possible."

"I will make sure you can wash it every day." His hands tightened around mine. "For you are coming back with me. Your new mistress will have to find someone else to finish serving at her supper party."

"I do not think she will mind overmuch, for you will have given her enough conversation to last for some days, I think." And I laughed again, for sheer joy, for the knowledge that Torric loved me despite everything, for realizing that he meant to set my aunt free, and that I would now go away with him to the palace, and my nightmare had finally become a dream come true.

After that he hastened us away in a dark carriage that carried no coat-of-arms, although the coach was surrounded by a contingent of ten guards. "I thought it best to be discreet," he told me, holding me close as we clattered over the stony streets on our way back to the palace.

"Well, as discreet as a great black carriage surrounded by a contingent of men-at-arms can be, I suppose," I replied, and he laughed and pulled me close, touching his lips to mine, letting me taste the sweetness of his mouth again. Perhaps we did get jolted by our rapid pace, but I noticed none of that, and only the magic of *him*, that lovely intoxication which seemed to sweep over me whenever I was in his arms.

He had brought a long, hooded cloak with him in the carriage, and he placed it around my shoulders and drew up the hood before we alighted. "For there are always prying eyes around the palace," he explained.

This I could well imagine, and I nodded and clutched the cloak tightly to me as he stepped out, then handed me down. From there we entered the building through a small door off to one side, and not through the great entry hall at the front of the building. Not too far off was an equally modest staircase, which I guessed was reserved for the servants' use. I did not mind such a humble entry into the palace, no, not at all, for at the moment my mind was still reeling with the abrupt alteration in my situation.

"Here we are," Torric said, and brought me into an elegant suite hung with shades of rose and claret, and with a welcome fire crackling in the hearth of soft blush-colored marble. "I hope you will be comfortable here. Only for a short time, of course, for I meant it when I said I would marry you as soon as I possibly could."

I glanced at the door, but the two men-at-arms who had followed us up the stairs had shut it behind us, presumably so they could take up a post outside. As Torric and I were more or less alone, I went to him and kissed him again on the mouth, pressing my body to him, hoping that he would sense from my touch how much I wanted such a thing as well.

It seemed I had communicated my feelings clearly enough, for after a moment he pulled away and said, "Gods, Ashara, if you do that much more, I don't think I shall be able to wait another hour!"

Yes, perhaps being quite so exuberant wasn't such a good idea, especially now that I realized I could see the suite's bedroom through an open door off to my right. It would be so easy to take Torric by the hand, lead him in there…

"Ah," I said raggedly. "I do see your point. So what is your plan?"

He smiled, as if he guessed all too well what I had been thinking. "My sister knew I was going to fetch you tonight, but your presence here is otherwise a secret. She has sent over a few gowns for you, as you are close enough in size that you can make do until we can have a wardrobe made. And that hair…"

"I thought it was very clever of me," I said, even as I reached up to touch the unnaturally black braid that hung over my shoulder.

"That is one word for it, I suppose." His mouth twisted a little, as if he were trying to hold back a grin. "I will also make sure that a bath is sent up forthwith. Lyarris' lady's maid will have to be let in on the secret, I suppose. But I do not want to present you as my affianced bride until you are…you."

"So concerned with appearances, are you?" I asked, my tone playful, but his expression turned unexpectedly grim.

"Yes, for there is already enough controversy concerning you and illusion. You need to look like the Ashara Millende everyone saw this past week, or it could cause even more trouble."

This observation seemed wise, after I considered it for a moment, and I nodded. "That probably would be for the best. And after all, just a few hours ago I thought I should never see you again. I will muster the patience to wait for you a week or so more, if I must."

"It will be a very long week," he said. "But I will bear it, for at least I will be able to come and see you while the preparations are made, and because I know that such a great reward awaits me at the end."

"And if you can bear it, I will, too." I paused, then stood on my tiptoes so I could kiss him on the cheek. "I do believe it will be just a little easier now that I am here in the palace, and know I will never have to polish Madame Cholmond's paneling again!"

He did not deign to answer, but merely bent and placed his mouth on mine, telling me with the kiss that there were a great many things far better in the world than having to polish paneling. And in that, he was certainly correct.

CHAPTER EIGHTEEN

Torric

After I had torn myself away from Ashara—doing so only because her bath had arrived, and although some part of me wished very much to stay, so that I might see even more of her, I told my aching loins that such a thing was certainly not seemly. What kind of Emperor was I, if I could not maintain my self-control for a few more days?

So I left her in the company of my sister's maid, and went instead to Lyarris' apartments. By then it was quite late, but I knew she would not yet be abed. Even when we had balls and gatherings that lasted into the small hours of the morning, she would often spend some time afterward writing. I had teased her about it on occasion, but she only told me that writing helped to settle her mind, to take her away from the day so she might sleep.

And that was how I found her, seated at her desk, her pen making slight scratching sounds that could barely be heard above the crackling of the fire. She had readied herself somewhat for bed, with her hair in a long braid and a heavy dressing gown replacing the ornate court dress she had worn earlier.

As soon as I entered, however, she set down her pen and gave me an expectant look. "She is all settled?"

"More or less. Your maid is attending her now, and helping to scrub some truly awful black dye out of her hair."

"Oh, dear. A disguise, I presume?"

"Yes, and one that obviously served her well for some time. If it were not for my one man-at-arms being suspicious of her story, and going to the Lady Gabrinne to inquire as to its veracity..." I let the words trail off. If not for tripping herself up with that one lie, Ashara might very well have been lost to me forever.

"Well, I can see why Ashara felt herself driven to such lengths. But it will be mended soon enough, and in the meantime I have already ordered up quite a few new gowns. My dressmaker was quite curious as to why I should suddenly be so enamored of russet and gold and warm green, as they are not colors that particularly suit me."

I could not help but smile at that, for the mischievous look in my sister's eyes told me she was quite enjoying this little subterfuge of ours. Luckily, the suite where Ashara was currently ensconced was just down the corridor from Lyarris' rooms, but far from the grand apartments several floors above that our mother called home. As the Dowager Empress preferred that we call on her rather than the opposite, the chances of her encountering Ashara were fairly slim.

No, at this point it was more of a waiting game...or perhaps a planning game would be a more accurate way to put it. For I had promised my betrothed that her aunt would be given her freedom, although at the moment I had no clear idea of how I might accomplish such a thing—not when it went against hundreds of years of law.

"You're frowning," my sister told me.

"Am I?" With a shrug I sat down on the divan near the fire and stared into it, as if the changing flames could somehow provide me with the solution I required.

"Rather fearfully for a man who just retrieved the woman he loves and has her safely under his roof."

Unlike me, Lyarris did not keep spirits in her rooms, so there was no decanter of port at hand. Pity. I could have used some at the moment. Of course she could have rung for the servants to bring a bottle, but I did not want to advertise my presence here that clearly.

Instead, I settled back against the divan's cushions and knotted my fingers atop one knee. "It is only that I promised Ashara I would free her aunt, and I can think of no good way to do so without upsetting my advisors by overturning a law that has been in place for more than five centuries, as well as giving the message that now it is perfectly all right to perform magic in Sirlende."

"I can see why that would be a thorny problem." She got up from behind her desk and came to take a seat in one of the two heavily upholstered chairs that faced the divan. "It is rather unfortunate that you, as Emperor, do not have quite as much power as most people think you do."

I scowled at her. "Thank you for that helpful insight."

Rather than taking offense, she merely chuckled a little. "Haven't you often complained of those same constraints to me? This is someplace where you must tread lightly, for while you cannot break a promise to Ashara, neither can you break the covenant you have with the people of Sirlende to keep them safe. True, the magic Ashara's aunt possesses seems to me to be a fairly harmless sort, but the same thing cannot be said of all mages, wherever they may be hiding these days."

"There were rumors of a particularly nasty one up in North Eredor some months back, but my spies could tell me nothing else. So you see why I must be cautious."

Lyarris appeared more intrigued by this intelligence than dismayed. "Truly? I shall have to ask Lord Sorthannic about that, for with his sister married to the Mark of North Eredor, surely she must have heard something of it, and has possibly discussed it with her brother."

"Well, if you can get any information from him, that would be useful, because the whole thing appears to have been hushed up. At any rate, it does show that we cannot afford to let down our guard too much, as I fear that for every well-meaning user of magic out there such as Therissa Larrin, there could be another just as inclined toward evil."

"I'll see what I can do." Her mouth pursed slightly, as if she were already thinking about that future conversation with the Duke of Marric's Rest.

Because I was preoccupied with other matters, I did not even bother to tease her about Lord Sorthannic as I otherwise might. "That may provide insight…or it may not. What I do know is that I require a solution now."

Lyarris' expression sobered at once. "Of course." She tilted her head to one side, as if considering. Then she said, "While it is true that any citizen of Sirlende found to be practicing magic is under sentence of death, can we make a claim that Therissa Larrin is not actually a citizen of this empire, as she has made her home elsewhere these past twenty years?"

I stared at my sister, struck by this insight. Sometimes I could only marvel at the quickness of her mind…and I hoped that Sorthannic Sedassa would appreciate it as much as I did. "That is an angle of attack I had not considered. Truly, she herself told me that she abandoned her homeland because she saw no future for herself here."

Lyarris continued, the words coming fast and almost breathless, as if she wanted to make haste before she forgot a pertinent detail, "Yes, she has had no residence here, has paid no taxes…I think you may make a very credible case for Therissa Larrin ceasing to be a citizen of yours some years ago. And if she is not a citizen, then it is not your place to hold the laws of this land over her head."

"This might just work." I turned the plan over in my mind, weighing it, attempting to poke holes in it before my advisors could have the opportunity. Yes, there was the chance that Keldryn would say that because she was born here, Madam Larrin was still a citizen. But I could counter that by saying she had willingly left and made her home elsewhere. Even so, I knew arguments would be made for some sort of punishment. If I let her go without any kind of consequences for her actions, then I knew I ran the risk of others seeing my leniency as weakness. I could not afford that so early in my reign.

"What is it?" my sister asked. "For you are suddenly looking quite grim."

I explained my misgivings to her, then added, "I fear I must mete out some kind of sentence for what Therissa Larrin has done. Nothing so extreme as death, of course."

"Your betrothed might find issue with a flogging or any other lesser punishment."

Lyarris said this simply, without any kind of remonstrance in her tone, but I knew she was right. I could not lay down a punishment that caused physical pain; it would be too much for either Ashara or her aunt to bear. An idea came to me then. I did not like it much, and I feared my beloved would like it even less. However, I did not have many choices left to me.

"She must be banished," I said at last, and Lyarris nodded, although her eyes were sorrowful.

"Yes, I think that is the only penalty severe enough to satisfy your councilors while still not doing any irreparable harm. It will be difficult for her to go, when she has just now met her niece after so many years away, but it is not as if she has any other attachment to Sirlende otherwise. She can return whence she came, and be glad of the Emperor's mercy."

At the moment I was not feeling terribly merciful, and wished I could have devised a better solution, but I could not think of anything else. I rose from the divan and said, "Thank you, my sister. It seems that once again I have relied on your counsel to see me through a difficult situation."

"I only wish I could do more." She stood as well, then asked, "Will you go tell Ashara now?"

I hesitated for only a second or two. "No, she is weary, and so I think it best to wait until morning, when she will be better rested. I believe we could all do with some rest." After reaching out and giving my sister's hand a gentle squeeze, I turned and left, thinking that for a man who had just solved such a difficult problem, I was not all that happy about it.

"Banished?" Ashara said blankly. For the space of a few heartbeats she said nothing, but only stared at me. The ablutions of the night before seemed to have had some benefit already; her hair was no longer raven-black, but a dull dark brown, with odd copper flickers within it. "Torric, she is the only family I have!"

Anger flickered within me. "Do you think I do not know that?" But then I shook my head and reached out to take her hands in mine. "My love, if there were anything else I could do, I would. She broke the law and has freely admitted it. Surely exile is better than death, or dismemberment. Would you rather her hands or tongue cut off, so she could not perform her incantations ever again?"

Ashara flinched, although I noticed her fingers only tightened on mine, instead of pulling away. "That's...barbaric."

"I agree, but I cannot change a law that has stood for five hundred years simply to serve the needs of one woman. Can you understand that?"

For a long moment she said nothing, but only sat there, holding on to me with the desperation of a drowning woman clinging to a rescuer's hands. Tears filled her beautiful amber-green eyes. They did not spill down her cheeks, however, instead glittering there, caught by her heavy lashes. I saw her mouth tighten, and a firmness came to her chin that I had not seen a few seconds earlier.

"I understand," she said at last. "You are Emperor, and you are a good ruler. You cannot make an exception simply for me. Of course it is better that she lives, even if it is thousands of miles hence in Keshiaar, or Purth. But oh, I shall miss her, although I have only known her for a week."

And she crumpled then, the brittle strength leaving her as I took her in my arms and tried to soothe her as best I could. She wept, but quietly, giving vent to her sorrow rather than trying to persuade me to change my mind. Oh, she would make a great Empress, this wondrous woman I had found. Somehow she understood matters that those with far more education and experience could not grasp. Perhaps it was luck, or the hand of the gods, but I thanked whatever fate had brought her to me. She would weep now, as she should, and then she would put that away and do what she must.

I could not ask any more from her than that.

CHAPTER NINETEEN

Ashara

My aunt's face went pale as I told her of her doom, but then she nodded briskly and said, "Ah, well, it was a risk I chose to run, and the consequences could have been much worse. It is not as if I have not lived outside the borders of Sirlende these past two decades. I daresay I can do it again if I must."

I had come here alone—that is, as alone as I could be these days. Two guards waited for me some ten paces away, studiously attempting to appear as if they were not listening to every word. Torric had offered to come with me, but I thought this might be easier without him. Now, though, I wished I had his comforting presence nearby. However, as I had made my decision and could not change it, I had no choice but to press ahead.

What my aunt saw in my face, I could not say, but she gave me a weary little smile and went on, "My dear girl, we have accomplished everything we set out to do. You are to be Empress of Sirlende, and you will be forever away from that terrible woman your father was foolish enough to marry. Please do tell me that at least *she* will not get away free in all this."

I shook my head at once. "Hardly. Torric—that is, I mean the Emperor—has said that because I was the one wronged, I should be the one to decide her punishment. I am sure she is in a state already, because his solicitors have been demanding to see my father's will, and to examine the lease on the estate, and a great many other matters having to do with the disposal of the assets that should have come to me. But I have not yet decided what I should do."

"Whatever you do decide, I know it will be the right thing."

My aunt stretched out her hands to me, and I went and took them, reaching through the bars to do so. From somewhere behind me I heard a muffled oath from one of the men-at-arms sent to accompany me, and the movement of heavy feet on the stone floor, as if he thought to intercede. I looked at him over my shoulder and shook my head, and he stopped where he was, although I noticed his hand still rested on the hilt of the short sword he wore.

Aunt Therissa's cold fingers closed on mine, and her dark eyes glinted with amusement. "You see? You are the Empress already, if not in name. When is the wedding to be?"

"Soon," I told her. "The preparations are already under way, and now that I have all that wretched black dye out of my hair, Torric says there is really nothing to delay us, save

Lord Hein wringing his hands and saying that he cannot possibly organize an imperial wedding in such a short amount of time."

"I can see how that might be difficult." Some of the light faded from her face. "I wish I could be there to see it, but I can tell from your expression that the Emperor wishes me to be gone soon, and quietly, so the scandal might die down as soon as possible."

"I fear so." I released her hands then, and said, "I knew it was quite out of the question to have you attend, but oh, Aunt Therissa, how I wish you could be there! You are the only family I have."

She blinked, and I saw tears glisten in her eyes. "Oh, my dear girl, you will have a new family now. I do not envy you your future mother-in-law, but from everything I have heard, the Princess Lyarris is a lovely young woman, and of course you will have your husband."

This much was true; we had only been acquainted for a short time, but I had already come to love the Crown Princess as if she were my own sister—which she soon would be. After suffering the cruelties of my stepsisters for so many years, it had come as quite a revelation that Lyarris looked on me as a welcome addition to the family, and not as a rival for her brother's affections.

"Yes," I said, although with some sadness, "that is true, but it would be better if you could be here as well."

"I cannot argue with that. But I will take up my wandering path and have a whole new set of adventures, so let us not be sad, Ashara."

The brave smile with which she said this made me blink away the tears that had threatened to form in my own eyes. "And will you write to me, and tell me of your adventures?"

"As best I can. Now go, my dear, and tell your future husband that I am quite content with my fate, and that he can smuggle me out of the palace whenever he deems wise. I will not argue with his decision, for I daresay it was the best solution he could think of."

I nodded. "Thank you, Aunt Therissa. Thank you for— well, for everything."

The gaze she sent me was warm and loving, and I knew I would hold it in my heart until the end of my days. "You are most welcome, my child. Go, and be the Empress I know you have it within you to be. Make me proud."

Her words made my throat tighten with unshed tears, and so I could only whisper, "I will," before I fled the dungeon, the two guards falling in behind me as I made my way to the light of the world above and the future that awaited me.

By that time my presence had been made known to all the denizens of the palace, so although I saw people staring at me and my escort, no one moved to stop me, or to ask my business there. Everyone knew that I would be marrying the Emperor not two days hence. Even so, I found it difficult to keep my chin up, to prevent myself from meeting any of their curious glances as I made my way up to Torric's suite.

He knew I would be returning to him there, and so had made sure to keep his schedule open so he would not be occupied with some meeting or another. Indeed, I thought he must have been waiting for me at the door, for he was there almost as soon as I entered. The guards closed the door behind me, and Torric took me in his arms, saying nothing, merely holding me, letting me simply be with him until I felt ready to speak.

At length I pulled away and said quietly, "She understands, and she is ready. If I were you, I would not delay."

"I had not planned to," he replied. He reached down to touch my cheek. "The preparations have been made. She will go in the escort of a troop of guards, who will see to her safety until she reaches the border with South Eredor. And she will go with a spare horse, and several changes of new gowns, and enough coin to support her for the next year. She will not be cast entirely adrift."

His words did far more than merely reassure me—they sent a wave of warmth through me, for this was proof, more than anything else he had done, that he wanted me to be happy, to know that my aunt should not suffer because of the punishment he was forced to give her. Truly, I could not have asked for anything more, save to have her stay with me, and I knew that was not possible.

"Thank you, Torric," I whispered.

He seemed to understand that I did not wish to speak of it further, and so he only gave me an encouraging smile and asked, "And…that other matter? Have you made your decision?"

"I-I think so." Truly, I had been avoiding the unpleasant topic, but I knew I must manage the question of my stepmother, and soon.

"Well enough. You should be Empress first, I think, so you have a few more days before that confrontation." His dark eyes warmed, and he bent to kiss me, his lips so very welcome on mine. When he began to pull away, I said,

"No, Torric. Kiss me. Kiss me again, so I might forget everything save you."

And, the gods bless him, he did just that…if only for a little while.

Gabrinne clapped her hands together and let out a little squeal of excitement, then said, "Truly, I do believe you are the most beautiful bride Sirlende has ever seen!"

I sent a fond smile at her, even as I shook my head. "I am not entirely sure of that, but I do thank you."

The familiar toss of her curls, followed by a beseeching stare in Lyarris' direction. "Your Highness, tell Ashara she is sadly mistaken."

"I fear I have to side with Gabrinne in this," my future sister said. "You are exquisite. But I do believe we need to stop debating the topic and go downstairs. Everyone is waiting."

At those words I felt a knot begin to form in my stomach, and I swallowed. Oh, yes, I wanted this. Rather, I wanted Torric, and if I had to take being Empress of Sirlende along with being his wife, then it was a sacrifice I would gladly make. I chose not to think of the throngs waiting in the temple on the ground floor of the palace, and instead of the man who would soon be my husband.

"I am ready," I said, and both Lyarris and Gabrinne came forth and threaded their arms through mine, so they might guide me to the temple as custom dictated.

As we made our way through the palace—followed as always by a complement of guards—I thought of how glad I was to have these two to stand with me as my attendants. Lyarris had been a treasure, helping me gather my wardrobe, giving quiet advice on how to manage the intricacies of court life, standing as a bulwark between me and the sharp tongue of my future mother-in-law. And Gabrinne had been no less important, her laughter buoying me up when I was weary, her mere presence enough to lift my spirits. Her own wedding was planned for the following week.

"And I have all but gotten Senric to agree that we must stay in Iselfex this winter, so you and I should have a jolly time," she'd told me just the day before, heartening me further, as I knew I would have another friend to stay by my side and help me through my first months as Empress.

I needed that courage now as we made the long walk down the palace's main corridor to the great temple of Minauth that stood at the far end. The hallway was choked with well-wishers who could not fit in the temple itself, and on every wall were swags of autumn leaves and berries and the hearty few flowers that still lingered at this season. Then it was through the great arched doorway, down the long runner of figured crimson that led to the dais where Torric waited.

With all those eyes upon me, I was more glad than ever of the exquisite gown of blush-colored damask embroidered with soft rosy pearls that Lyarris' seamstresses had somehow managed to create within the space of only a few days. My hair, now returned to its usual burnished russet, streamed down my back, held in place by a circlet of rose gold and pearls.

Once we reached the dais, Lyarris and Gabrinne broke away from me and took their seats, leaving me to approach Torric alone. This was how it was always done, to show that a bride had now left the shelter of her family and friends and gone willingly to her new husband.

I could not let myself think of my Aunt Therissa, for as happy as I was, I knew I would weep at her absence. Better to stare up at Torric, at the elegant strength of his profile, the width of his shoulders in the fine doublet of wine-colored velvet, and to think of how he made my heart beat faster every time he turned that dark, long-lashed gaze upon me.

What followed afterward was a blur—the speaking of the ritual words, the drinking of the wine—everything save the pressure of his mouth on mine as he kissed me at the end, kissed me and then announced to everyone that they now looked upon the Empress of Sirlende. And the oddity of everyone bowing, and realizing that they were bowing to me, Ashara Millende—now Ashara Deveras—who once was no more than a scullery maid, and yet now by some miracle had been made their Empress.

More blurs, as the company moved on to the great banquet hall, where a feast had been laid out for us all, and from there to dancing and drinking, swirling in Torric's arms, everything a whirl of color and light and sound. Until at last we broke away from the celebrations, and made our way upstairs to his apartments—my apartments now as well, I realized— and he pulled me close and kissed me, his mouth sweet with wine and desire.

But then he stopped, his dark gaze searching my face. "It is finally here," he said.

I understood what he meant. That first kiss in the woods, every embrace which had followed…they had all led to this moment. Perhaps I should have been afraid, but I knew something of what was to come next. A shiver went through me, but not of fear.

Anticipation.

"Make me your wife, Torric," I whispered.

At once his arms were around me, lifting me, taking me out of the sitting room and on into his bedchamber. Then his hands were on the laces of my gown, until the fabric slipped away to lie in a shining heap at my feet, and he pulled at my chemise, lifting it over my head so that I stood naked before him. But I wasn't cold, no, not with the heat of need coursing through me. Unashamed, I unbuckled his belt and let it drop, then undid the buttons of his doublet, and of his shirt underneath. How beautiful his body was, lean and muscled, with a light dusting of dark hair that trailed down beneath the waistband of his breeches.

He let out a breath, said, "You are a glory," and leaned down to kiss my breasts, to send every nerve in my body alive with desire, and then lifted me, setting me on the bed before he unbuttoned his breeches, and there was nothing more between us, only our bodies pressed together, aching with want, until finally at last we were one, joined in a way

I could never have imagined, all the emptiness of my life before this finally filled.

He loved me, and made me whole.

It would have been so pleasant to spend our days abed, to forget the world and everything in it save one another. But that was not our destiny…and I had one task which still lay ahead of me.

"You are ready for this?" Torric asked, and bent to kiss me at the nape of my neck, pushing aside the mass of my hair.

Once again shivers worked their way over me, and I marveled at how this body of mine, one I thought I knew, could give me such pleasure. How I wished Torric could trail those kisses lower, pull away my gown, take me to bed once more.

Later. For now we were expected in the audience chamber.

"As ready as I can be," I replied. "But it must be done. Then there will be nothing tying me to my past."

He nodded, dark eyes warm with understanding, and took my hand. We left our chambers that way, fingers twined around one another's, as the guards fell in around us to provide an escort down all those staircases, through all those corridors, until at last we entered the grand hall where the Emperor and Empress conducted their business.

It was already full. No real surprise there; word had gotten out, as it always did, and the waiting onlookers had the greedy, expectant air of those about to observe someone else's downfall. I felt my mouth twist with distaste, but there was nothing for it. This thing must be done, and if those watching took enjoyment from seeing someone else's misfortune,

I could not be responsible for that. I had asked Torric if this could be done in private, and he had said no, that he wanted everyone to witness this punishment, and learn from it.

When I had further inquired why he wanted this punishment to be public, when my aunt had been quietly whisked away, he had only shaken his head and said gravely, "It is far more likely that there are those in my kingdom who wish to scheme and steal the goods and lands of others, rather than practice magic, and so I believe this particular set of consequences will hit home with far more people."

I could not really argue with that observation, and I had agreed that the deed would be done in the audience chamber. My stomach still knotted at the thought of confronting her, but after this, I told myself, it would all truly be over.

Torric did not release my hand until we had both seated ourselves on our thrones. One final squeeze of my fingers, and a reassuring smile, and then he turned to Renwell Blane, his captain of the guard. "Have them brought in."

That had been the first disagreement of our marriage, for I had not wished my stepsisters to be present for this. However, Torric overruled me, saying that while perhaps they had not been involved in my stepmother's original scheme to deprive me of my wealth, they most certainly had never spoken up for me, or done anything to make my lot at all easier. That was nothing more than the truth, and so I had not protested further.

Now, though, I felt my fingers grip the carved arms of the throne in which I sat as the doors at the far end of the chamber opened and my stepmother and her two daughters entered. At the sight of them, I felt the breath seize in my throat—a foolish reaction, I supposed, since I was now far beyond the reach of Bethynne Millende's harsh words and petty vindictiveness. It was not as easy as I had hoped to shrug off a decade of such treatment.

Not that any of them were looking terribly intimidating at the moment. They had dressed soberly and plainly—I guessed that my stepmother wished to avoid any obvious evidence of her misuse of money that was never hers—and while she held her head high, both Jenaris and Shelynne appeared thoroughly wretched, their gazes cast resolutely toward the stone floor they now traversed.

I waited until they had paused at the bottom of the dais where Torric and I sat, and then rose, aware of the watching eyes upon me. The crown I wore upon my head suddenly felt very heavy. I cast a quick, sidelong glance at Torric, and he nodded, his eyes earnest on mine, even though his sober expression did not change.

"Bethynne Millende," I said, and to my wonder, my voice was clear and strong, carrying to the farthest corners of the audience chamber, "the Crown's investigators have found irrefutable evidence that you plotted to deprive me of my inheritance, and that you took the proceeds from this inheritance to support yourself and your daughters, only to leave me to work as a drudge in the very house which should have been mine."

To my surprise, she lifted her chin and glared at me, saying, "You had a roof over your head, and meals every day. I deprived you of nothing."

Anger blazed through me, that she should continue to spew her falsehoods, even here before her Emperor. Beside me I heard a hiss of breath, and the creak of the throne on which my husband sat. I knew Torric wished to rise, to tell her exactly what he thought of her lies. But it was not his place to do so.

It was mine.

I laughed, and I saw her eyes widen in shock. I knew then that she had perhaps expected she could still cow me, even now when I was Empress. She had spent too many years in control of her household and everyone around her; it was clear that she still had not grasped how drastically her situation had changed.

"A pallet in front of the fire in the kitchen, and stolen mouthfuls of food, yes," I said. "Not precisely what I should have inherited, however. Therefore, I am now taking back everything which should have been mine—the estate in Larenston, the townhouse here in Iselfex, whatever remains of the money you have squandered for your own luxury over the years."

Her face paled, and I could see the rouge standing out on her pallid cheeks. "Am I to be thrown on the street?"

"Not at all," I said sweetly. "For I know your sister, the Baroness of Delanir, has given you much advice and succor over the years, and so I am sure she would be only too happy to shelter you now in your time of need."

No protests at that pronouncement, although I saw her lips compress and her eyes narrow. I had a feeling the Baron might have some choice words about her coming to live with him and his wife, but that was no concern of mine.

"And my daughters?" my stepmother asked, and now an almost whining, cajoling tone had entered her voice. "Are they to be left with nothing? For they are blameless in all this."

A few paces behind her, both Jenaris and Shelynne looked up for the first time. I could see the worry and fear all too plainly in their faces. Although I did not much like them, I did feel sorry for them.

"As for 'blameless,'" I said, "I am not so sure of that, for certainly they did nothing to make my life any easier. However, I know how cruel this city can be to a young woman on her own, and so I do not wish that fate upon them. Jenaris shall be given the estate in Larenston, and Shelynne will have the house here in town. All monies left of my inheritance will be divided equally between them. I myself will appoint managers to oversee both properties and to ensure that the funds are spent wisely. They will not be cast out, and they will have sufficient wealth to perhaps attract worthy husbands. But you are to leave them strictly alone and have no further contact with them."

Even as their mother looked aghast, Jenaris and Shelynne appeared distinctly relieved. Perhaps having Bethynne Millende removed from their lives wouldn't be quite the hardship she herself thought it to be.

"And sisters," I continued, fixing them both with a direct stare, "if word reaches me that you have spoken to your mother, that you have used any of the funds given to you to support her in any way, then you forfeit my generosity, and will be thrown on the sufferance of your relatives. Do you understand?"

"Yes," they both replied at once, and nodded vigorously.

"Very good," I said. "Lord Keldryn is overseeing the transfer of the properties to you. Until the estate's renters can find another property, you may both stay here in the townhouse. But your mother is to be removed immediately to her sister's home. Say your farewells now, for this is the last you will see of one another."

My stepmother began to weep, and turned toward her daughters, hands outstretched. They, however, backed away, all but throwing themselves into the arms of the guards surrounding them, who appeared distinctly uncomfortable.

"So, she has poisoned your minds against me already?" cried their mother. "Think of everything I have done for you. It was all for you! All of it!"

They both shook their heads violently, and cast entreating looks at the men-at-arms, who obligingly led them away after I nodded. Noting their unceremonious departure, my stepmother took a step toward the dais, fury etched in her brow.

"I knew I should have killed you when you were a child!" she spat. "Useless, worthless, scheming little *whore!*"

The watching crowd, which had been silent up until that point, sucked in a collective breath, and Torric finally stood.

"You are speaking of your Empress," he said, "and what you say is treason. You will have no comfortable exile at your sister's estate. Guards, take her!"

They surrounded her and pulled her away as she screeched and hurled insults. Aghast, I could only stand there and watch until she and her escort disappeared through the doors to the audience chamber. My fingers trembled, and Torric stepped close and wrapped his warm hand around my icy one.

"That is the end of today's audience," he announced.

At once the remaining guards began to herd everyone out. There was much murmuring and muttering, but of course no one dared go against their Emperor's wishes. At last we were alone, and he pulled me against him, holding me, saying nothing, but lending me his strength.

Finally I murmured, "I had no idea she hated me that much. That is, sometimes I wondered if she ever thought of killing me, but to hear her say it out loud...."

"Think no more of it." He gently lifted the crown from my head so he could place his lips against my hair, his breath warm and reassuring. "She is an evil woman. Indeed, I am rather glad she spoke out as she did, for then she gave me a reason to imprison her. I thought you were being far too lenient by allowing her to simply go to her sister."

"And what are you going to do with her?" I asked, pulling away so I could meet his gaze. "Keep her in the dungeon forever?"

"As much as I would like to, no." One of those brilliant heart-melting smiles, and he continued, "I think letting her cool her heels there for a few days might assist her in pondering her misdeeds, so that when she is released, she will be suitably chastened and will reconsider her future actions."

"Very wise, O Emperor," I said, and grinned back up at him.

"I have learned from your wisdom, wife of mine. And I hope I will continue to learn from you for the remainder of my days."

"Only if you will teach me as well," I replied.

"Always."

He took me in his arms and kissed me on the steps of the dais, and I knew then that he would always be there for me, and I for him...and the both of us for Sirlende.

And perhaps, just perhaps, we all would be the better for it.

᷈ Tales of the Latter Kingdoms ᷈

A SERIES OF LOOSELY RELATED NOVELS set in a world that never was, a world that has survived the destruction and chaos of the mage wars in ages past. These "Latter Kingdoms" have rejected magic and grown prosperous once again…but magic still lurks in the corners and shadows, if one knows where to look for it.

ALL FALL DOWN

Healer Merys Thranion has been trained to fight disease and wage war against ignorance. Her training comes to the ultimate test when she is captured by slave traders in a neighboring country and brought to the estate of Lord Shaine. Her task is to heal the brooding lord's injured daughter…but that is only the first of her trials. As the deadly plague raises its head again and threatens to wipe out everyone on Lord Shaine's estate, Merys must summon all her skills to protect those she has come to care for…including the man who has become much more to her than simply her master.

"One of the most original and creative works of fantasy I've read to date."—Jack Sheppard, author of *The Marlowe Transmissions*

Fantasy romance • 102,000 words
Publication date: September 2012

DRAGON ROSE

The shadow of the cursed Dragon Lord has hung over the town of Lirinsholme for centuries, and no one ever knows when the Dragon will claim his next doomed Bride. Rhianne Menyon has dreams of being a painter, but her world changes forever when a single moment of sacrifice brings her to Black's Keep as the Dragon's latest Bride. As she attempts to adjust to her new life...and to know something of the monster who is now her husband...she begins to see that the curse is far crueler than she first believed, and unraveling the mystery of what happened to the Dragon's Brides is only the beginning.

"This is Beauty and the Beast as it is meant to be, at once wreathed in fantasy and magic, and grounded in the hard truths of reality and love. Christine has a style unique and totally her own, both suitably archaic and elegantly modern. She can conjure the peasant towns and drafty castle of the Middle Ages, the magic and folklore reminiscent of influences like J.R.R. Tolkien and Tad Williams, as well as the insightful understanding of human psychology and love anchoring this potent and compelling tale. If Dragon Rose and All Fall Down are indicative of the caliber of stories we can expect from the 'Tales of the Latter Kingdoms,' then fantasy fans should eagerly await every new release from this author."— Amber Sweetapple, author of the "Houri Legends" series

Fantasy romance • 74,000 words
Publication date: November 2012

BINDING SPELL

A case of mistaken identity takes Lark Sedassa from her family's estate and into the power of Kadar Arkalis, the ruler of North Eredor, who thinks he's captured a much greater prize. Although he soon realizes his error, he makes Lark his bride anyway, still hoping to capitalize on her family's connections. Escape is nearly impossible, and before long Lark is not sure whether she even wants to leave. As she struggles with her growing feelings for her captor, she must find the strength within herself to draw on powers she doesn't even realize she possesses. Without those powers, she cannot hope to face the evil rising within the kingdom…or save the man she now calls husband.

"In Christine Pope's *Binding Spell*, the reader is drawn back into an elaborately realized fantasy realm visited in the author's two previous books in this series (*All Fall Down* and *Dragon Rose*). In each installment of the Tales of the Latter Kingdoms, the author skillfully weaves bits of history and snippets of backstory into tightly focused historical fantasy. As always, her writing is deft and precise…This is a story strongly rooted in the land's history, geography, and disparate cultures,. I think I said this in my last review of Ms. Pope's work, but…don't miss this book!"—Jack Sheppard, author of *The Marlowe Transmissions*

Fantasy romance • 93,000 words
Publication date: March 2013

About the Author

A native of Southern California, Christine Pope has been writing stories ever since she commandeered her family's Smith-Corona typewriter back in the sixth grade. Her short fiction has appeared in Astonishing Adventures, Luna Station Quarterly, and the journal of dark fiction, Dark Valentine. Two of her short stories have been nominated for the Pushcart Prize.

Christine Pope writes as the mood takes her, and her work encompasses paranormal romance, fantasy, horror, science fiction, and historical romance. She blames this on being easily distracted by bright, shiny objects, which could also account for the size of her shoe collection. After spending many years in the magazine publishing industry, she now works as a freelance editor and graphic designer in addition to writing fiction. She fell in love with Sedona, Arizona, while researching the Sedona Trilogy and now makes her home there, surrounded by the red rocks. No alien sightings, though...not yet, anyway!

For more information on any of Ms. Pope's individual books, as well as upcoming works in the Latter Kingdoms series, visit her website at www.christinepope.com.

Made in the USA
Lexington, KY
13 April 2014